1,001 Las Vegas Nights

Angelique St. Chase, Jr

ISBN-10: 1517686806

ISBN-13: 978-1517686802

10 9 8 7 6 5 4 3 2 1

First Edition: November 2015

CONTENTS

CHAPTER 1

"Oh my God, Scott! You feel incredible!" I whispered into his ear with my hot breath cascading down his neck. Having met only two hours ago, I could feel him climax for the fourth time inside of me, and showing off sexual skills most porn stars had yet to discover. My back arched just as my body felt like it was being struck once again by lightning. I felt the electricity travel from neuron to neuron starting at my groin and radiating to every cell. As a Psychology Professor at the local University, he knew how to read me as very few people ever had. The seduction had started over the internet when he responded to my online profile. 6'5" and in his early 40's, Scott had an ageless soccer player's body. After a week of relentless emails and messages, I had finally agreed to meet him in person for coffee that day. As the time to meet drew nearer, I was rethinking the wisdom of meeting in such a public place. Being a well known casino executive in town, privacy could be an issue. As such, the thought of a crowded coffee house with people listening in at will was less than appealing. While grabbing my keys to head to our agreed to meeting spot, I decided to book a room at a nearby hotel instead. Given my work, I looked upon hotel rooms as convenient extensions of either my office or home depending on whom I was meeting. Without ever having seen me in person or having spoken to me on the phone, Scott agreed to the change in venue.

I was not sure what I had expected to happen. I had placed an order with room service for some wine and food, so that much I had been planning on, along with some flirting and conversation. The odds after all of his getting me naked within the first 10 minutes of stepping foot inside the room were the equivalent of winning the *Power Ball* on the first try. I should have bought a ticket that day.

Our initial encounter started with my opening the door and leaning in to greet him in the typical European fashion of a kiss on each cheek. I guess they do things differently in Texas, though, since he instead of going for the air by my cheeks, took control by kissing me fully on the mouth. Then, in one fell swoop, pinned me against the foyer wall while cupping my breast before the door had even finished shutting. "Well, that settles the chemistry question," he noted upon coming up for air and moving further into the room. Within 10 minutes, our clothes lay crumpled on the floor and 5 minutes later round one of several that day was well on its way. It was a whirlwind of activity for the next few hours as we attempted to outdo each other in our adult version of *show-and-tell.*

Then it happened. The flashbacks I had been trying to avoid with such a meeting. It seemed that even Scott could not stop my thinking about *him.* Why did I have to recall his touch, his scent, his kiss at the most inappropriate of times?

***

CHAPTER 2

Ken screwed the cap back onto the fountain pen with which he had signed the divorce papers just moments prior. The only thing left was the judge's signature and stamp to make it official. He was admiring the pelican shape of the clip so as to avoid looking at the person to whom he had been married. The person, with whom he had had children with, had been financially responsible for and shared residences with for over a decade and a half.

It had been a long time coming. The meeting today in the lawyer's office to witness their signatures was simply a formality. There was no anger or great sorrow, other than for time wasted. They had been living their own lives for close to a decade now. Separate bedrooms had been just the start of their relationship decline. With the children going off to college and becoming adults in their own right, and living their own lives, it no longer mattered if appearances were kept up or not.

They were free to pursue the people that had made them happy after they came to realize that it would not be each other. She had her boyfriend living across town, and he could finally follow his heart to Las Vegas.

As he stood up to thank everyone for their time and shaking hands, including his soon to be ex-wife's, his thoughts turned to his future. He had not spoken to Pandora Richardson in close to a year. How would he find her again?

***

CHAPTER 3

Scott Himmel was a godsend. There were plenty of men in this town willing and eager to have sex with me - or any number of other women - but few were worth the effort. If you were a woman in Las Vegas under the age of sixty and weighed less than 300lbs, the easiest thing in the world was to have sex with someone - anyone - at any time. While looks certainly did not hurt, they were truly not necessary considering the simple law of supply and demand. Already ranking as the U.S. city with one of the, if not the highest available male to female ratio, these numbers, while high, still did not provide an accurate reflection to what degree the selection process was skewed in the favor of women in Las Vegas. Not only could visitors outnumber residents but also most visitors to this charming town were business convention attendees - and the majority of these were men. Either way, though, be it for business, escapism or a little of both, travelers flocked from all over the world to visit this Mecca of Indulgence year around. It was synonymous with the Mob, money, entertainment, drinking, gambling, and of course sex. While the LVCVA (Las Vegas Convention and Visitors Authority) had not created this image initially, it sure had done a fantastic job of keeping it polished and shiny. It was for all those reasons and along with many others that I had decided to call this city home once again after having traversed the globe.

It had been less than an hour since Scott and I had left the hotel room. I was basking in the afterglow of it all while sitting and sipping on a glass of Riesling at *Fleur*, one of my favorite restaurant/bars in the *Mandalay Bay* on the infamous Las Vegas Blvd (aka the Strip). Watching the latest batch of visiting conventioneers, I was reminded of why people watching on the Strip was one of my pet hobbies. Thank you, drunk tourists, thank you. I had arrived barely in time to hear Sandra, my darling bartender, put on her best industry face as she answered the questions of the woman on the barstool next to me. I could hear her patiently describing such exotic foods as 'fingerling puree' and 'creamy polenta' to someone who apparently thought that any restaurant that did not have a drive-through was *'fancy.'*

Tuning out the budding food critic as she finally placed her order, I looked into my wine glass as if it were a crystal ball that held all the answers and my thoughts turned back to Scott. He was sensual, take-charge and addicting - both in and out of bed come to find out. I could still feel his right hand on the small of my back as he had pulled me towards him, his left hand behind my head entwined in my hair, and that look he would get in his eyes every time he was about to seduce me. However, that was not my favorite memory. My favorite memory was afterwards: after the sex and the dialogue that would ensue. Like the first time he sat completely naked, and oh so striking, with no inhibitions across the table arranged by room service before his arrival with a selection of cheeses, fruits a bottle of wine and two glasses. All it took was food, wine, and conversation to change my life forever.

CHAPTER 4

"I have to admit that I am still a bit stunned as to why a successful, independent, beautiful, single woman winds up online looking for a Friend-With-Benefits, " he said as he sliced a piece of cheese and put it confidently on a water cracker.

"The Internet is my wheelhouse. I spend more time online than anywhere else and ... isn't that how everyone meets these days anyway? Besides, I work long hours; would rather sift through the data on my computer than the hurt feelings in person; and after the last relationship ended as badly as it did, I am not looking to jump out of the frying pan and into the fire. I am one of the best friends a person could ever have; just do not ask me to marry. I will make you miserable if you do," I responded as I sampled the fruit spreads that accompanied the cheeses.

"I am not the kind to fall for someone easily."

"That's what they all said."

Taking a sip from his glass to wash down the cracker, he asked, "All? Is it a common occurrence? People asking you to marry them?"

"I don't know how to answer that question since 'common' is a relative term. I don't think any marriage proposal is common, even if you have been proposed to by a total of 14 different people," I answered as I combined the apricot spread with the Gouda cheese.

"14?" Crumbs flew out of his mouth.

"Yes," I replied in a matter-of-fact tone.

He grabbed the water to ease his cough from having mis-swallowed and after taking a sip asked, "Only 14?"

"Well, at last count. Not that I am keeping score." I paused to do a mental calculation in my head. "Yes, 14. Or, I should say those were the serious proposals. I am not including the times when they did not have a ring." I carefully balanced cracker, cheese, and spread, and brought it to my lips.

"Are you a hypnotist or something?" he asked laughingly.

"Maybe," I answered with a shrug.

"But seriously. Do you think you do this on purpose?" He popped one of the grapes into this mouth that he had plucked a moment ago.

"Do I do what on purpose? Have people fall in love with me; spend two month's salary on a ring; get down on one knee in a public place; and ask me to marry them within four months of knowing me? No ... never on purpose."

"Within four months of knowing you? Really?" His eyebrows rose as he combined a piece of Asiago with one of the grapes in his hand.

"Well, it's not always four months." I stole the Asiago and grape combo off his plate and smiled as I bit into grape and cheese stack.

I saw the relief on his face as his eyebrows went back to normal height. "I was starting to get worried. Even for a shotgun wedding, four months seems a bit fast."

"Usually it is less than that. Four months is just the longest amount of time it has taken for someone to ask me to marry him, if he is going to ask me to marry him, that is. Both of my ex-husbands proposed within two weeks of having met me." I explained before he could finish cutting the second piece of cheese to go along with his grapes and have it accidentally go down the wrong pipe.

"Two weeks?" He had put down the knife to focus on my answer.

"Yes."

"Indeed." Leaning back in his chair so he could take the information in a bit better, he asked, "What, pray tell, did you do to the 14 serious, and the other not so serious, men that made them propose to you?"

"You would be in a better position to answer that than I."

"I'll get back to you within the next four months then," he replied with a laugh. "So, 14 proposals and two marriages. How many times have you fallen in love? 20? 30? 100?"

As I prepared to take another bite of Gouda and Apricot, I stopped my hand mid-air and looked into Scott's eyes. *Should I tell him*? I wondered. He has those eyes and that smile like: *this is someone I can trust. This is someone to whom I can tell all my secrets. This is someone who will understand what I have been going through for the last few years.* No wonder he is in the field he is in. I placed down the cheese, picked up my wine glass instead, took a sip of courage, looked into his eyes, and confessed. "Once, and sadly it was not with either one of my husbands."

"Why marry them?" I saw curiosity on his face.

"The first time because I did not think that I would ever fall in love, so I married the person I thought would be the best work partner," I answered as I picked up my Gouda and apricot again. Taking a thoughtful bite and enjoying the sweet, salty, and tangy sensation on my tongue I closed my eyes. Opening them up again after swallowing, I continued. "The second time, I knew better it's just that I felt that I would never find it again, so I married the person I thought I could help the most," I concluded with another sip of wine.

"You could help the most? Were you doing penance for something?" he asked as his fingers entwined under his chin.

"I told you I am a great friend. I have hurt a lot of people though in my life ... usually ... well, usually the ones who fall in love with me," I said thoughtfully while tapping the edge of my wine glass.

"Why do you think that is?" I could see that he had completed the transition from curious small talk to full-blown analysis mode.

"You are familiar with my namesake? The myth of Pandora? The first woman formed of clay by the Gods, who through her charm and beauty was to bring misery upon the human race?"

"Yes."

"Well, it has nothing to do with that," I smiled self-satisfied at my comedic timing. Scott was not going to be dissuaded and his eyes showed that he was seeing past my efforts of sidestepping his questions by way of humor.

"Who is it that hurt you so deeply that you felt the need to take your revenge and lash out at every man within perfume distance of you? Which, by the way, is delightful," he added with a wink.

"*Chanel* does know their stuff, don't they?" I asked a bit coquettishly, grabbing on to the odd tangent.

"Like I said, it is intoxicating just not the answer to my question." Scott could steer the topic quite adroitly.

"No, it isn't," I agreed with a sigh, knowing I would have to come clean, however, not sure that I wanted to just yet.

I could see his face softening as he picked up on the extent of my discomfort, even if the source was still a mystery. Leaning forward a bit before feeding me a grape he said, "OK, how about this Pandora. While your namesake did let loose a lot of harm upon mankind, I personally like to remember her for having also released hope. After all, all's well that ends well."

"Do you think there is hope for me?" I asked looking him in the eyes wondering if I would ever have redemption.

Leaning back into his chair again with a smirk he answered, "That depends on what specifically you are asking. If you mean is there hope for you to go from an outstanding to sub-par lover in bed? Then the answer is sure."

Wanting to smack him but only being within reach of his lower region and afraid of hurting his exposed private parts, I held back and said instead, "You know what I mean."

Turning into the thoughtful analyst again he said, "I think that we have the ability to get over anyone in our past ... If we want to."

"What if I don't want to?" I knew the question made me sound like a 3-year-old. The only thing missing was the stomping of the foot and the tossing of the head. However, unlike a 3-year-old, my tone was not obstinate and instead one of self-reflection and sorrow. I had suspected that this had probably been the truth for some time now despite my vows to the contrary in past discussions and self-appraisals.

"That is entirely your choice. Of course, it makes me wonder what sort of man is able to hold your attention for all this time? What makes him so special?" His long academic fingers formed a steeple in front of his mouth as he asked the question.

"You're being such a psychiatrist right now! I have the feeling that I am part of a case study." I responded twirling my glass while a hint of a sad smile played on my lips.

"No case study Pandora - Just a friend having a friendly conversation. Yes ... a friend with a professional background and in-depth knowledge of human behavior and therefore probably able to ask better questions ... but a friend nonetheless." Scott answered as he sliced the Camembert gently and smeared it onto the cracker.

The sad smile deepened as my eyes took on a faraway look. "Well, the short answer is he wrote me love letters. No one had ever, ... at that point, or.... actually anytime after, written me love letters. The long answer ... hmm ... how long do you have?"

"There is no expiration clause on friendship Pandora. I'll listen for as long as you want to talk," he answered sincerely as he looked into my eyes, no longer focusing on the cheese or cracker.

Propping my feet up on the ottoman I sank down lower in the overstuffed chair and took a sip from my glass. "Ok ... this isn't easy for me to discuss ... And, honestly ... are you sure you're up for this? I mean, this is another man I have had sex with that we are talking about. Not some story about a car purchase or vacation horror story. Can you maintain objectivity?"

"Well ... my nickname is *House*, as in *Dr. Gregory* from the TV Show ... if *House* had been a psychiatrist instead of an M.D., he would have been me ... although maybe that is not the best thing to mention given his faults ... Either way, though, maybe now it makes sense when I say that I promise to be completely unemotional about the matter. These types of puzzles are what I live for solving and hold a personal interest to me," he answered popping cheese and cracker into this mouth.

Nodding, I decided to trust him. Ultimately, I did not really know him all that well and things such as these were often times easier to discuss with a relative stranger as opposed to a fast friend. I decided that Scott would have to read the letters - those darn letters - to understand fully. He would be the first to do so other than myself. I knew them by heart, of course. I could probably have recited them aloud! Nevertheless, the full impact would require seeing those words and their letter shapes. I felt the familiar weight of my convertible laptop/tablet computer while lifting my briefcase, which had been leaning against my overstuffed chair. The computer served as my digital modern day attic of personal memorabilia -

minus the cobwebs - and contained everything necessary to help explain the current state of my mental quandary.

"August 2nd is the first date of several that will live in infamy in my mind. It was the day he first contacted me. I had no idea then that this would be my own personal Pearl Harbor of emotional invasions until the damage had already been done and assessed months later," I said with a nervous laugh as I fumbled with the zipper. "What I thought was an innocent friendship at first, wound up shaping the rest of my existence." As my hand moved to power up my computer, my mind was already moving back in time. I was seeing scenes of my life moving at lightning pace, and experiencing the full range of emotion with each flash of memory. I felt like a time traveler or a CPU downloading information. While these scenes were all familiar to me, having lovingly re-experienced each memory hundreds of times during my quieter moments, - especially the painful ones - Scott's presence and questions were causing me for the first time to look at them, not as emotional time capsules, but analytical data. It was as if a switch had been flipped and I was accessing a different part of my brain. Shuffling through my memories and reorganizing the data with this new perspective, I wondered aloud, "Of course, while that was the first time we interacted, just like trying to find the point of origin of anything, where did it actually start? With my marriage? With my mother? The big bang and the origin of the universe."

"Hmm, I know I said to take as long as you like, but could we start maybe some place between the origin of the universe and August 2? Preferably closer to the August 2 than the origin of the universe," he replied with a smirk.

With a sigh, I tried hard to slow the rapid chain of events my brain was reconstructing, just as a video game had to rebuild the confines of its world every time it was powered up. We were sitting across from each other, and I could still see him, but in my mind, the room was spinning and melting around me. I felt like *Professor X* from the *X-Men* while the Professor was in the chamber. In the back of my mind, I could hear my inner voice asking *Why ... why ... why* and with each why a new scene would pop up. "Had it not been for 100 different things happening exactly the way they did, I would never have met Ken, and you and I might not be sitting here today. I see life as a wonderfully complex chain reaction. For example, I would not be doing work-wise what I am doing today had it not been for my 6th-grade teacher. I would not have had this 6th-grade teacher without my mother falling in love with a married man and moving to the town we did. She would never have been in the same business as this married man without her ex-boyfriend Peter, and on and on it goes. Where to begin?" My computer had finished loading.

"Well then, at the risk of sounding cliché, why don't we start with your childhood?"

I turned my head and knew where I had to look to find the memory I needed.

***

CHAPTER 5

Believe it or not, my life is based on a true story. I grew up living both sides of the fairy tale - the dark and the light. Adored and fawned over one minute and physically beaten and ridiculed the next. I knew that my mother loved me; just sometimes, I wished she loved me a little less. Growing up, I was luckier than most I suppose since my abuse was at least in nice surroundings and would alternate with hugs, kisses, and words of praise. Love and its expressions had therefore always been confusing to me from the start. Unlike many others, I did have my Grandmother, who would protect me when she stayed with us. She would stand up for me with quiet determination. Maybe having her as an example was what gave me the strength in the end to do what I needed to do.

I was considered a child prodigy in ballet, tested at a genius IQ intellect, and more often than not, had adult responsibilities thrust upon me from a young age on. I wore make-up since I was three while on stage but was not allowed to do so in my personal life until my mid-teens, and rarely did so now. Tall my whole life long, I topped out at 5'10" in middle school. My stepfather, always the soul of gentility, would call me a brute. I was never what could be considered a petite and delicate little flower but being called a brute from age 12 on by an authority figure, was a bit harsh. I had a volleyball player's frame, with a DD chest. Fortunately, my two redeeming features of femininity outside of my chest were: my long hair and the ballet grace that had been drilled into me for hours on end until it became second nature.

I was in my mid 20's when Ken and I met. Despite having been married for a few years, having traveled the world over several times, having dined with royalty, diplomats, heads of Fortune 500 companies and calling more than a handful of celebrities friends - all before the age of 21; I was naive and inexperienced when it came to relationships. This, like everything else, was a dichotic existence growing up for me. On the one hand, I was sheltered from the romantic relationships. Never even having had the time to have a boyfriend while in high school, no idea how to start a relationship, I had no idea how to attract a man other than what was written in the teenage romance novels. On the other hand, I had learned about the 'Birds and the Bees' when I was three years old and would vacation on nude beaches with my mother and was able to see sexual images in most magazines growing up. My first real kiss from a boy was on the evening of my 16th birthday, and my first long term relationship that lasted longer than a few weeks was my first marriage.

My first husband and I had met in Florida and started a company together that dealt in rare and collectible books. I was his second marriage. His first wife had left him for someone else. In addition to this ultimate form of rejection, he had a bit of an insecure personality already anyway; this would result in his repeated accusations of my cheating on him and looking for ways to leave. The irony of it all was had it not been for his accusations I would have never thought of leaving him, much less actually left. Despite being innocent and despite my best efforts to soothe his fears, these insecurities of his, not to mention, anything else I excelled at over him - which was a lot - would be a point of contention for our entire relationship. He was jealous of my looks, my intelligence, and my magnetic personality and while he would have no qualms to use my talents to his advantage, he would predictably and consistently fight with me over perceived slights and tell me that I was worthless. It was not until much later that I realized that while many women married their father, I had married my mother. It was a mentally abusive relationship and after years of trying to make it work and having a beautiful son together, I had started to come to the end of my rope. He was possessive and controlling. My life had become one of a conjoined twin with him. Rare was the occasion when we were not in the same room at the same time, even at home. For someone who had started flying alone at the age of five, I felt suffocated.

We had moved from Florida to Las Vegas earlier that year and the fights had gotten progressively more frequent and the accusations more ridiculous. Chief of which was always the accusation of infidelity. The allegations became so fantastically absurd that I had to wonder about his mental state. While alone in our home together, he thought I was cheating merely by being out of his sight, such as being in the kitchen while he was in the living room - with no one else in the house. The deranged delusions achieved their apex when he accused me of immoral relations while I was standing next to him in public. I doubted even Houdini would have been able to pull that one off, but the mere fact that a man had smiled at me was cause enough to give me the third degree. This ultimate fantasy turned out to be my breaking point.

Despite my legendary flexibility (both physical and otherwise), I found myself to have limits and had already left him twice before this latest separation. Being the kind of person who usually avoided conflict in every fashion possible, I never really knew where I got the strength from each time. Somewhere deep inside I must have had reserves of which even I was not aware.

I had never stepped outside of our marriage, even during our separations, even with his arguments to the contrary. The same could not have been said of him, which possibly also helped to clarify why he was so quick to accuse me of it. Each time I left, he would badger me into returning with promises of change and compromise. I would be worn down and eventually return. Albeit, there would be change and compromise at the start, it would repeatedly be renegotiated, to the point where my wants and needs were compromised completely out of the picture a few months into my return. It felt like everything I was and had ever been I needed to change just to make him happy. I didn't realize until much later that there was no making him happy for even when I changed and morphed myself into everything he told me he wanted, he was still not happy.

Emotionally it was difficult to come to the decision to leave. However, once I had made up my mind and despite not having family or local friends to lean on, it took only a matter of days to separate myself physically from Aaron in a somewhat permanent fashion. I had stayed at one of the Las Vegas Strip hotels for less than a week before I signed the lease to move into a small two-bedroom apartment. Dividing the business, work and finances was another matter altogether, though. I was in my mid 20's and at a significant crossroads in life again. Technically married with a young son, my work life had become so entwined with my husband's, he had made sure of that throughout the years, that at the outset, I did not have a way to support my son and me other than to continue working in the business Aaron and I had founded. Moreover, the company required both Aaron and I for it to be profitable. It would take some time to find projects through my contacts that would not be in direct competition with Aaron as well as to find a way to fill the hole that my exit would create. I might not have wanted to share my life anymore with him - that though did not mean I wanted to hurt him financially and bring operations to a grinding halt. It was quite a balancing act. Separation, for the time being, was no different for me therefore from being married, other than it did cut down the amount of negativity I was exposed to by escaping to the safety of my apartment at night. True to form, Aaron, my husband, attempted to win me back even though I had left little doubt as to my intentions. I never did understand exactly why he would go to the lengths he did to coerce my return to him, when once he had me, all he would do would be to tear me down again. I was doing my best to avoid his advances without taking more drastic measures when I met Ken.

The business was divided into two areas, product knowledge, which was all Aaron, and everything else. I handled the *'everything else'* part, from operations to marketing. I wrote the business plans and the software, controlled the website, print production, graphic design, copywriting, technical issues, partnerships and customer service among other things. Part of the innovation of our customer service, at the time, was being available online. When it came time to decide, who would run this new and novel feature, the choice was a no-brainer. Aaron had a difficult enough time finding the on-switch to his computer. I not only had a natural aptitude but also had a minor fanbase that would seek me out online due to the monthly publication of my humor and opinion articles. This, therefore, like so much else, became my bailiwick and had me online most days for 12 hours straight, fielding questions and making sales and being available to just simply add that personal touch. Sometimes I would be logged in from the office and other times I would be logged in from my apartment. I never could have guessed how this minor idea to improve customer relations would affect my life for years to come.

I did not pretend to know what Ken searched under for my profile to appear; maybe it was as simple as "female las vegas." He would never tell me even when I asked. However, one day unexpectedly I received an instant message from him and we just started joking around. I cannot remember for sure what he said. It was a week or so after a satirical article of mine had been published. The article was on the misguided self-appraisal of collectors and their collections and the feedback had been resoundingly positive. A copy of which was on my profile page. However, I also had a profile picture along with the article and knowing him, there was doubtlessly a comment or two on my appearance as well. Most people would observe on how my eyes would change from fiery green to cobalt blue, particularly when viewed in person. I had received remarks about their color and intensity ever since I could remember and had decided a long time ago that part of what made them stand out so was the long dark hair contrasting the lighter irises.

Ken was initially just another name on my computer screen. Granted a witty and flirtatious name, but all in all just another in a crowd of names. I was not looking for a tryst or any kind of romantic relationship and my online presence, while entertaining at times, was work driven. In the face of so much change, I was trying to simply keep it together and focus solely on my son and providing for him and my obligations as a whole. The fact, therefore, that during those first few weeks he knew what I looked like but I had yet to see a picture of him did not bother me in the slightest. All the same, after about two weeks he sent a picture of himself on a beach in Tahiti wearing a straw brimmed hat. The picture showed that he was tall, built like a linebacker, and fair skinned. Any kind of detail outside of the hat and landscape was difficult to make out, though.

Even if the photo and visual description of him were vague at best, spending 8+ hours together online on an almost daily basis, made for ample opportunity to get to know him in other ways. I knew he lived in Scottsdale, AZ and that he was in big business finance, what exactly that entailed I was not sure of yet. He visited Las Vegas for work and loved to play blackjack. Naturally, all of these were just words on a screen. He could be anyone. Even though it had not been all that long ago when all access to the internet was metered and charged at an hourly rate, stories of online deceptions were already time immortal and plentiful. Despite being aware of the high likelihood of fraud, I took delight in the fantasy of it and had to admit to myself that I was enjoying the banter. I found myself smiling again much more often - no matter who he really was - the banter was one thing that certainly could not be faked.

As the days passed and his presence never waned, the instant messages moved from innocent jokes to risqué ones which moved to flirting outright. I could feel myself blossoming just because of his virtual presence and the words he chose to type out on the screen. After a while, I was not only daydreaming about him but also habitually looking for him every morning when I logged onto my computer. Feelings of attachment were forming rapidly. Fortunately, despite the emotions and despite his clever wordsmithing and my being in a vulnerable state, there was a part of my brain that still knew better than to fall outright for some electronic impulses on a screen. According to the news, being catfished was more the norm than not. The internet was rife with people pretending to be something other than what they were, which made it easier to deem our conversations no more than fun diversions. Then, one day, weeks after his initial contact, he called. The first time I heard his voice, it felt like a bolt of lightning had struck me. I was now able to confirm that at least I had been interacting with a guy online. His voice was so deep, smooth and sensual; even James Earl Jones sounded grating in comparison. This was definitely not a woman or a teenage boy. When he laughed, it was like a mountain shaking off a blanket of snow. It was that moment - with that voice - when it dawned on me, I might be in trouble.

***

CHAPTER 6

"Ugh! Where did the day go? My presentation is first thing tomorrow and I have yet to finalize it. I keep changing how I want to stage the material ... Not to mention PowerPoint can be cumbersome at times," Ken said with a sigh.

"Hmmm, looks like your presentation will be an exercise in extemporaneous speaking then." I was working on filling out some mailing labels while talking to him.

"Is that a long word for seat-of-my-pants?" I could hear the smile in his voice and had to laugh in response.

"I am delighted that I have been standing up for you after all. You really aren't at all as stupid as you look. I think you will do well on the pop quiz yet."

"As long as I get off my extemporaneous," he said in a by-and-by voice. "See! I used it in a new sentence!" I could almost hear the innocent pride of a preschooler in that one. Like a son showing off his first 'A' to his mom.

It took a moment for my mouth to relax enough from the smirk to allow sounds to form. "Two more times and it's yours. Remember to picture yourself naked in case you get nervous ... or is that picture your audience naked?" I asked with an unabashed coyness that surprised me.

Playing right along and upping the ante, his voice dropped an octave, which given its already natural depth I would have thought impossible, and became ultra breathy when he countered, "Maybe, I should picture you naked?"

I was thankful that this conversation was happening over the phone or he would have seen how bright red my face was turning at the thought. Bluffing in personal relationships was so not my forte. In a nonchalant voice as possible I answered, "Will that make you less nervous?"

"Nah ... actually that will just distract me," he responded in an almost off-handed tone with his pitch going back to normal.

With a mental sigh of relief, my nervousness abated and then it struck me that he had just admitted to my having an effect on him. *Me?* Bolstered by his admission of my influence and smiling at the thought of him becoming distracted by my image during his presentation I pictured all sorts of *'male wardrobe malfunctions'*, and could not help but retort. "Not to mention that then there goes your 'extemporaneous', either up into a tent or falling down to the floor."

"Yes, I would have to have some strategically placed file folders or jump into an interpretive dance to distract them from my hard-on." I could feel his laugh resonate through my whole body.

My ears perked up at the word dance. "I didn't know you danced," I responded a bit curious once I recovered from how attracted I was to the mere sound of his laugh.

"I don't." He changed his inflection from playful to disarmingly frank. I could almost see him getting closer in my mind's eye. As if I was being invited to share a part of him few would receive an invitation to, he clarified, "But I would love to watch you dance. Something makes me think that you are probably at your happiest when you are dancing."

His insight caused me to pause. Had I said something along those lines in our conversations in the past? I did a quick rundown of the IM's I could remember and concluded, no. He must have come up with this observation on his own. That was another point in the plus column for him! I decided to confirm his statement. "It is like being in a different world for a few hours. I go into an almost trance-like-state and just act out the music. Sometimes I focus on the lyrics, other times on the melody, countermelody or the beat." I tried to think of a way to draw a parallel to which he could relate. "The only way I can explain it is dancing is for me, like sitting outside sipping on a martini during the twilight is for you." We had spoken about sunrises versus sunsets in the past.

"That light does tend to bathe everything in the most beautiful colors doesn't it? Although that could just be the view through the martini glass talking," he answered thoughtfully and with a reminiscent smile in his voice.

"No, it is not just the martini glass. I think it is due in large part to expert PR and marketing firm the sun hired." I could not help but steer the conversation back to silliness. Humor was one of my many stocks in trade.

"The sun hired a PR and marketing firm?" I heard the confusion in his voice not knowing quite where I was going with this.

"Well, the sun is a star! It only makes sense." If my mind would have had legs and shoes, the tap dancing would have been unmistakable as it attempted to stay half a step ahead of my mouth, stretching my B.S.ing skills nimbly. "I took a trip to Austin, TX and went to this restaurant along Lake Travis. They would make the biggest hoopla over the sunset. People were cheering and banging on things etc. as the sun was dipping down into the water. How else would you explain those actions?"

"You're right. Cleeeearly, it must be the marketing from the sun and not the restaurant," he replied with an amused tone. We were like two school kids sitting at the lunch table and flirting by poking elbows into each other.

"After all, the second most profitable form of writing is advertising copy."

"Only the second? What is the first?" I could hear the creak of the chair as he was leaning back in his office, probably putting his feet up on his desk.

"Writing ransom notes of course!" After a pause, another flash of intuition came to me. "Although if you write the advertising copy accurately, it is pretty much the same thing. 'Give us $50 and we will hand you back your self-esteem in the form of pre-packaged colored powders that you can use on your face.' "

"Hmmm ... speaking of, have I told you how gorgeous you are without any make-up on?"

Taken a bit by surprise with the compliment, I could imagine him looking at a zoomed in picture of myself on his computer as I replied; "Now I am blushing. Don't you have a presentation to finish?"

"I do, but I would rather listen to you. I love figuring out how your mind works." I could hear the long audible sigh on the other end of the connection as the disarming honesty of that statement reached across the desert.

Our conversation lasted for hours longer that day, since Aaron had decided to go out, and I did not have to be concerned on being walked in on. I was still anxious each time I occasionally had to place Ken on hold, worried he might become offended at the interruptions and hang up. However, my fears were uncalled-for; he was always there when I returned. Each kind word he continued to speak was like another drop of water for my parched soul after having received so many ugly words for so many years from Aaron. I was surprised at how quickly the emotional connection between us deepened. How much I had been looking for validation and belief in me. I told him about my mother and growing up and my failed marriage and my concern about my being a good mom and we debated everything from religion to politics to the stock market. Long after the streetlights had come on and despite having spoken for hours, I was still reticent to say goodbye and could feel the sadness before my finger hit the disconnect button. As soon as the silence of the office engulfed me this strange sensation of missing him was everywhere. It was obvious that I needed more of his words and emotion and breath - regardless of having never met the man in person. At least I knew it was a man I was talking to, though. So, he had that going for him - which was nice. When I went to sleep that night, all I could think of was that voice!

The next day when I woke up, I could hardly wait to log back in and see his name online. The mere thought caused my pulse to quicken, my stomach to flutter, and the corners of my mouth to curve up in a perpetual smile. I had never felt quite this enraptured before and I did a quick jump and then spun across the room to reach my computer keyboard. As soon as I realized what I had done and why I had done it, I squashed the thoughts back to their depths. I knew better than to let emotion rule my world. I had successfully been able to discipline my sentiments in the past. Ballet had taught me that. Refusing to cry when my mother would beat me even into high school had taught me that. Surely, I could get these butterflies under control. I threw myself into my work. That had normally been able to accomplish it in the past.

Yet, I kept looking to see his name online and I could feel my disappointment turn to worry as minutes felt like hours. With each move of the clock hand, my heart sank a little deeper. After about 15 minutes of suffering from an exponential increase of disappointment and fear, I mentally smacked myself over my own stupidity. Had we not spoken in depth about his presentation and the long string of meetings ahead for him this day? In my selfish excitement, I had completely forgotten that he would not be online for most of the day as a result. I was being such a stereotype moon-eyed dope! With a sigh, I concentrated on my list of things to do again until I heard those three little Pavlovian words from my computer that made my amygdala salivate if it could have salivated ..."you've got mail."

Subj: hmmmmmmm.........
Date: 8/17 3:42:13 PM
From: FinanceGuy
To: Pandora

My dream.......or should that be Hope.......since you are Pandora........or should that be sexy or delicious friend..........hmmmm.........I think we will go with......

My Hope:

Wonderful hearing your voice ......and while I do apologize for not being able to write to you sooner and for taking so much of your time yesterday afternoon ....I have to tell you that I have not had such a wonderful and meaningful conversation like that in some time.

What happens when fire and intensity........turn to hunger.......is that we become insatiable.......and......well.......I am hungry.......thought I would give you some food for thought.....

I hope that you have a relaxing evening........and here is hoping that if you don't dream.......you continue to at least have a daydream or two........hell try having 69 of them.......there is a good number to shoot for.....

Pardon the pun.........call me crazy..........just as long as you call me......lol

Thinking of the possibilities........

C

###

I was giddy and lightheaded with excitement. Had I been a Southern Belle, I might have fainted with the sudden change in blood pressure I experienced. No one had ever written to me like this before. Those words 'thinking of the possibilities' had my brain reeling and doing the same, despite my best efforts to the contrary. This level of emotion was alien to me and I had to stop myself. My psyche was wandering into areas it had no business sticking its nose into. I should be put in a padded room with a white jacket and a butterfly net, for just merely *'thinking of the possibilities'* with this man that was causing my lungs to expand and contract irregularly just with his words. It took 20 different drafts before I finally hit the send button and decide to exercise extreme restraint.

Subj: Re: hmmmmmmm.........
Date: 8/17
To: FinanceGuy

Thank you for your very sweet and inspiring letter. By the way, I just realized in all of those wonderful hours of conversation, I don't even know your name. I am not sure why it never occurred to me to ask.

As to the hunger, don't they feed you during those meetings? lol

Waiting with bells on to hear your voice again.

Pandora

###

Subj: Re: hmmmmmmm.........
Date: 8/18 9:58:29 AM
From: Finance Guy
To: Pandora

I will call you shortly
My name love........is Charles

###

And that was lie number one!

***

CHAPTER 7

Scott had switched over to the bed and laid there holding my computer, which had been folded into the tablet state while reading the file that contained all the aggregated emails Ken had written me and I him.

"I thought you said his name was Ken," he asked looking up.

"Yes, he lied about his name at first." That statement had not lost its sting even after all this time and I had to bite my lip to bring my emotions back in check because of the chain of questions it would always bring up in my mind. "I should hate him for it, and I do, but still, it's strange how I miss him even now as I am rereading these letters."

"What do you miss most about him?" Scott was in analyst mode. Distancing myself from my emotions I responded by digging deeper into the why's than I typically had in the past.

I split myself mentally into two people again, the person back then who was experiencing the full range of the emotions, and the impartial person sitting in the room with Scott observing my former self. The answer came like a bubble of water on a string from the past to the present. As it arrived, I was able to translate the concept into words and reply to Scott."The way he made me feel. I felt so safe and wanted. He made me feel like I could conquer the world - conquer my situation. I miss that friendship." I could see myself in my mind's eye looking at the person I had been to verify I had gotten it right. I could feel my former-self smiling back and nodding her agreement.

"Why did it end?" For Scott this was a logical follow-up question, for me it was a question I had asked myself probably more often than raindrops fell in Florida.

After countless hours of contemplation, there was only ever one answer that I had been able to come up with. "I'm not sure it ever did. I officially broke up with him - again - for the fifth or sixth time ... I have lost count by now ... about a year ago ... and even though we haven't spoken in all this time ... I expect that we will reunite again at some point. Consequently, it feels like we are still in a relationship. I guess it just went on hiatus as the writing team is trying to figure out how to change the storyline."

"What keeps you around for the next resurrection?" Scott was focusing intently at my face as he stroked my hair while sitting up in bed. I had moved to lay down with my head in his lap staring into space.

"I don't know." I paused to think while he continued to stroke my hair with one hand. He had asked me to look towards the future and I was no longer in need of my past-self. Without thinking about it, my past-self faded out of my mind's eye, leaving only the analytical version of me. "We have undergone so many changes since we first met and it has been interesting trying to figure out how to make the new pieces fit with the old pieces. I know I have changed. He has changed. Both of us have changed." My eyes were intent upon the ceiling as if it held the clues to the answer."Maybe I miss who I was when I was with him back then more than our relationship." I bit my lower lip while deep in thought. "Being with him maybe gives me hope of being that same person again that I once was." The stucco pattern of the ceiling was blurring. "I was happier then and a lot more trusting. I didn't always see the ulterior motives at the time, I guess." Scott had started to massage my hand with his free hand, digging deep into my palm with his thumb while our fingers were entwined as if in prayer and the energy changed. His thumb, which should be therapeutic, was causing my breathing to become shallower and my palm to tingle.

"Do you feel that I have an ulterior motive?" asked Scott as he stopped caressing my hair to lean over and place the tablet on the nearby bedside table without losing contact with my hand. Breaking my intense focus on the ceiling, I became conscious of the warmth spreading from his hand and my palm to the rest of my body. I lifted my head from his lap to allow him to turn and wondered what had caused this shift in energy. Taking advantage of the movement to reposition myself onto the headboard pillow as opposed lying crosswise on the bed; I took back possession of both of my hands and folded them across my midsection as I puzzled over what was happening. There was one aspect of the male psyche that I had a difficult time wrapping my head around - the concept of romantic competitiveness. Personally, displaying interest in someone else was the quickest way to have me lose interest and shift my attention to a more fascinating topic, such as the mating habits of the fruit fly or how long it would take for fingernail polish to be actually dry as opposed to appearing dry. Men, however, for the most part, seem to be pre-programmed to establish dominance over another male even if that male was a mere memory. It was probably why the whole *I'm-only-doing-this-to-make-him-jealous* thing came about to begin with. My intent had not been to use my pain or my longing as an aphrodisiac and then I remembered what he had said at the outset of this conversation. Something about being like that *House* character and having a personal interest and drive in solving puzzles. So maybe that was one of the reasons why he got turned on by sexual history. It would explain why Scott's observable reaction to it all was as if I had hand fed him a bucket of raw oysters.

He turned onto his side to face me and started to caress my arm lightly. When I turned to look him in the eyes, I knew that this had to be the feeling people described when they were recounting an alien abduction, and I could see the answer to my question right there. His eyes were like tractor beams that had locked onto mine and from which, I felt like I could not turn away. Any footing I had gained towards self-possession just moments ago was teetering again.

"No, your motive is quite clear." I was struggling to bring my emotional armor back up. Why was he reacting in such a possessively dominant manner when he hardly knew me? "You want uninhibited sex and my soul and outside of those two things you are reasonably content." What was it about him that made him so irresistible? Was it transference from having just talked about Ken? It could not be that. It had to be something about his eyes, or maybe knowing what that mouth could do once it touched my skin. Whatever the case, he was doing a fabulous job of getting my mind off my longing for Ken, which had seemed all encompassing just moments prior.

"Is that so bad? To want your soul?" were the words that came from his throat as he leaned closer to kiss me. I could see his pulse quickening in his jugular vein and felt mine respond and match his beat. My breathing changed and my eyes, focused on his lips, closing as they tracked his mouth coming closer.

How did he do this? I could feel the searing heat of his body through my robe as I was contemplating my visceral response. How could he go from perfectly ordinary conversation to full out sexual seduction in 2.5 seconds? His lips were so close you would not have been able to fit a sheet of paper between us.

"Is it so bad to want to be inside of you and feel you all wet and wrapped around my cock?" he asked as his right hand reached for my neck and forced my mouth those final few micro-millimeters towards his. I could feel the heat now radiating from my mouth down to my thighs. I could sense myself getting instantaneously wet as his hand traveled from my neck, down my spine to the small of my back and pulled my body towards his. My hands, as if moving of their own accord, shifted to the side of his face so I could kiss him deeper in answer to his questions.

All logical thought had left my brain outside of, *'my God, his lips are soft,'* as my thighs rose up to meet his and my robe parted to expose my lower half. This supersonic-like speed from the mundane to the full-blown attraction was fast becoming our sexual signature. My body required about as little prep time with him as a fighter jet required runway space during a takeoff from an aircraft carrier. He should have been a Navy pilot instead of a psych professor who still maintained a practice. I could feel his hard cock pushing against me, using the weight of his body to pin me to the bed. Finally, he released my mouth and while raising his upper body up on his arms, his hips kept pressing against mine in a wave-like motion. His right hand undid the belt to my robe and exposed my breasts to him. Still propped up, the hand that had just undone my belt moved along my stomach, up towards my breasts, and started massaging them with a soft circular motion. Using those Svengali-like eyes of his, while he was pressing against the wet lips surrounding my clit, he said, "I want to feel you squeeze down on my cock like you did before. I want you to scream until my ears ring, "and with that last statement he pushed himself into my dripping wet pussy. Before I knew what was happening, he was all the way up inside of me again. I could feel my first climactic wave course through my body. My left hand came to my mouth to help quiet my scream, but Scott pulled my hand away in one smooth move and followed it up with, "I want to hear you."

Highly orgasmic anyway, it was normal for me to have four or five to the guy's one. However, even with my propensity towards multiples, I was not expecting that I would be well into double digits by the time Scott finally decided to have mercy on my body and shoot his cum up inside of me for the second time that day within the span of about an hour. There was so much cum, I could feel it dripping back onto my thighs. In one final euphoric contraction of mine, his juices were pushed out and onto the bed.

Getting up carefully, so that the room would only tilt instead of spin, I walked to the bathroom and ran the washcloth under the hot water faucet. Bringing it back, I wrapped it around Scott's still hard shaft and proceeded to clean it and his thighs from our recent encounter. Walking back to drop the washcloth off in the bathroom as well as getting myself cleaned up, I put the robe back on which had come off during our latest sex session. Scott was pouring the wine for both of us and while handing me, my glass said with a smug tone, "So tell me more about Ken."

And, it was back to normal conversation just like that.

***

CHAPTER 8

The curtain of reminiscence I had drawn about me fell off with the arrival of the waiter. I was just finishing my glass of Riesling at *Fleur* as my Tarte Flambe was placed in front of me, a flatbread dish with the consistency halfway between a pita and a cracker and topped with: onion, bacon, truffle, asparagus, crème fraîche. Sandra, always vigilant despite her packed bar, caught my eye and I nodded in her direction. Yes, I would like a refill on my wine. "Another long day at the office?" she asked with a sympathetic smile as she poured my refill. She did not know, of course, that on this particular day, I had actually spent the majority of my time in a hotel room not too far away from here, getting my sexual psyche worked on by Scott instead of my typical workday. "Oh, nothing Shakespeare couldn't turn into a really good play" I answered with a shy smile not actually lying but also not telling the truth either.

However, Sandra would have been right on the money most other days. Being the V.P. of Internet Marketing for one of the familiar casino-resorts located on Las Vegas Blvd., I was known for spending anywhere between 12 to 16 hours a day in the office. I usually arrived by around 5:30 a.m., this way, despite my long hours I could still make it out at a decent hour, spend some time with my son in the early evenings, and have a social life before sleep claimed me for the usual 4-5 hours a night. While Sandra's work differed from my own, not to mention working for an entirely different establishment, casino workers were known for a bond much like those shared by sororities and fraternities. We even had a secret handshake called 'clapping out.' It involved showing the tops and bottoms of the hands to the cameras usually located above and then clapping them together. Anyone who handled casino chips was required to do this move to prove no chips had been palmed. Later this became an inside gag, if not oft used move, when away from the tables covered in felt.

Living in Las Vegas, in general, took an unusually flexible character, however, working for a casino and lasting past the initial 30 days, required that along with a solution driven, and not easily shocked personality to make it. People who worked for a Las Vegas casino saw and experienced things on a daily basis most people only ever read about in books or saw in movies. The Las Vegas reputation, while wild, was nothing compared to the actual occurrences in this town for while Mark Twain was talking about truth, in general, he might as well have been talking about Las Vegas in particular when he said: "It's no wonder that truth is stranger than fiction. Fiction has to make sense." One of the more stellar examples of truth in advertising: "What happens here, stays here." - a slogan utilized in ads by the LVCVA should probably have included something along the lines of "for you wouldn't believe it anyway."

It was common to rub elbows, and other body parts, with everyone from famous entertainers to billionaire tech company CEOs. Of course, that was not even counting the masses who just wanted to live as if they were famous while here on vacation or a convention. Las Vegas was a town that allowed the everyday office worker to have a few days of the red carpet treatment, otherwise impossible to achieve to this extent in any other city but this one. To make all these fantasize reality, required a fast-paced environment, no matter if you were on the front lines or in the office; and necessitated unusual improvisational skills to make life during the customer's short stay with us, appear as if it were a well-choreographed dance.

There was a time when living in Las Vegas automatically meant you worked for a casino. These days, however, while the casinos were still considered the major employers in town, they were not as predominant as they once had been. With the population expansion over the last 20 years, many more industries had cropped up. Therefore, the neighborhoods had expanded further and further away from the Strip mimicking life in other cities. Whereas once proximity to the Strip was quintessential for an efficient commute in a three-shift town, there were now areas marked with stucco homes and cul-de-sacs. These areas had children riding their bicycles and playing on swings in the parks, just like any other suburban neighborhood in a dry mountain town. Some people lived in these areas who despite having a Las Vegas or Henderson address barely made it out to the Strip once a year. Other than seeing the Luxor *Sky Beam* on a nightly basis and utilizing it as a handy tool to navigate by when the GPS would go out, while they went grocery shopping at 2 a.m., they would describe Las Vegas as any other town. Well, any other town that also had a 42.3 billion candela light shooting out of the top of a building, hailed as the strongest beam of light in the world, which could be seen from space, and using it as one would a compass needle. And just like any other town that had slot machines in grocery stores and at the airport and more than the average number of 24-hour stores of all varieties along with being able to buy alcohol at all hours of the day - every day (no 'Blue Laws'). Yes, suburban Las Vegas was just like any other town.

For those of us who worked in the casinos, however, our life was everything people had ever heard of and so much more that our confidentially clause in our contracts would not let us talk about - well not without changing the names to protect the innocent.

After some small talk with the conventioneer sitting next to me, I paid my bill and headed to pick up my son, Troy, from his friend's house where he had been working on a school project. I was not sure why I was surprised to have the first words out of his mouth be "What's for dinner," despite having been fed by his friend's mother. If it were not for his height, I would have thought he was a Hobbit. We stopped off at *Pizza Rock* for some award winning pizza where he proceeded to polish off the entire large pie by himself - as usual. When I ate, it went straight to my hips, when he ate, it just kept adding length to his legs. It almost seemed as if with each 16" bread disk he consumed, he gained another half inch in stature. At age 14, he was already taller than I was and with a stride that would make most runners and climbers jealous. Unfortunately, unlike my son who was used to having multiple breakfasts and dinners and still had his ribs poking through when he lifted his shirt, I was still full from my meal of 30 minutes ago. I opted for some iced tea while keeping him company. Of course, none of the wait staff minded. Not only had we become regulars, but Troy's order alone was the equivalent amount as most would have ordered for two anyway.

"So, Mom. I wanted to ask you a question" he started out with an innocent bat of the eyes.

"How much is it going to cost me?" I replied with a sigh.

"Do the Hallmark people know about you? 'Cause you're a natural! Why do you automatically assume that I am asking for a video game? I mean I am, but why automatically assume?"

"Because you are my son and I have lived with you for 14 years. When you really just want to ask me a question you do instead of prefacing it with 'I want to ask you a question.'" I said in a calm tone as my elbows moved up from my chair to lean on the table, my hands intertwined, and my chin moved to rest on my fingers while staring challengingly into his eyes.

Squirming in his seat he said, "I could have been on an entirely different train of thought such as: Did you know that dolphins are so smart that within a few weeks of captivity, they can train people to stand on the very edge of the pool and throw them fish?"

"So you wanted to ask me about the manipulation psyche of dolphins?" I answered without blinking an eye.

"No, but I could have been." He batted his eyes.

"If I agreed with you then we would both be wrong. So out with it, what is the game and how much will it cost me?" I sat back in my chair with a sigh.

"It's this game that I have been playing with my friends on their account. It will only cost about $45," he said in a rapid-fire voice.

I shook my head. "I don't know Troy. I just hate to see you waste your time on some of these things. "

"Well, I'll blindfold you then," he said with a smile and a twinkle in his eyes.

Ok, I had to admit that the apple had not fallen far from the tree with that one. "Well played! Although you should remember that, it is actually flattery, which will get you everywhere. Did you clean your room like I asked you?"

"Yes," he blinked his eyes in rapid fashion signifying that he was not telling the entire truth.

"When you say yes to having cleaned your room, does that mean that you mainly just cleared a path from your bed to the door?" I asked in a slightly vexed yet amused voice.

"Yes." he replied sheepishly while looking down at the table and back up to me.

I took a long pause debating what to do next. After all, I could not just let him get something for nothing, despite how much I really wanted to give him the world. However, I also did not have it in me that day to hand out one of my infamous hour-long or more lectures. So instead, I just sat and enjoyed watching him squirm. After what must have seemed like hours to him but could not have been longer than a minute or two, I replied, "Ok, I tell you what; you either bring me the head of Alfredo Garcia ... or ... get your room cleaned up to my standards if you would like the money."

"No lectures?" he said elatedly.

"My blood sugar is low. I will have some tiramisu and get back to you." I said dismissively but with a slight smirk.

"Thanks, Mom! I'll do it as soon as we get home. I promise!" He sealed the deal with a warm hug and kiss.

We ordered dessert, paid the bill and proceed home. Troy, true to his word got his room in working order to my standards and I made good on providing my credit card, although, due to the lateness of the hour, Troy only had time to start the downloading process. We both had a 9 p.m. bedtime.

With it almost approaching the time when I turned into a pumpkin, I went through my usual nighttime routine and sat my laptop to charge. As I plugged in the cable, my memory was prompted once again and I thought of Scott and how his long academic fingers looked while holding my tablet. I loved studying his face while he was reading Ken's emails. Sometimes I would read over his shoulder so I knew how to introduce the next one.

***

CHAPTER 9

"What is your favorite sexual position?" asked Ken in his inquisitive and off-handed way. As if, he was asking me about my favorite color. This question, of course, came after having already quizzed me on my sexual history and having examined a good chunk of my likes, dislikes in various online and phone conversations. It was unbelievable how he was able to bring up the topic without even so much as a *by your leave.*

Being European and comfortable with sexual discussions, be they with strangers or friends, as long as they did not end in heavy breathing or wanton touching, I was not fazed by his topic choice. I was though amused that it was a theme he was bringing up with more and more regularity and ever increasing the degree of detail as the emotional and sexual tension grew between us.

"My favorite position you ask? That would be the one I climax in," I replied with a smirk. Humor was the best emotional armor I knew followed only by logic. Both had always served me well to compartmentalize all sorts of emotions. With humor and philosophy as ready weapons, sex was easy for me to discuss due to the lack of sentiment I would attach to it during what I saw as healthy debates on a xxx topic.

"You are a rare find Pandora," said Ken with a smile in his voice.

"A woman who likes sex, Charles? You know there must be at least one or two others around or we would not have the overpopulation issues we do," I replied with a chuckle and my armor was up.

"You are a rare find because you can go from discussing the latest business trends to describing your orgasm in vivid detail without skipping a beat." Well, he might have had a point there.

"I just pay attention to the particulars. That's all. For example, even though no one is officially talking about it, I think these two entertainment companies are a good buy in stocks right now," I said sending him a link over the instant messenger. With my logical armor, still very much up and changing topics to something less Dr. Ruth Westheimer like.

"What makes you say that?" I could hear the amused curiosity in his voice since not only was he used to my tendency to answer his more loaded questions with deflections by now but that I was doing so by broaching a subject which after all was the very world he dealt with day in and day out. What he had lost sight of though in his single-minded pursuit in attempting to make me squirm was that I had dealt with the entertainment industry since I was knee high to a grasshopper and had business insight someone who dealt just in finance would not necessarily have.

"Simply based on the things I have seen in the news. First, some of the biggest exports of the United States are movies and music. Second, not that anyone has made any official statements or anything, but I think both of these companies are going to be purchased by respective larger corporations, and soon. Typically this involves stock swap which will enable you to essentially get a higher value stock for less money."

"Is this the kind of stuff you think about before you go to sleep at night?" he said a bit taken aback despite having just complimented me on my intelligence. I found it curious that people would be surprised that someone with my face would have more on their mind than just manicures and fashion spreads.

"Sometimes, but not lately."

"What have you been thinking about lately?" I could hear the shuffling of papers in the background.

"You. And how you are quite possibly the solution to the clean energy question." The shuffling came to an abrupt halt as I was practicing the age-old strategy that sometimes the best defense is a good offense. It was time to make him squirm. My way!

"Pardon?" His voice had gone up an octave.

"Well, every time I think of what it would be like to have your hands on me, my body starts getting this electrical charge like a battery," I said in a clinical voice and creating emotional distance while acknowledging the elephant in the room. Or rather, the elephant on the telephone wire since we had yet to breathe the same air. It was also my way of conveying information that I might otherwise never have the guts to do. Yes, I could be quite grade-school about the whole grown-up relationship thing.

"Really?" The pitch had not come down yet. Ha! Let's see how he liked them apples.

"Yes. Imagine how much electricity could be harnessed this way if you just went from person to person and gave them an erotic rub down. We would have enough electrical capacity to power the grid for a month easily." It was as if I were making an argument for ethanol vs. petroleum while keeping my emotional armor mostly intact. In the end, conveying romantic interest while using humor made it a lot less scary and reduced the chances of getting feelings hurt in the process. It was also much easier to take it back afterwards under the guise of *"I was just kidding"* or ignoring it all together.

Once he stopped laughing, he said, "I'm not sure that it works quite that way."

"They thought that about the light bulb too until Edison made it happen and practical." I loved making silly arguments in a logical manner. This was how creative people came up with innovative ideas.

"I think you're forgetting about a major component." His voice had gone back to a normal octave.

"Oh? What would that be?" I asked innocently.

"Attraction," he answered matter of factly.

"Hmmm, true. I hadn't thought of that."

"You think?" I could hear the amusement in his voice again.

"The woman's attraction to you might be too high and when merely coming within her vicinity could possibly cause her to implode, actually shutting down the grid." I could have been recalling an article from Scientific American for all the emotion my voice conveyed.

It took a good minute before he could stop his laughter enough to reply, "I don't think that has ever been a problem."

My mind was already working ahead. "You have been too busy concentrating on your IPO's in the male-dominated business you're in to notice the puffs of smoke as the women disappear one by one from sight." Pushing the content into the ridicules took more and more emphasis off the initial confession making it less awkward on my end. It was one thing to admit to an emotion in an email and quite another in actual conversation.

"And here I thought it was just the cologne I had been using." It was inconceivable to me how someone of his caliber would not have a bevy of women around his office door.

"No, I am pretty sure that it is the sexual heat of yours. All self-made individuals have it," I said while taking a step further in our risqué banter.

"Self-made people have sexual heat?"

"Of course! Nothing is quite as attractive as confidence. And it takes confidence not to rely on others to take care of you." I was making a mental bow.

"This is starting to sound like 'Six Degrees of Kevin Bacon,'" he said with an audible sigh.

"One of the nicest guys I know."

"You know Kevin Bacon?" He was evidently surprised that the connection could be made in less than six moves.

"Well, we have hung out at a couple of parties. So, I would say yes. I know him. We've talked anyway." My mind was recalling swapping family stories with Kevin as I answered Ken.

"You are just full of interesting facts."

"Speaking of, did you know that his dad was the seventh cousin to Richard Nixon?"

"The President?"

"No, the rock star. Yes, the President. He is also related to Mark Hamill."

"His dad?"

"No, Kevin Bacon."

"Uhu."

"Speaking of breakfast foods ... "

"Bacon?"

"Yes, so speaking of breakfast foods, here is something my friend Penn Jillette told me." I felt that the Kevin Bacon subject had been exhausted and it was time to move on to the next topic since I doubted he would be a fan of *Footloose* despite my fancy footwork of moving the topic way from sex. I was amazed at how well grade-school tactics worked into adulthood. *'I like you'* followed up with a shove and then running away.

"You're friends with Kevin Bacon and Penn Jillette? Any other names you would like to drop?" His voice had gone up an octave again.

"No, I'm friends with Penn Jillette. Kevin Bacon is just someone I happen to know and who happens to know me and you're the one who brought up Kevin Bacon," I answered patiently while sticking my tongue out at him in my mind.

"I see, ok so Penn, the talking half of the *Penn & Teller* magic team, gave you some spiritual insight into breakfast." I could feel his brain still wrapping itself around that concept as he slowly spoke each word.

"Well, more of an insight to the power of marketing. Did you know that orange juice was not considered a breakfast drink until the orange growers got together and decided to market it as such?" Personally, I had always been amazed at this tidbit of information.

"I feel like less of a rebel now when I drink it after 12 noon without any vodka. Like I said Pandora, you are quite the rare find," he said with a sigh.

"I am certainly glad you seem to think so since I am desperately unable to concentrate on any of the work I brought home with me. There goes my gold productivity star," I sad with resignation in my voice.

After a slight pause, I could almost hear the gears spinning in his mind, as he asked, "You seem to be always so upbeat even now when you are talking about my taking you away from your tasks at hand. Do you ever get down?" I could feel the probe past my emotional armor. Why did he have to pick this one? The topic of sex would have been much easier and less sensitive to maneuver through. I took a moment to choose my words carefully.

"All the time! That is why I am so upbeat." I knew that this statement would not make much sense to the average person as soon as I had said it.

"What do you mean?"

This was one of those times when it helped to have the anonymity of the phone. Much like laying in the dark and talking with a friend, I closed my eyes and peeled back the preverbal layer of skin. If he could handle this answer, he could handle most any answer. "There are so many things that stress me out on a daily basis and so many ways that I fall short of people's and my own expectations on a daily basis that sometimes it can be overwhelming." I paused and took a sip from my tea as I went against character and confessed to my weaknesses. "Most days it is overwhelming. But, that is where my ballet training comes in and I push past the pain and I focus not on my own existence but my responsibilities instead." I was searching for the words until they just came to me. "I think of my son and his needs. The business and its needs, and I just put one foot in front of the other and try to look on the bright side of things. Sometimes that requires not getting any sleep, as I am sure I won't tonight." I had to pause once again as a somewhat painful memory came to mind. "Aaron has called me Pollyanna more than once, but I don't think he meant it as a compliment." I shook the memory off with a laugh. "However, if I don't do those silly things and take a *Monty Python 'Always Look On The Bright Side of Life'* like approach, I would probably just curl up and never get out of bed ... instead of staying up for 72 hours straight and complete a project while still getting to talk to you."

"Well, you know what my mother would say."

"Absolutely not," I answered, in an attempt to recover my emotional equilibrium with a bit of humor.

"That which does not kill you only makes you stronger and Pandora, it sounds like you have the strength of Hercules." The unreserved friendship and admiration in those words was unmistakable, even at this distance.

"Not sure if I have his strength or lack of intellectual fortitude, but yes I suppose I have one or the other." It was not always easy to accept kind words from people.

"Considering you are one of the smartest people I know, I will go with strength."

The conversation lasted well past midnight before my voice finally gave out. With a hoarse, "good night" I hung up the phone, poured a cup of coffee, before attacking the mountain of work that had to be completed prior to the next morning. Tired and yet invigorated, the latter probably due to the 3 cups of coffee I had downed within the first hour, I knew there was a smile on my face without having to look in the mirror. He had viewed a weakness of mine and had done the unexpected: instead of shying away, he had not only understood but also drawn me closer to him. I could feel my armor on the verge of crumbling all together and allowing him into the deepest parts of me - physically and emotionally.

Despite the euphoria created in stacking: emotion, lack of sleep and caffeine; there was a nagging feeling in the back of my punch-drunk brain that he had left something important unsaid as of yet. I decided it was just the lack of sleep that had me all addle-brained before I closed my eyes to grab an hour catnap prior to having to be up and about again.

***

CHAPTER 10

Scott had developed a nervous habit back in high school of twirling a highlighter or pencil while reading whatever book had been assigned by the teacher for the class. Ever since, it was difficult for him to read for any extended amount of time without keeping his hands and fingers busy in the process, even when there was no need for quickly highlighting passages or making notes for quizzes and tests.

Having Pandora across his body as he dug into her history, he found himself with one breast in his hand while the other held the computer as he would a book. The breast turned into an excellent substitute for his ingrained habit. Instead of twirling a pencil, though, his fingers kept thumbing her nipples seeing as her breasts were within easy reach and had a great bouncy quality to them.

It was a difficult choice in deciding which part he was enjoying more, the unrestricted access he was getting to Pandora's heart or the unrestricted access he was getting to her feminine physicality. All he knew was that he had not felt this relaxed and yet aroused with interest with anyone ever. It was something worth contemplating once time allowed.

Taking only a moment to watch one of the waves the massaging of his thumb had caused, and feeling the hypnotic security-blanket-like effect it had on him, he turned his attention back to the emails.

***

CHAPTER 11

Subj: a good morning.........
Date: 9/21 10:03:24 AM
From: FinanceGuy
To: Pandora

My Love:

As I know that you are most likely on your way to begin your busy day......and, of course, I must get to mine as well, I wanted to take just a moment to wish you the best of days today and a great weekend ahead.

Thank you for the wonder of you in the morning, I think I can almost feel your smile from here.......as I know I can feel how tired you are. This, of course, is something that I will bear the blame for, for the more time I spend with you, the more difficult it becomes to bid you adieu. Even if it is just for the night. I hope that your incredible energy level will return very soon and you will regain the productivity that we missed together yesterday. But then again, yesterday was productive.....emotional productivity is nowhere to be found.......other than in the heart. There is no transaction......no IPO.......no debt deal.......no saving of a troubled company.......that will ever replace.......being understood.....being alive with lost emotion.......and the wonderment of knowing someone amazing.

So there you have it.........the rest of my good morning to you. Be safe...... I hope you slept tight........and don't forget to look at the stars....for someday you just might see me there.......looking right back at you ....it could happen.

Meet me in my dreams...........

###

Subj: Re: a good morning.........
Date: 9/21
To: FinanceGuy

Hmmm ... meet you in your dreams? I keep trying to explain to you that I gave up dreaming a long time ago, but I suppose if anyone could make me dream again, it might be you. When I think of you, I hear water in my mind. Like a brook - calming and energizing at the same time. I no longer worry about that day's particular list of things to do, although there, it's not as all-consuming as it was before. My mind now has time to think about things outside of the immediate tasks ahead of me. So, maybe, in that way you have caused me to dream again.
Of course, that might be the sleep deprivation talking. I think you must have worked for the government at some point and learned the finer arts of interrogation, of which sleep deprivation is thought of being better than any synthetic truth serum (in my opinion anyway). NOT that I would have any experience administrating truth serums outside of the sort found in the occasional wine shaped glass :-) .

Through it all, though, I still don't understand what about all of this ... all of me ... attracts you. You are single and the world is your oyster. You can do anything. Be with anyone but you are deciding to pursue me. Me! Who does not even live in the same state much less the same city. Are there no women left in the Scottsdale or Phoenix or heck the state of Arizona as whole? You are successful, tall, handsome, and write as if Shakespeare had been your apprentice and the Kama Sutra was just a pamphlet you threw together. I wish I knew what to do with you.

I guess for now I will just enjoy the sound of running water and soft piano music.

Pandora

P.S. I hope that pictures I attached are not too much.

###

***

CHAPTER 12

I have heard it said that a picture is worth a thousand words and that a word is worth a thousand pictures. If there was ever a statement that could sum up my relationship with Ken, particularly in those first few months before we met in person, this came as close to it as any. During our time together I must have sent him what amounted to hundreds maybe even close to a thousand different pictures of me. Ken, in turn, replied in just as many if not more so words. Words of appreciation. Words of longing. Words of delight. Words that instilled confidence in me I thought I had lost - if it had been present ever. Words that would penetrate time and again through my well constructed emotional armor of distancing humor. After all, I was one of the millions of women who fought weight on a daily basis and all the mental anguish that went along with it. Luckily, here was where for once my height was in my favor. My height combined with my genetic predisposition to distribute the weight evenly made the additional weight easier to hide while in clothes.

My picture taking started back with Aaron. Throughout our marriage, despite my weight, he had consistently been after me to take risqué photos for him. Self-conscious though about the extra padding here and there, I had typically refused. About a year prior to meeting Ken two things had happened, I had lost around 50lbs and had purchased a digital camera. Pictures no longer required being developed and seen by your local drugstore clerk and I had a new wardrobe to show off. It started out as a Christmas present for Aaron, prior to our move to Las Vegas, and turned into a monthly photo journal. All it took was a tripod and the extensive use of the timer on the camera to start creating some photo magic. I would take the picture and then run to see the image on the preview screen and either delete or keep it based on how attractive I thought that particular angle or pose was. Since I was now both photographer and model, and I could make corrections on the fly and see the results almost instantly. As such, the learning curve of the optimum way to stand, the best lighting and background, props, bevel, and tilt was a small one. All the skills I had learned back when I was younger and modeling came back to me. However, back then I never considered my attractiveness. Now, being older I could see I was photogenic. With my cadet-chin, cinched-in waist, and curves in all the right places, it was difficult to find a bad angle. Even still, some poses were more flattering than others and despite deleting more pictures than I kept, those that remained in a session, numbered higher than a standard roll of film would have typically held. I could see that I looked better than I had when I was 18 and accordingly I started to lose some of my old inhibitions. Aaron was so amazed at the quality that he had kept a boudoir-style print on his desk even after our separation.

People had been telling me my whole life long that I was beautiful. Positive statements, particularly when one had been raised by exacting teachers and parents, were not always the easiest to believe about yourself. It was not until I started taking those pictures of myself - on my own - that it dawned on me that they might possibly be saying nice things about me for a reason. I was becoming an early trailblazer for the selfie generation and the psychological mindset and borderline addiction that accompanied it. After a while, it had become such a habit of mine, that albeit the initial purpose was to provide a present for my then husband, it had turned into an act of self-affirmation.

Once I separated from Aaron, it seemed as if I was taking pictures purely out of habit and for really no reason other than to look at them myself. Well, and to possibly document my appearance for when I would be 80 years old and providing proof to my grandchildren that their grandmother had once been younger. There was no one to share them with - that was until Ken came along.

There was being told you were beautiful. There was being told you were beautiful by someone that mattered and whom you respected. And then - there was being gushed over by someone that mattered and whom you admired and felt the same way about in return. That last one had been foreign to me until Ken and wound up being the most exhilarating feeling in the world for me. Within less than two months of knowing him, Ken had become my personal designer pharmacologist - setting off chemical reactions in my brain as neurons fired in areas that were ordinarily unused. I had never thought of myself as being able to captivate by my sheer presence. Ken, within a matter of 50 days, made me feel feminine and light and yet still strong and competent and cherished. Through his words, his thousands of words, both on the computer and in our ever-increasing phone conversations, I saw my pictures differently. As I came into my own through his eyes and his molding of me, I could feel this strange kind of power growing inside that I had never appreciated or consciously used before - I knew I was sexy. I would hear and read words on almost a daily basis directed at me I had only read in works of fiction prior. I felt caressed and kissed without ever being touched and this confidence within me was budding with every response to batches of pictures I would heap upon him week after week.

Subj: amazing.......
Date: 9/21 9:57:51 PM
From: FinanceGuy
To: Pandora

You completely gorgeous creature:

I sit here.......somewhat dead tired.........yet wide awake........and all that I can come up with is amazing as I am looking at your pictures. Rest assured that once sleep deprivation finds its cure with a solid night's sleep........amazing just might be replaced with a more precise definition of you.

I wanted to express both a sincere thank you.......and a gift of my conscious to you this evening.......an evening that will most appropriately be filled with a strange hope.....intense thoughts of magic.......of chemistry.......and of this overwhelming mystery that is you.

I feel enlightened by this day, but this, of course, has always been the case with you. I am captured, but at the same time free. My imagination........my hunger.......my passion all have this strange new energy.........energy of possibility.......energy of hope........and the definity of this day.......a day somewhere in the not too distant future.......when this man.....will have the silent whisper of you.....with perfect eyes.........and everything else that is amazing.........simply saying hello.

Capturing emotion in words........is not one of my strongest suits.........however......I must say this with all sincerity........I love the way you dance...........and I love dancing this dance with you........ even if it is while we are not in the same room.

As my eyes keep refocusing on the snapshots of your soul that you sent today ...... it becomes clearer that ....While you may be every man's fantasy.......... to me....... you just might be every best part of every dream I have ever had.......

Beautiful evening to you gorgeous.......

Sweet dreams.........

###

Subj: Re: amazing.......
Date: 9/22
To: FinanceGuy

Charles,

I woke up to an email that should have had a warning label attached. How is it possible to have someone who is driven and successful in business be also this eloquent and seductive? I read your emails and they take my breath away - literally. I just simply forget to breathe as I read them. It takes my automatic nervous system to knock on my lungs and remind them to expand for my brain to register: 'oh yes, it might be a good idea to actually use those nostrils to move some oxygen from the outside in'.

I am not sure how many IQ points I will lose with each email of yours knowing how I keep depriving my brain of an adequate oxygenated blood supply, but whatever it is, I feel it will be worth it. You make me smile in ways I had not thought possible.

I am counting the seconds until I hear your voice again.

Pandora

###

Scott's hands started a patterned rhythm of caressing and squeezing as his breathing adjusted to the pacing of the words he was reading. Pandora, enjoying the caressing touch, shifted slightly so as to allow for a more natural angle for Scott's arm.

***

CHAPTER 13

"Tell me about the last time you masturbated," asked Ken.

"It's always back to sex with you isn't it? I am a mother and don't have a sex life. You, on the other hand, are a single guy and should be swinging from the rafters having wild orgies every single night," I answered trying to deflect the question.

"Hmm, somebody neglected to copy me on that memo. Any idea where these wild orgies happen?"

Banter I was comfortable with. Banter I could do. Banter allowed my armor to stay intact. "Not sure but according to Jeff Foxworthy single people have the best sex stories."

"My sex stories are boring. You, on the other hand, are sensually fascinating and I love to learn what makes your inner goddess tick." I would hate to be up against him during a negotiation. The seductive quality of his voice was making it more and more difficult to sidestep the question, but I tried nonetheless.

"My inner goddess is quite practical," I answered.

"How German of you." I could hear the soft laughter. "So, tell me how a practical person masturbates. What do you think about?" Like a dog with a bone, that was Ken and this line of questioning.

"I guess it's a jumble of things." Should I tell him? Would disclosing the truth make me seem 'easy'? It was one thing to joke about the past sexual exploits. Admitting to the present was a step closer to intimacy I was not sure I should take. Of course, chances of ever meeting in person were slim anyway. Adopting a deep breath but keeping my voice as non-emotional as possible I dove into the wave."You have been entering my mind frequently." *There it was! I said it!* "Of course, these types of conversations are not helping the matter any."

"I have? Hmm, maybe it is because you have me all adrift as well." He took a pause and I could hear his breath before he continued, "I see your eyes every time I go to sleep at night."

"Wait ... what?" I replied somewhat hesitantly and incredulously. "I have that much of a hold on you?"

"I look at your pictures more often than I probably should." He laughed at his own folly. "I have my laptop out, lying in bed and working and yet just can't help myself but pull your images up from time to time." Another pause before he went on. "You and I have shared a glass of wine together this way a few times."

I had to let that last part sink in for a moment. I was not quite sure if I should feel creeped out or flattered. I decided to go with flattered. "I can honestly say that you are the first man to have told me that. I hope the vintage was a good one." I had to smile at the thought. "I have never had drinks with your photo,... but I have traced the outline of you with my mouse on the screen imagining what it would be like to touch you." I was going to stop there, and it would have been perfectly acceptable to stop there, but, what the hell, in for a penny, in for a pound. "And when I do, I keep wondering what it would be like to kiss you." I could feel my face getting bright red at the admission and was just thankful that he could not see me. Here we had discussed various sexual anatomies as if we had read an article about a study in *Scientific American*, with no qualms. However, admitting that I wanted to kiss him turned my cheeks a fiery red.

"You do? Hmmm ... I think if I would ever get the chance to kiss you, it would be about as close to heaven as I could get without actually dying."

I had not realized I had been holding my breath. After taking in, some much-needed oxygen replied, "Why is it that you are not taken again?"

I could hear the big sigh on the other end of the line and the creak of leather as he was probably leaning back in his chair before answering, "I'm a machine. I tend to spend a lot of hours in the office." I could hear another deep intake of breath as he continued, "I was in a relationship not too long ago."

"You recently broke up with someone?" This was news that could explain a lot of things.

"Yes."

"What happened?"

"I found pictures of another man in her drawer. Come to find out she had been cheating on me for a while." This explained a multitude of nagging issues I had had and made this internet search a bit more plausible now.

"I am so sorry to hear that." My heart went out to him as I said it. It was never easy being passed over for someone else and at that moment I wished he were in the same room so I could hug him or even just squeeze his hand in comfort.

"Story of my life," he replied with a laissez-faire sound in his voice. "I have never been that good at relationships. In college, I typically would lose the girl to the guy with more money, better looks, bigger dick ... whatever. I became a pro at being second best. It is probably what drove me to work even harder in business because I hated the taste of silver and bronze in my mouth."

"Hmm, referencing the metals when you are talking about losing. Did you play a sport?" I had to change the topic to something less charged and go back to my safeguards of logic and humor. Compartmentalization was the key to a happy life after all.

"I did the typical gentry sports: lacrosse and rowing." I could hear the tension lessening.

"No football?" I asked a bit surprised since he undeniably had the built for it.

"No, I wasn't good enough for college ball. Played some in high school, though."

"Where did you go to college?"

"*Stanford.*"

"I've heard of the school. That is one of those newer upstarts isn't it? I mean compared to some of its east coast counterparts like *Harvard, Princeton,* and *Yale.* Honestly, I am surprised that they even bestowed it with the University designation instead of College. So what happened? Couldn't get into a real school?" I hoped I had not pushed the envelope too far, with my rib poking. *Stanford* was an amazing school by all accounts, but there are those that felt the only real education to be had was on the east coast. Others would argue that there was no education to be had in the Americas at all - if education was judged on founding dates. *Stanford* was founded in 1885 while *Harvard* was established in 1636 and *Oxford* was so old that no one can remember when it was established although the evidence did show that teaching existed there in some form in 1096. The Titans probably had their children, the Greek Gods, educated there. This would explain the British accents Zeus and the like would take on when portrayed in movies.

Fortunately, Ken was not taking offense to my trash talking and instead decided to volley the banter right back at me."It costs less to move from L.A. to *Stanford* than all the way across the country. And I had the added bonus of not having to get a new license. Just had to mail in my address change."

"Of course. I hadn't thought of that. I think given the choice between a great education and not having to go to the DMV, I would pick not standing in a DMV line for half a day, too. Great thinking!" The ball was squarely back in his court.

"Not having an Ivy League education has its advantages sometimes. *Stanford* teaches you to think for yourself being the rebel upstart and all." Point and match went to Ken on that one.

"Understood *Mr. Pompous Stanford Guy*," I replied as I was conceding the verbal sparring match.

"That's my Indian name, but on my license it just says *'Sex God.'*" Of course, it did.

"Is that the meaning of Charles? Sex God? I love learning new things." If he wanted to be sophomoric about the thing, I could accommodate. "So *Mr. Sex God*, what is the craziest sexual thing you have ever done in your life?"

"There was this one time, in Lacrosse Camp ..."

I interrupted, "Uhh, I take it Lacrosse was a co-ed sport during your time?"

"No. But the parties were."

"Good point. So this one time at camp ... "

"Yes, this one time at Lacrosse Camp I was on my computer and instant messaged this girl named Pandora in Las Vegas."

I could not help but laugh, as I replied, "Not funny!"

"Is that why you are laughing? Because it's not funny?" he asked innocently.

This time, it was my turn to be the bloodhound on the trail, though. "Fess up, wildest sexual experience."

There was a long pause as Ken was evaluating which story to share with me. "I had a threesome with one of my teammates, a very good friend of mine, and this girl who was in our psychology class."

"A groupie?"

"A study partner," he replied with suppressed laughter as if the thought of a young girl fawning over a college athlete was as farfetched as seeing a real life griffon."All three of us in close proximity in the library, after study drinks talking about human sexuality and things just kind of happened. We were young, dumb and full of cum." Taking control of the conversation again he asked, "What about you?"

As every good lawyer and interrogator would, I had my answer prepared prior to having asked the question. I replied with no hesitation whatsoever, "Can't say I ever did the threesome thing, but did have sex in the stairwell of a mall once and also on top of the hood of a car in the middle of a cornfield."

"Ever thought of doing either again?"

"No, once was enough. Sometimes the fantasy is more exciting than the reality when it comes to sex."

"What have you been fantasizing about lately?" he asked leading the conversation right back to its start.

I was, however, not ready to go back to the emotional soul-bearing of earlier, so I flipped a mental switch and became a rational observer. I knew what he was looking for and decided that the best way to take control of the conversation again was to take the sexual discussion to another level. "Ramming your cock down my throat," I replied in a voice as if I were talking about ingredients for bread baking.

"Schwing." I could hear him gasping for breath at that statement.

"Breathe," I replied laughingly taking pleasure in his reaction. It was strange how my saying the things I had, made me feel more distant from him while his response pulled me back closer, effectively canceling out my attempt to create an emotional gulf.

"Wow, you didn't pull any punches on that one." His voice sounded slightly off balanced.

"Sometimes I have to shock you." I never changed my inflection from the analytical conversation tone. Pulling back once again I continued, "Like telling you that last night as I went to bed, and I could feel the sensation of the sheets against my body, I couldn't help myself but run my hands all over my skin as I was thinking of you."

While the emotional level of my voice stayed at the same intensity as discussing the weather, his reaction was quite clearly not as even keel when he exclaimed "Oh my God!" under his breath.

Since I was doing well, I decided to stick with my near monotonous delivery. "I then took out both the dildo and the vibrator and leaned back onto the pillows as I turned on the vibrator in one hand and imagined what it would be like to feel your skin and taste your mouth."

He audibly whimpered in response. It was like listening to a wounded animal.

While remaining completely emotionless, I continued, "I tried to imagine what it would be like to look into your eyes and have yours looking into mine. Without meaning to my other hand took the dildo and pushed it up inside of me while the vibrator was still working on my clit."

"Holy shit!" I could hear the distress in his voice as he was, what I could only assume, trying to maintain his composure on the other side.

"My back arched up and my eyes closed. I wanted to bite down on my finger, but I didn't have a free hand, so I just turned my face into the pillow as, what felt like a million volts of electricity, coursed through me."

My analytical side remained in control as I elaborated on the story, his rational side, by the sounds of it, had escaped him a few minutes back. "Wow!" was the only response I gave him time for, before pressing on.

"I started to move the dildo in and out of me very slow at first. I could see that my outer lips were sticking slightly to it as I pulled it out ever so gently before I pushed it all the way back in with a thrust."

"I think I am starting to leak pre-cum here."

"I did that a few times, slowly out and hard back in. I could feel my walls squeezing down on the dildo making it more and more difficult to push it back in and almost not wanting to let it go as I was pulling it out."

"Amazing description."

"Eventually there was less and less time between pulling and pushing and it changed to just a steady rhythm of in and out."

"What a visual."

"I could see my cum already on the dildo, all creamy and white. Some of it was getting on the vibrator that was still working on my clit."

"Wow, you are amazing ... Just amazing," I heard him say over what sounded like a zipper being lowered.

Never missing a beat, though, and with my voice as even keel as ever, I continued."Finally, I couldn't stand it anymore and I took the cream covered vibrator and positioned it to rim my other hole while the dildo was still in my pussy."

"You are ... sexual napalm." I could tell that he was close to conceding.

"Had it not been for my need to cover my mouth with the pillow so as not to let the whole neighborhood hear what was going on, I would have seen myself gush all over the dildo."

"Yup ... that just ... confirmed it." There was a shakiness to his voice that had not been there before.

"I did, however, see all that creamy whiteness once I pulled it out and cleaned both the dildo and the vibrator off," I said as if I were discussing cleaning the dishes.

"Did I say that you are a rare find?" There was a softness in his tone which was new. While I had maintained my equilibrium, it was obvious that I had thrown his. Funny how men reacted to sexual descriptions while women could form shopping lists in their minds.

"A little sore, but very satisfied I put on a long shirt, slid back into bed and fell asleep thinking of having you wake me up with your dick inside of me."

"Uncle! I give up!" His self-control had reached its limits.

Laughingly I decided to allow myself to respond with a smile in my voice instead of my robotic accounting and said teasingly, "I tooold you I was detail oriented." Before he could respond, reversed back to my grade school antics of taking it all back and said, "And if you believe the story I just laid out for you, then I have some oceanfront property in Arizona I would like to sell you." Little did he know, though, what I had described was an actual play-by-play of events. I would not have been able to give the vivid descriptions of it otherwise.

"That is quite the gift of storytelling you have then. Sure you are not Irish?"

With a laugh, I answered while affecting an Irish brogue, "No ... Not that I know of."

The longing was unmistakable when he said, "In my next life I want to come back as your sex toy."

***

CHAPTER 14

Pandora had to be the most interesting psychological puzzle yet! Magnetic! That was the best word Scott could up with as he sat reading through Pandora's email correspondence and listened to her background explanations. Maybe the word was hypnotic instead, as his eyes tracked the movement his hand had caused in her breast. Watching the waves was as strangely relaxing as the proverbial pocket watch used to induce trance-like states. With his thoughts traveling back in time, he was thinking of when he had seen her profile for the first time. Her *je ne sais quoi* had stood out even when all he knew about her were a few words on a screen. Her written summary of herself had been a mix of sensuality and intelligence, qualities not easily found together in such a medium. While her words had gotten his attention, her eyes were what had kept it. He had not known what she looked like when he contacted her initially. Once she sent him what she considered a common work profile picture, he knew without a doubt that those eyes should have been registered as lethal weapons. Her eyes seemed to leap out of the screen and grab his soul. To gaze into their depths alone required using a mental safety harness or risk losing touch with reality. Fortunately, he had been up for the task. It was invigorating diving into her in such a manner and having garnered her trust by his sheer semblance. None of those things, though, the impression given by her writing or image, had prepared him adequately for meeting her in person or gazing at her as she was lying in bed with him.

With his eyes still utilizing her breasts as a hypnotic focal point, his mind had been debating the hows and whys of her attraction even prior to their meeting. Genetics certainly had played their part from her body in general to even the shape and color of her eyes. It was the pain, though, a pain he had only guessed at at first, but had recognized the instant she had opened the hotel room door, that made them so compelling. He should know. This was not only what he did for a living, but what he had actually lived. Scott and Pandora were like mirrors of each other. As he was reading and listening to her history, he discovered that this woman who appeared to the world around her to be unshakably strong and sure of herself, a rock to tower above and to which others clung to, needed protection more than most people would have ever thought. It was this pain and the resulting strength of having born it for so long, that had called out to him and drew him in. For he knew firsthand the strength such acts required to live with day in and day out.

He had been able to identify the pain of rejection, abandonment and betrayal long before he had honed his professional skills and added letters of certification to his last name. Long before he had even graduated from elementary school. He, of all people, knew that this type of emotional pain created a push and pull. It pulled the nurturer closer to the afflicted and caused the afflicted to press the nurturer away. Unless - unless there was great trust. Only then could homeostasis be created, something he had yet to fully achieve for himself.

Scott knew the game well - that endless spinning of want. That need to be fulfilled while fearing it at the same time. It could be enough sometimes to have one quite the endeavor altogether such as his vow of bachelorhood after his fiancé had left him for a fashion photographer back in college. Claudette had been the last straw for him after a long and distinguished line of relationship failures. He had not allowed himself to fall under a woman's spell after her. Of course, Claudette alone, while tragic, did not cause him to become an emotional ninja. Had it just been her and maybe a forlorn love or two or even three while, in high school, he might have been just like everyone else. Fortunately for his students and patients, the depth of female betrayal started long before his first sexual encounter, long before learning how to drive or even learning the times tables. Back when he had lived in Texas.

His own mother had abandoned him and his sister as children for a year while getting married to their stepfather. He was 7 years old at the time and had just started the second grade. While living in a weekly rental, she did have the conscience to stop by and drop off some food every other week or so, even if it was not usually enough, and check on her children to see if they were still alive. Looking back, he had wondered if she secretly longed for them to meet with some terrible accident to free her from motherhood. Unfortunately, they were survivors. Despite the odds, they would hang on, day after day, week after week, month after month. During that year, school became the only safe haven for Scott. It was at school that he knew he would receive at least one government-subsidized meal a day and maybe some handouts from well-meaning students. Food and hunger became the tools that would shape his life's preferences. Unlike other children his age, he detested the weekends for the hunger pains could get overwhelming. Was it any wonder that he never minded going to school and that his positive association with learning and school would last him a lifetime? Unfortunately, his distrust of women would as well as would his juxtaposed and almost pathological need for female approval. It was a psychological catch 22. With no solution in sight, he believed that he was destined never to be sated.

When Scott turned 8, his uncle by sheer accident discovered what his younger sister had done and came to rescue his niece and nephew who had been on their own for the better part of a year by then. The reunion should have been joyous. Unfortunately, just as hope had entered back into his life, his mother would almost obliterate what was left of his psyche. Remarried and her secret exposed to the entire family, his mother took his older sister Emily to live with her and her new husband but refused to take her only son. She treated her son much like male lion cubs were treated when their mothers took on a new male partner and before the cubs had achieved an age of maturity. With few options open to Scott, and after many broken promises, he was eventually taken in by his paternal grandparents. This was how he came to live on the ranch and inherit it upon his grandfather's death.

Some considered ranching a hard life, for Scott it was an easy burden to bear. In many ways, it was just like school and as such, he never thought of it as hard work. There was a clean, direct line between cause and effect. He understood the expectations and successes were quickly defined and thusly obtained. There was no guessing needed. He would labor side by side with his Grandfather, tending the animals and learning about his responsibilities. It was during their shared work and the never-ending stories that poured out of his Grandfather's mouth where his life values were instilled in him and the bond between the two was forged that would withstand the test of time and death. He would hear that raspy voice in the back of his mind as it guided him through difficult choices and periods long after his Grandfather was no more and long after he had moved away from Texas and anyone who knew his sordid history. The boy who had not been wanted by his own mother.

In high school, he found an easy way to garner the female validation he sought - sex. Being good at sex was empirical for the most part and just as school and ranching had been, there was a direct and clear line between cause and effect. He would touch here and she would moan like so. It was difficult to deny the physical evidence of a woman's enjoyment when she would leave opaque trails on his cock. Her satisfaction of the act was self-evident, was a total result of skill, and did not require having a traditional mother and father at home. Each time he saw his cock covered in gobs of female cum it was like getting a pat on the back and hearing the words "well done - well done indeed" in his mind.

Unlike sex - love and acceptance (or at least his own perception and impossible Hollywood like expectations of them) would elude him time and again no matter the partner choice. Scott accordingly took an interest in psychology to understand those who kept rejecting him. His only successful relationships were one-night stands for when he would attempt to traverse a path of trust it would inevitable dead end in a cul-de-sac of betrayal. His repeated failures when he did foray into the emotional bonds as a teenager and young adult taught him that a person's perception of someone else consists of more than just their direct actions and tangible assets. And assets Scott had plenty of ever since high school. Not only was he tall, intelligent and personable, but he also had money now and due to ranching, was skilled at almost any sport he became a part of; and yet girls would find reason to leave him time and again in those impressionable early days. They would never mention his family, but he knew that was the main reason why.

There was no denying Scott's destiny to enter the psychological profession. While some could argue that the events set in motion before he was even a pre-teen could have been adjusted later in life, by the time he became a sophomore in college and upon the devastating break-up with his fiancé, it was the only career path that held any interest for him. He knew that he would probably never forgive Claudette or his mother, and by extension all women, or escape the numbness a lifetime of female treachery and abandonment had generated. While his family history had not been directly to blame for his break-up with Claudette, he concluded after hours of introspection, that his family history had not allowed him to learn the social skills and bonds others had. As such, his brain had never created those crucial neural pathways necessary for successful romantic relationships in adulthood. He had to accept that his brain was damaged in this way - that he was damaged. It was freeing and devastating to recognize about himself.

Afterwards, every time someone would come close, he would look for a reason to find the "*aha,*" that moment when he found a fault so great that he had to leave, that he had to lash out, that he had to get even before they had a chance to discover his brokenness. That was until now!

Pandora, while having a different background, had the same pain as he did and it called to him and cut through those stellar defenses of his, which he had built over the years, usually incorporating humor. He felt protective of her and something else he could not quite put his finger on - possessive maybe? He had never felt possessive of anyone after Claudette. He could smell the danger of it - the possibility of his emotional annihilation - as he could feel his brain trying to shake off the hypnotic state he had slipped into. As more of the grey matter was waking up, he could see he was becoming invested again. However, the question loomed in his mind if he could be strong enough when she would turn her back on him as everyone else had? A part of him hoped he would never need to find out. History had taught him though that the only sure success for him laid in the lack of his emotional attachments. That when those irritating chemicals that brought about love and affection were coursing through his veins, that they clouded not just his blood but his judgment as well. There was only one problem with all of this. After years of having sidestepped great pain with his cognitive control, he had deprived himself in the process of great joys as well. One only came at the risk of the other.

He knew, unlike his propensity to shy away from exposing himself to such risk in the past, with Pandora he had to try at least. Feeling fully awake now, he felt like he had had a double espresso and there was this need to formulate a plan of attack to assure mutual emotional success. While not typical, the first sure sign that there was valid reason for his sense of hope was how quickly the trust had been built between them. Trust that neither had given to people who had known them for much longer than they had known each other. Trust was most easily built upon common experiences and acceptance which with Scott's and Pandora's histories explained why there had been little deep bonding with others. Few had experienced the depth of deception like he had - like she had - like they both had. Their kind of pain brought the rest of life into stark clarity and in the retelling of it, bound them to each other. It was as if they had been in the same trenches battling a losing war of acceptance and understanding until they met and their mental and sexual energies combined.

A thought dawned over Scott's cerebral horizon as the solution became clear to him. Pandora was his best chance at normalcy and he felt that in turn he was hers. He could already feel himself falling for her and was wondering what steps he could take to solidify their already strong foundation and not have his fear of abandonment color their reality? The first agenda item would be to help her do what she had asked of him, to help her get over Ken. After all, was it not Zig Ziglar who had said that if you help enough other people achieve success that it will help you to achieve your own success? The next part required a bit of manipulation of *Mother Nature*. In the process of exercising the ghost of Ken's memory, he would flood Pandora's (and by extension his) system with oxytocin, the "*love drug*" produced by the body during orgasm. The accompanying guilty conscience he would have to face was nothing a Hail Mary or two could not help clear. Besides, he was exposing himself to the same relationship super glue.

Excited at having a tangible goal, Scott's mind was quickly sketching out the details of his plan as his hand reached for his security blanket, her breasts, and started again playing with her nipple absentmindedly. Already feeling the dopamine hitting his bloodstream as the powerful, visceral need intensified, his hand distractedly reached past her nipple and past her abs. He was letting his fingers do the walking so-to-speak as he was drawn to exploring that g-spot of hers that seemed to be within such easy reach every time he slid into her.

CHAPTER 15

Subj: some wonderful thoughts.........
Date: 9/25 9:44:07 AM
From: FinanceGuy
To: Pandora

My gorgeous creature:

To say that I had a carefree past few days, days without wonderment, without emptiness........without craving ....would be simply put....a farce. I have this strange hunger......strange urgency with you. I sit here, just simply wanting you.....wondering if you are dreaming, wondering if you can still hear my voice running through your soul. Without being too melodramatic, I could not sleep the last few days. Sure I normally toss and turn.......but at some point.....I do crash....but not these last few days. Even after a relaxing day at the spa......I still could not have a clear thought......without it including you......surrounding you.......

It is safe to say that you encompass me today........and for that matter yesterday.....and the day before. For the first time in a long time, I am actually wanting to lift a woman with emotion, to touch an inner piece of her and to make a difference in her daily existence. Sure...it may be that these are just flurrying emotions, somewhat out of control.........but...............a larger piece of my heart tells me that I am not. So this, in some measure, is what I hope to do to you today.....to lift you.....to give you this mental safety net of comfort, mixed with a little pleasure and the warmth of a smile.

You have given me many gifts that I am not sure you are aware of. Without realizing it, you have touched my heart.......maybe lightly......but with impression. You have caused me to think......and to care. You have caused me to walk differently and with an unusual confidence. You have made me simply feel. You cause ecstasy and passion........you cause intensity and Eros. Amazing.

I do dream.......and whether you will admit it or not.......I know that you do to. Maybe we dream at different levels........maybe we dream at the same level.......but we still dream. I desire for that moment with you. A moment where I can hold your perfect face in my strong hands.......just before I kiss you hello. I dream that someday.......well someday I might just hold your hand........or just look into your eyes. I would love the honor and the gift of making love to you.......as I know you are coming to grips with the understanding that it would be beyond words as paths have crossed with you and me. Today is another day.......meant to be shared in some small way with each other.

So today..........smile for me, take an occasional deep breath and enjoy the feeling of the sun on your face. Take a walk (if you have the time) and take a very special moment of your day to watch your son smile......make him laugh......compliment something he does just for you. But most importantly.......look in the mirror.........for there is where I will be smiling right back at you......

You are an amazing woman ....so beautiful..........so utterly gorgeous.........someday I will just whisper this into your ear.....this is ....just after I kiss your neck........

Talk with you soon.........toes still curling???

and one more thing...........just before I go.........(scroll down)

I
Want You............

BADLY.

###

"What would happen if I just showed up at your front door some night to surprise you? What would I see?" It was a topic that had weighed on my mind for some time.

"A 10,000 square foot home with an unfinished backyard filled with rocks and two *American Bulldogs*," Ken replied a bit amused.

"No girlfriend?" How I wished, I could look him in the face while asking these questions.

"No girlfriend." He laughed.

I was not convinced, however. "And I can show up at any time?"

"You are welcome whenever you can make it over this way," he answered patiently as any boyfriend would answer to an overly paranoid girlfriend.

I was somewhat mollified but still had a difficult time accepting his answers. "Why do I rarely hear from you on the weekends?"

"I tend to shut my mobile phone and computer off so I have a chance to relax and just catch up on things I miss out on during the week due to my schedule." That answer stung a bit. After all, was I not supposed to be one of the things that aided his relaxation? I decided to let it slide for now.

"No children?"

"No children," he answered with a sigh. I could feel his patience starting to wear.

"You have a stellar education, great job, wonderful home, two dogs and are single. What is wrong with you?" I asked with a laugh trying to lighten the mood but still not feeling 100% satisfied.

"I ask myself that question every single day," he replied with that dynamic laugh of his to which I could listen to for hours. "The best answer I can come up with so far is that I tend to focus on my work too much. People in my life can feel neglected at times. It seems to be the general consensus amongst my exes, anyway. Every single girlfriend that has ever left me usually has complained about my work." His voice had such a profound sadness in it when he said the last sentence; I lost all will to pursue my line of questioning, which I felt I had exhausted already anyway.

"Because of your work? I personally never understood that reasoning, but then I come from a mother who was anything but stay-at-home."

"So many women want, I guess, a guy who is independently wealthy. They want someone who can provide all the luxuries of life without having to spend a single minute working for it. It was a lesson I learned early on." He took a long pause as if to work up the courage to tell me another truth about him. "Unlike everyone else who had a wealthy mom and dad, I came from nothing and had to pay for my own education. So I started my own limousine service company to pay for school."

"That was pretty ingenious of you," I answered. I could identify with him. While I had grown up with the luxuries of life, I had to learn early on to provide for myself if I wanted to escape the abuse my mother was fond of disseminating. I was 17 when I struck out on my own.

"Yes, I thought so too until I found my girlfriend screwing one of the drivers in the limousine to get back at me." His voice never broke, but the hurt he felt over that act came through loud and clear by the very lack of emotion he had while sharing the story with me.

"Ouch." I could feel his pain and rejection as my own.

"Yeah. Story of my life," he said with a defeated-sounding sigh.

Subj: Sometimes it comes in waves
Date: 9/28
To: FinanceGuy

I have typically prided myself on my ability to read people well and understand them better than they understand themselves. A large portion of this self-perception and confidence stems from the fact that, from the time I was old enough to speak, people have come to me for solutions and advice of all sorts - from personal to professional. When my ballet teacher would leave the class for whatever reason, I was tasked with teaching the class. I will meet someone for the first time at a party and within 30 minutes, I will be their confidant handing out objective advice.

Then I met you. I try to approach my understanding of you as I would of someone who has come to me with a story asking for my objective advice. I can do this without even thinking about it, separate myself from my emotions, from my physical situation, and just let the facts speak for themselves. I become an observer, impartial and stoic. But, when I try to use these tools to look at you, it is like a computer code with an error that creates an endless loop. You are, without doubt, a living, breathing and walking plethora of contradiction. In many ways, you are a dreamer and have the soul of a poet, and yet, you actually seem to have some sort of concept of reality, financial obligations, and ambitions. You spend most of your time with me either instant messaging or talking on the phone Monday through Friday, but Saturday and Sunday you go off the grid. You are one of the most open and passionate people I know and yet I have this nagging feeling that there is much you have not told me yet about things I should probably know.

I think the biggest difficulty I have is trying to reconcile your romantic side with your business side. I was raised with a mother who consistently attempted to beat the 'dreamer' side out of my personality and develop the 'doer' side of my life instead. After having been smithed by this fire for the better part of 17 years, I was still never able to rid myself of my 'dreamer' side entirely, the one she despised and reminded her of my father, and as such, I am still (despite all her efforts) an amalgam of both. I never met anyone else who could do the same.

Being someone who can move from ethereal to factual within a blink of an eye, I have sought to help those I have run across by giving them a more balanced view of the world. After many failed attempts, I came to realize that the majority of people are not like me. Those who are artists are artists and those who are methodical producers are methodical producers. I had learned to accept this as fact and me as a statistical outlier.

Now here you are, with what would appear to be unyielding characteristics of both. Neither side dominant over the other, and honestly I don't know what to make of it. That is to a large degree where the second-guessing and the doubt comes from. Where I ask myself, is he for real? He must be lying about something because no one behaves this way. No one spends the hours on the phone and instant messaging the words he does. Well, no one who also knows how to balance a checkbook that is.

I think the scariest part of all of this is that you are feeding the 'dreamer' side of me and making it stronger and I am starting to feel out of balance. I am still trying to decide if it is becoming dominant or just feels like it is. If it was just so suppressed in my marriage and by my mother that bringing it back to be of equal measure to my practical side makes it feel dominant as a result. Nevertheless, and anyway you slice it or any explanation you choose to go with, it seems strange and is scary and I feel myself losing my usual objectivity.

If someone came to me with this story, I would warn him or her to stay away, and yet I cannot seem to help myself. At night, I dream about you despite my not wanting to, and during the day I try to find the reasons why I should not dream. A vicious cycle. And yes I stay awake at nights, thinking about what you are like. You inspire all of these emotions which I had prided myself on not having, or when I had them to a lesser degree of being able to control them.

When I see you online, my heart skips a beat ... and when you call, my body relaxes and a smile crosses my face. I keep telling myself that I don't really know you all that well and that cooler heads should prevail. And yet, despite my counsel, it is getting more and more difficult not to think of you. Trying not to think of you is like trying not to breath. Only accomplishable for a few minutes at a time.

My rational self, my observer, is giving me excellent advice. She is saying: "Stay away from him." Unfortunately, the hope you have awakened in me, the dreamer who is wiping the sand out of her eyes, that person is unable to follow that advice. As such, the conclusion I have come to is that, no matter what happens in the end, the journey of finding out who you are, down to the very last cell and the most trivial thought, is one I am looking forward to.

Pandora

###

***

CHAPTER 16

Ken had just finished rereading Pandora's email to him for what must have been the thousandth time and years after he had initially received it. Her email brought out such emotion; it made him both eager and hesitant to reach out to her again. She had been perceptive even back then - there had been no hiding from her. He had wanted to confide everything and that simple realization had scared him as much back then as it still did. Things had moved so quickly for them both - much more quickly and into deeper emotional chambers than he had anticipated - and indeed quicker and stronger than any relationship had prior. It was as if the brake lines in the car had had been cut and there was no stopping. There was something about Pandora that had always drawn him as a compass was drawn to the North Pole - and he had had just about as much control over his direction as a compass needle did. Unfortunately, he had started his relationship with Pandora based on a lie. He never expected things to become as involved as they did. It was just supposed to be a diversion maybe a fun night out while in Las Vegas. That is what it is was supposed to be and then - he got to know her. Ken remembered wrestling with the pain and possibility of Pandora rejecting him back then if he revealed the depth of his deception to her. It was for this very reason he had kept his secrets close to his chest for as long as he did. Even though, he could not help but wonder now as back then: how would his life have turned out had he met Pandora even just a few years earlier than when he had?

Ken came from upper-lower-class beginnings. Raised by a single mother, whom he adored, he never knew his father until he was an adult and even then, only got to know him for the last year of his life. Ken had consistently felt like the outsider staring into the windows of those happy homes with the 2.1 children having dinner around a table every single night. Unlike others who would let themselves be defeated, Ken was that guy who never sat still and was forever striving for acceptance to reach his mix of J.P. Morgan and Norman Rockwell-like ideals. He worked hard in school, despite being made fun of for his weight. His mother, whom he adored, made just enough money for them to pay their bills, but not much more, working as an accountant in a retail flooring store. On the other hand, her skills in accounting and bringing her work home many nights, turned out to be instrumental in his future success. They only had each other to lean on and their situation, both emotionally and financially, and such it drew them closer than his friends with happy homes were to either one of their parents. As an only child, and being the only male in the household, he felt the weight of the world on his shoulders from a young age on. It was a lonely existence, for the most part, but it fueled his single-minded need for making more of himself than the standing he was born into would have predicted.

There had consistently been this hunger inside of him and this endless call for proving himself. He had for all time known that he was meant to be more than he was and he fought every day to achieve that goal. Money had usually been the best way to keep score of who was winning, so he had decided early on to surround himself with it and the symbols of power it could provide. It was a joyous and sad day when he received his acceptance letter from *Stanford*. It was joyous for the reason that he had made it against the odds, and sad as that success in this pursuit stacked the odds that much higher in opposition of his favor. His mother could not afford the books much less the tuition. In real American ingenuity fashion, Ken did not let that stop him. He started his own limousine company and scraped enough money together to pay for the school and living expenses without any assistance or loans. He attended the *Stanford Business School* and received his MBA among other degrees.

It was at *Stanford* where he achieved what some might term a Ph.D. in fitting in with the upper echelon. He learned not just what to wear and whose parties to attend, but where he also met two of the most important people that would impact his adult life: his wife Vicki and his best friend,

Scott. Scott, unlike Ken, did not have to worry about paying his bills since his family covered the costs. While not having exactly an idyllic childhood either, which would become the bond between them that not even time could break, Scott had grown up on the family ranch doing everything from wrestling cattle to breaking horses. In contrast to growing up with money in a big city, though, he was Texas through and through with none of the refinement one learned when surrounded by status symbols that did not include oval belt buckles. His mostly solitary rural life during high school alternated between bouts of physical labor and periods of nothing to do but read. After four years of this, he had arrived at *Stanford* with a body that had developed in ways few inter-collegiate sports could have brought about, and a mind that had developed with an academic fervor few professors even possessed. In many ways, Scott and Ken were like the yin and yang of each other while their shared childhood pain was the line where they touched. Had it not been for lacrosse and rowing, they might never have even met.

Scott, not being too concerned with clothing labels other than to discern the size of the garment and even then only upon the initial purchase, had never cared much for Vicki, Ken's wife. Vicki was as close to American royalty as one could get. She was a Rockefeller descendant and everything good and bad that went along with it. Scott, being the quiet observing sort, saw all the hoops Vicki made Ken jump through just to date her, much less to actually possibly marry her. Ken's hard work and sheer determination paid off not just for his social climbing design, but in his fast-paced work promotions as well. Within the span of a few years, he went from an accountant at *Price Waterhouse* to a VP position at one of the premier private banks in the Midwest. Somewhere in-between was when Vicki finally agreed to marry him and Ken had to beg and plead for Scott to come to the wedding in support of Ken if not his marriage. After all, her side of the aisle would be overflowing with family and his side was going to be something closer to *Grapes-of-Wrath* sparse. While this was not Scott's cup of tea and not a choice he would have made for himself or a choice, he agreed with Ken for having made, he knew that in a strange way it was a symbiotic if twisted match. Each was getting something out of this and he could not fault Ken for valuing social prominence as highly as he did.

Ken was finally marrying into the social prestige he had always yearned for and Vicki's immediate family was getting some much-needed infusion of cash. It was a match made in heaven or an Excel spreadsheet, which to some was the same thing.

With each promotion, the house would become bigger, the cars would become more luxurious, and the shopping trips would become more extensive. By all accounts, Ken had achieved the *'American Dream'* but still could not live up to his wife's *K-2* like expectations. He would see her disappointment on her face every morning knowing she had to slum it in a 10,000 square foot home. It was grating to her that unlike her friends she had a budget to adhere to of no more than $50k per month to spend on incidentals. She would remind him every chance she had that she could have married better. Like all marriages, the actual price of their initial mutual agreement became apparent only after years of being together and they grew apart.

Unlike the rest of the country, divorce was not something easily accepted in this social strata, and while both would possibly lose status, the money would be hers in the invisible prenuptial contract as defined by social and court norms. For Ken therefore while legal separation was not the answer, separate bedrooms and lives were quite tolerable and the only solution if he wanted to keep his social and monetary gains that he had sacrificed so much for. Ken found himself now in a fairy tale marriage that resembled something closer to the original dark leanings of the *Grimm Brothers*, than the effervescent *Disney* versions.

It looked like nothing but darkness and dragons for the rest of his life until one bored afternoon, upon the suggestion of a colleague; he browsed through profiles and ran across one that perked his interest. That was where he met Pandora. She had not fit into any of his carefully charted strategies. He had not planned to fall in love with her. He was just looking for some sexual diversion on his next out of town trip that happened to be Las Vegas. She did not fit into his common criteria for a woman he could *'fall in love with'*, chief of which was to hail from a longstanding and prominent family. And yet, she was beautiful and engaging and captured his imagination as no one had done in his life. At times, he had felt like she could see right through his soul even when he had not divulged his secrets.

Even though it had been years, and his emotions were still as intense as they had been the first time they met and it was causing him to question the wisdom of honoring her wish to stay out of each other's lives. During his weaker moments, he had felt like throwing caution to the wind and to follow his heart and seek her out despite the lack of contact with Pandora or confirmation that she still felt the same way about him. However, he was able to keep it together by reminding himself that he was only days away from signing the paperwork anyway.

He felt like he needed to talk to someone and Scott seemed like the only person who would understand particularly since he had been blissfully ignorant of everything else going on. Even though their individual choices after graduation and certainly after Ken's marriage had kept them more apart than together, theirs was a friendship that was not hindered by time. Scott had known him before he had become a CIO or wore $300 socks. Back when everyone knew him as *Sunny*. A name he had not been called, or personified, in quite some time. Picking up the phone, he dialed the familiar, if not often used, Las Vegas number. He heard Scott's prerecorded voicemail message before the beep that signaled for him to speak.

"Hey House, it's Sunny! I know it has been a while ... but ... well ... I have something important I need to talk about and it would be nice to see your ugly mug again over some adult beverages ... well ... anyway ... call me and let's get together."

***

CHAPTER 17

"So you were suspicious from the start?" asked Scott while crossing the room to pluck a grape off the plate and pop it in his mouth.

"Well, I never would have guessed that he was lying about his name, but I knew he was hiding something. He would be so open and yet so closed off at the same time." I had to pause and come up with the appropriate words to explain why. "The thing that would always bother me the most was why was he never available over the weekends? Again, it was early in the grand scheme of things so I was trying to give him the benefit of the doubt, and to keep things light and him at somewhat of a distance, but something was just not adding up."

"How were you planning to meet in person? Were you planning to meet in person?" His eyes were intently looking into mine as he asked the question. His lips had ever so slight a smile around them.

"Yes, as a matter of fact, I remember his first trip to Las Vegas after we started talking, it was right around this time, he had arrived in town unexpectedly and I had prior obligations so I could not meet him." My mind was pulling up the images so I could describe them to Scott. "However, at the last minute I did catch a break and called him on his cell phone so we could see each other for a few a minutes. He did not answer and I was on an unfamiliar emotional rollercoaster ride." I could feel the disappointment of that memory as if it had happened yesterday. "Come to find out he had been playing Black Jack and had left his phone in his room. When he got back upstairs and heard my voice messages, he threw the phone at the wall for having missed the opportunity. I think it broke. Melodramatic I know, but it sounds like him so I believe that story. Of course, I wouldn't have been able to do more than say hello and goodbye so it was probably for the best."

"Were you in love already at this time you think?" The faster he could get her to work through her emotions the faster he could get her to see past this jerk.

"Hmmm. In love?" I had to look at my former self and jump into her heart and mind before answering. "Probably. I would have to say, almost borderlining on pretty darn sure." I looked into the mirror sending out a questioning tendril as I poked at the memory of my old heart. "Maybe it was more infatuation than love at the time I wrote those emails, but even still, I had never been this infatuated for this length of time with anyone ever. It snuck up on me. Before I knew it, this mix of feelings grabbed me by the collar and kissed me on the mouth. I had never been emotionally dependent on anyone before ... and his emails and phone calls seemed to be all I would think of at times." Before I could stop myself, I said, "I felt tricked into it, really."

"Like *Tom Sawyer*?" asked Scott laughingly. It seemed that trickery was essential to falling in love. Falling in any case implied a lack of knowledge, which was a fundamental part of the experience.

"Yes. I suppose just like *Tom Sawyer*. Although there was no fence painting involved," I said smirking at his reference and not really knowing what had made me say such a silly thing to begin with. Then it came to me why I had chosen those words. "I did feel tricked into some of the sexual conversations we were having. He would continually push me to go into more detail. He would ask me things like: Did I masturbate that day? What did I use my fingers or a dildo? He would ask me to describe it. How it felt. What I would think about etc." The unease was as intense as if it were happening right now. I felt myself splitting further to continue. "I didn't know at first how to answer those questions, so I would approach them with almost a clinical-like depiction. Like a scientist describing an experiment or a police officer detailing an accident. Removing myself from the story telling so to speak. I think part of me thought that by doing so I could keep my heart at a distance as well."

"Did you enjoy pushing the envelope of experience with him?" asked Scott as the look in his eyes became a little more hungry seeing an opening. It was obvious that the time I spent recounting my time with Ken had had an effect on him. I was starting to doubt his promise of objectivity, but also felt myself not caring quite as much as I should. I had expected my discussion of a former lover to mute his sexual desire. Instead, it seemed to have brought out the insistent side in him. Of course, he had prided himself on his sexual skills even prior to our meeting, so it would only make sense that he would feel the need to prove himself instead of walking away. Merely seeing his body starting to strain with what I could only interpret as desire combined with my already emotional state brought on by reliving my past and no place to dissipate the energy to, triggered an autoerotic response of my own. We were both in bed. I was laying with my head on one of the many pillows, naked and he was lying crosswise on the bed with his head on my right side and his body across my legs.

I could feel my heartbeat quicken as I was attempting to suppress the build up and tried to keep my voice as normal as possible. "Yes and no. I was definitely not inexperienced in sex. After all, I had been married for several years and had had a healthy sexual relationship with my husband. Add to this that I was not a virgin by any stretch of the imagination prior to my marriage." I paused and thought for a moment if I should continue telling him the full truth. Admitting this next part was difficult. I decided to risk it nonetheless. "And yet, Ken made me feel like I had never had sex before. Not in an awkward sense, but as if everything else had never even existed and that the first time I had been genuinely touched by a man was by his virtual hand since we had yet to meet in person. And while I have had other lovers since then, no one has been able to match much less surpass that level of intensity and focus - virtually or physically." I could feel Scott's energy getting stronger and reaching out for me reflexively - as if to engulf me while picking up the gauntlet I had unintentionally thrown down with my statement. He recognized the importance of what I had said even before I could fully register the impact of my words and he was already moving to eclipse the distant emotional imprint made by Ken with his personal physical proximity.

"Did talking to him feel anything like this?" asked Scott as he spread my legs apart slightly before I could fully comprehend his intent of redirecting my emotions away from Ken. Using the broad side of his now very soft tongue, he slowly created a line between my ass and clit.

I gasped. With a slightly strained voice and trying to recover my thoughts, I answered, "Yes ... something along those lines. Do you have to do that?" I knew that Scott prided himself on his raw sexual talent and this appeared to be his way of not just competing with my memories but working to outright obscure them. It reminded me of a line from *My Best Friend's Wedding* where the character *Kimmy* had said 'He's got you on a pedestal and me in his arms.' The virtual pedestal I had placed Ken on was no longer looking quite as steady as it once had as Scott had me not in his arms but instead on his tongue.

Ignoring my question he created another slow, deliberate stroke with his tongue with, "How often would you masturbate while thinking of him?"

It was becoming ever harder to answer his questions. It took a few seconds for me to process what he had said and answer in an increasingly strained voice, "I can't remember." If this was a new therapy technique, it seemed to be working, although not sure about the ethical aspect of it if used in a real therapist / patient setting.

"Try" was all he said as his tongue took another trip along my London Bridge and clit. My back arched again and my hands went to his head and attempted to pull him up. Before I could, though, he had grabbed both of my wrists, held them against the bed, and continued his sweet torture.

"How often would you masturbate while thinking of him?" he asked in a breathy professor voice. I could just imagine being a student in his class and him trying to draw out the correct answer out of me, the answer that would get me an 'A' for class participation.

The room was starting to spin, his voice was sounding far away, and I could hear myself answering, "About once a day."

"Are you thinking of him now?" as he punctuated the word 'now' by letting go of my wrists and pushing his index and middle finger up inside of me making me cry out in the process from pleasure. Scott was either a mind reader or a magician as he literally and figuratively placed his finger on the matter - something no one else had ever been able to do - ever. "Yes, I am thinking of him now." Yet strangely, it was not the same intensity as I had thought of him before. The memory was becoming more distant. It was as if all this conversation and by just asking that very question, Scott was helping me face and exercise the ghost of Ken as Scott's mouth and fingers became the center of my focus and replacing those memories that had plagued me for so very long.

This unconventional therapy seemed to be working, as it was difficult to focus really on anything else. If I had any thoughts of escape or restraint, they soon left my brain. I was fast succumbing to my semi-drunken state of pleasure, and becoming his finger puppet as I had earlier that day. How easily he was once again taking control of my every nerve and thought. He continued to use his tongue and hand, trapping me with the fiery sensation of desire. Every time I would try to move up and out of his reach, he would adjust his positioning or grab me by my hips and pull me lower to his mouth. It was a tug of war of control and I was losing ground. By the time, he finally decided to relinquish his hold on me I had already had multiple orgasms and coated his mouth and hand. As he lifted himself up and moved north along my body with a sly grin on his face, I could see his very hard cock between his legs moving closer towards my lathered clit. I could feel the tip of his shaft now resting just outside, his chest level with my face, as his mouth came closer to my ear, and he asked the question again in a whisper, "Are you thinking of him now?" Just as he started on the word now, he pushed himself fully inside of me causing half my body to lift up off the bed from the sheer pleasure of it. Holding himself there, he could feel my walls closing down on him in a pulsating rhythm. Pulling himself out slowly, he asked the question again since I had not answered it to his liking. "Are you thinking of him now?" Again, he thrust himself deep inside of me, and again I could not help but arch up off the bed. My hands grabbed his back to pull him on top of me, but being much stronger than I, his upper body did not move. His lower body, on the other hand, kept thrusting itself into me, at first very slow and deliberate, and then, as I refused to answer him, his rhythm increased its pace. I had definitively lost this tug of war and had already fallen off the cliff; he just did not know it yet. I could feel his body starting to tense. His breathing became shallower. His cock pulsating within me and just as he begun to cum inside of my already overly drenched pussy, I could not deny him anymore and so I whispered in his ear, "No, I am only thinking of you right now." I could feel him orgasm with his entire body. As the last drop made it to my back wall, he finally pulled out slowly.

The room had just started to calm down for me after spinning quite rapidly. I watched Scott cross the room unselfconsciously picking up our two glasses of wine, walking back to the bed, still rock hard, handing me my drink, assuming his position again across my legs on the bed and asked, "So, how did he seduce you?"

***

CHAPTER 18

If manipulation is being able to make someone do what you want them to do and make them think it was their idea, then Ken was a master manipulator. Our discussions were becoming less and less banter and more and more soul bearing until our proverbial sleeves were stained red. They were no longer studies of past exploits and silly extremes, but our fears and hopes and plans of our lives - lives that we envisioned spending together. Of course, before any of those plans could become reality, there was the hurdle of our first meeting - a meeting that was the topic of many of our discussions. We would talk about our expectations for that first magical time when we would be sharing the same air. What we would feel, see, do. It seemed like that meeting would never happen until, one day and quite unexpectedly, Ken instant messaged me with the news that he was headed back to Las Vegas on the second week of November - a little over a month away. The dream was about to morph from fantasy into actuality and my heartbeat quickened. My brain started spinning faster and faster with what it would be like to feel the heat from his body and it was as if there was an endless flood of endorphins coursing through me.

I was allowing myself to become truly vulnerable, which was ever entirely uncharacteristic of me. Once it sank in that the realm of possibility was inching closer with each passing second, the mere idea of him had such a strong gravitational pull that my heart had no hope of escaping anymore. It was a classic episode of *Catfish*, I had fallen hopelessly in love, for the first time ever no less, with a man I had never met and of whom I had only a general physical description and an even vaguer photograph. I had fallen in love with his words and the voice that would deliver them from time to time. Consequently, I was confiding in him thoughts I would not have written even in a diary much less expressed to another person. Of course, he would build upon my words, match them and then surpass them in a fashion that challenged me to want him even more.

Subj: to a world class flirt........
Date: 9/29 10:27:14 AM
From: FinanceGuy
To: Pandora

Good morning love:

My extremely gorgeous world class flirt........yes you. Thank God you are also an exquisite lady, elegant and full of warmth as well.......without which your world class ranking would, unfortunately, be diminished.

Having said this........what sparked it? Hmmmm.......as you always seem to grab me just as you say goodbye.......you sufficiently grabbed me beyond reason last night. Yes ....with the words......" I would love to make love to you "........my heart......my mind........my body........went racing.

So absolutely.......the major chills......the highs of passion......and the desire that I have for you exceeded anything that I have definition for last night. Just when I thought I could not get any more seduced.......aroused.....you name it.........I find myself at a higher place at this moment......all because of you.

Unusual? For me........yes.........for you.......maybe.......for us.....absolutely. So to close this little thought bending good morning to you.....I will leave you with this........

I hope that I see the day........when I can show you without a deep voice.....without a tuxedo tie simply hanging around my neck.........without words........but with only my touch.......my character........my heart........and the intense level of passion that I have for you.......what it really means to make love......to touch you......to hold you......to taste everything about you.

I just hope afterwards......I don't die.......for it will be the closest thing to heaven I will have experienced in my lifetime.........

You simply force me to sit down.....

###

"Are you thinking of me?" I was in the office and his voice had a wistfulness I had not heard before.

"Well, we're talking on the phone so of course I am thinking of you. What else would I be thinking about?" I answered as I was working on compiling numbers in a spreadsheet. One of those tasks I could do blindfolded.

"Making love to me." I had raised my cup to take a sip of coffee only to spill it slightly on my hand as I was trying to recover from what he had just said.

Putting down the coffee cup and dabbing at the still hot drops on my desk and hand with a napkin I answered, "Ahem ... I think that would still construe thinking of you."

"Can anyone else make you feel the way I do?" It was too early in the morning to be having this conversation. What was causing him to behave this way?

"We have never even met in person Charles, how am I supposed to answer that question?"

"Honestly."

"I have never thought about someone as much as I think of you. Will that work?" I hoped that my answer would appease him since I still had a busy day ahead of me.

"No, I want more."

"How much more?" I asked with a sigh.

"I want to hear about all of your fantasies so I can make them come true when we see each other next month."

"You mean the fantasies where the laundry folds and irons itself?" I asked with a laugh trying to change the subject.

"No the fantasies where I make love to you and you can't get enough of my being inside of you." There was a sound to his voice that left no room for doubt that this was exactly what he was hoping to do.

"Ahhh, I see ... Those fantasies." I was starting to feel a little uncomfortable having this type of conversation in the office with Aaron being able to walk in on me at any time. We might have been separated, but this was after all a place of business. Besides, I was still a bit ill at ease with the concept as a whole of having a love interest at all, much less flaunting that fact in front of Aaron. Our working relationship was amicable and I was not looking to upset the apple cart.

"I want to slowly drip cognac on your skin and lick it off one deliberate stroke at a time." He had barely finished his sentence before I could feel an energy surge like a lightning bolt hitting my body at the mere thought of what he had suggested. Unfortunately, I could also hear Aaron walking around the office. *This was torture*! I wanted to just concentrate on Ken and let myself sink into his words and what he was saying, but not being able to because I was sitting on pins and needles with Aaron around.

"That would be ... ahem ... enjoyable I think." I was finally able to finish taking a sip of coffee.

"Are you as hungry as I am?"

I was working hard to keep my wits about me and with a sigh answered in a softer and lower tone, "Starving."

"Do you still think of me when you masturbate?" It was that moment when Aaron picked to walk into my office looking for a copy of a catalogue we had issued the prior month.

Adjusting my tone to one of a professional conversation I answered, "That is one of the scenarios, yes."

"Is Aaron in your office right now?" I could almost hear the wheels in his mind working as he asked the question.

"Yes." I was thankful he had picked up on my verbiage as well as my tone of voice.

"What do you use more often? Your hand or your toy?" I almost coughed up my coffee at the unexpected question.

"The latter." In my mind I was thinking, *'Just you wait Henry Higgins. Just you wait!'*

"How deep do you put it inside of you?" Thankfully I had no coffee in my hand or mouth.

"That would be the base," I answered as Aaron seemed to be taking what felt to me like an excruciatingly long time to find the catalogue.

"Can you take a picture for me the next time?" he asked with a wicked laugh.

Clearing my throat I answered with a straight face, "I am sorry, that is against company policy." Aaron heard this and gave me a quizzical look. Covering the mouthpiece, I moved my lips to say, "C.O.D." With an understanding nod, Aaron turned his attention back.

"I want to kiss your neck right now," he continued in a breathy whisper.

"So it would seem." I had to adjust myself in my chair as I could feel myself getting wet at the prospect.

"If you could only see how excited you have me at this moment."

"I can only imagine," I answered in as matter-of-fact a voice as possible.

"I love you Pandora."

He was making it impossible for me to get coffee from the cup to my mouth without some sort of spillage happening that particular morning, and certainly not after a statement like that. Constrained with Aaron listening in on my half of the conversation, I answered, "Thank you. That is kind of you to say."

"I have fallen in love with you," he emphasized as if I had not heard him the first time.

"So I have heard. Is there anything else I can help you with?" I wanted to smack him upside the head for making me squirm and saying something of this magnitude when he knew I was a hostage to the situation.

"I want to see you," he said with a sincerity that came through loud and clear.

"I think that is happening in November," I replied in a bit more of a conversational tone.

"Do you want to see me?" I had already answered this question multiple times in the affirmative.

"Of course, that would be my pleasure," is all I could say while Aaron was still within listening range.

"Would it?" He was just enjoying this too much.

"Distinctly so." I had to get Aaron out of my office so I could bring the conversation to a close. "Here is the price list for the catalogue you are looking for."

"As I kiss you and make love to you like no one else has?"

Aaron had finally left the room and I could speak freely again but not knowing when he would be back I was eager to get off the phone."Yes. I love you too, I really need to get off the phone now Charles," I said under my breath.

"I want you to be only mine." He always had to push the envelope.

"I am. But you know I am going to get even for this," I answered in a half-threatening half-laughing tone.

"Looking forward to it." I could hear the smile in his voice.

Subj: On your way home
Date: 10/13
To: FinanceGuy

I sit here still basking in the warmth of your voice. It's funny how talking almost every day is starting to not be quite enough. Every time I pick up the phone and hear you on the other end or I see one of your amazing emails in my inbox, it is as if I have been instantly transported to a remote section of Hawaii. I am on a mountain or on the beach, feeling the caressing sensation of soft rain on my skin, closing my eyes and feeling the wind hugging my waist and combing my hair.

I say these things because you seem to need constant reassurance on how much you have become a part of my everyday thoughts, wants, and desires in such a short amount of time. I have never fallen in love before Charles, and you have accomplished the unaccomplishable in record time. When I think about this logically, I just sit and shake my head, for not only falling in love with you but for something even more difficult, trusting you. I am not sure I have trusted someone this deeply, this completely, ever before in my life. It is this same trust that acts as a platform, or maybe rather a fertile ground, for these emotions to build from, grow from. I am just simply amazed at the garden you have been able to create within me where before was just desert.

Knowing this, can you now understand why I am looking forward to our meeting with a fervor and intensity that just might outmatch yours? I know it is strange for you to fathom such an idea. Your constant questions are laced with doubt posed in such a way as to elicit reassurance. You have been hurt in the past and I have doled out a lot of hurt to others. I suppose it is only natural for you to doubt. I just wish at times that I could open a portal to my brain and my heart sometimes, so you could feel what I feel and see what I see. Then you would understand that your doubts are unfounded.

If you need any more reassurance ... take this as a thought .... I am counting the minutes until I can feel you inside of me. I am looking for opportunities to shorten what seems like an excruciating wait so that I can create trails with my hair on your skin. When I look at my calendar, the first thought that goes through my mind is, how many more days until I can kiss his neck, his fingertips, his mouth, and feel him swell up against me? How much longer before he entwines his hands in my hair to pull my mouth towards his? Will I be able to live up to his idea of me when I push him down on top of the bed? Will he shut up when he sees that look in my eyes and understand that no words can really express what is coursing through the body at that point? Will he let me lovingly explore every inch of his skin? Using my fingertips to caress every injury, every documentation from his life, every weak spot, every peak and every valley? Will he understand that I will try everything that I can to make this a reality? Does he understand that I am excruciatingly frightened, but that nonetheless I want to feel all of this and more? Does he know that I will probably tremble when I first see him? That I want him to feel, once he leaves, that even though he has seen me now, experienced me now, like some punishment out of *'Dante's Inferno'* or Greek Tragedy, fulfillment only begets more hunger? That his desire is 10x worse after having satisfied his curiosity than any desire he had felt before he saw me? I want him not to be able to leave. I want that when he smells my perfume on his clothes or pillow to remember what happened and to wish it to happen again. I wonder, if he is starting to understand when I keep telling him I want him mind, body, and soul, what that means? I wonder if he knows that it has gone from not a week, to not a day, to not an hour when these thoughts go through my head? These thoughts of: being held, holding, tasting his mouth, his skin, and feeling that even though we have been as close as two people can, that there has to be a way to get even closer?

And if you were to send me a few pictures as you have promised throughout this time, I could reassure of all this and more in more specificity.

Take that

###

Subj: Re: On your way home
Date: 10/16 9:51:48 AM
From: FinanceGuy
To: Pandora

My Love:
An amazing letter.........for now......I am speechless. As your thoughts radiate through my soul......I find myself gasping for breath.

As I am limited for time at this moment........I will assure you that today is picture day........and some will be floating your way later in the day.......

Hope you are smiling........

I miss you.........yes more than that

###

***

CHAPTER 19

Ken, up until that day, had sent a total of maybe one or two picture of himself, taken from a vast distance. True to his word, for the first time, he sent something more in line with the variety and quantity I had sent to him. He must have sent at least 20 pictures, each better than the last. With each file, I downloaded and opened, I became even more enamored with him than I had already been. I did not understand why he would not have taken these earlier. Of course, he had mentioned having fought weight most of his life so there might have been a trace of self-consciousness. As I examined the close ups and head-to-toe shots, I was able to see the details, which had unfortunately never been available in the past, such as his thick head of dark hair that set off the bluest eyes I had ever seen. I adored his football player's body, but it was his smile that just melted me to the core. When I would stare into his face close-ups, his eyes just seemed to cut right through me, I had to catch my breath. For the first time, I understood what he (along with others) had been talking about when they were trying to describe my pictures back to me. If there had ever been any doubts as to my physical attraction to Ken they were washed away with the mental drool, I had to wipe from the corners of my mouth as they became my favorite screen savers. Next month, when we would meet for the first time face to face, we would most certainly not be playing pinochle.

My thoughts, which had been easily led down the path of fascinating exploration already, were now running ramped with desire. It was getting more and more difficult to rein Ken in during our phone conversations. I could feel myself losing control, which in many ways had always been a double-edged sword. It took the loss of control to feel the real depth of an emotion, but the aftermath of guilt and self-flagellation I typically went through was also the onset of my running from the relationship. I had left men for less than what had already occurred between us.

The first real test of our relationship happened the next day on 10/17. Ken and I had what started out as an ordinary conversation. It was early evening and I was relaxing on the couch at home talking about this and that. Like a teenager talking to her boyfriend. The conversation, as all of our conversations of late - no matter what their start - wound up in the realm of sex and our mutual desires. While, in the past, I had been able to avert delving any further than factual discussions and such, that night, I lost control over the content. Maybe it was the lateness of the hour, maybe the depth of the connection and finally having a detailed image to put with the voice, but that night he was the mentalist and I was his hypnotic subject.

"What are you doing right now?" His voice had the same soothing quality as if he were getting ready to read me a bedtime story.

"Hmmm... laying on the couch with my eyes closed, enjoying the sound of your voice," I answered with a content sigh as I stretched out like a cozy cat. I was utterly relaxed. It felt like we were on the couch together and I had my head in his lap getting ready to doze off instead of being in different states and on the phone.

"What are you wearing?" a standard question of his by then.

I opened my eyes so I could describe it correctly. "Long plain white T-shirt, panties, and socks." I closed my eyes again so as to fully focus on his voice and slip back into my half-awake, half-asleep trance-like existence.

"How is your pussy feeling?"

"It is doing fine. Thanks for asking." I was amused and too content conjuring his image in my mind in full detail, thanks to the new pictures, to steer the conversation back to a legitimate topic.

"Are you wet?"

"Why?" I asked with a sigh.

"Just curious." He was hiding something. I could tell.

Trying to appease him, I answered, "I can feel a high level of humidity in that general vicinity ... yes."

"I want you to check for me." That was a request he had never made before.

"Pardon?" I was a bit shocked and not entirely sure I had heard correctly, but also not shocked enough to come fully out of my sleepy-cozy state.

"I want you to take your hand and feel how wet you are and tell me." I felt like I was at a bit of a crossroads. This was going a step further than we had in the past. This was a giant leap further than any phone conversation I had with any other man, ever.

"Really?" I was still debating the wisdom of complying with his request.

"Please." His plea had such sincerity and need imbued in it. I could not refuse without hurting his feelings. It felt like a game of *'Double Dare'* and I thought, *'What was the harm in acquiescing?'*

"Fine." With a deep sigh, I slid my hand under my panties and let my middle finger explore. "Yes, it's definitely wet."

"I want you to take your hand and tap your clit lightly."

"Charles! Seriously?" I was torn between truly feeling comfortable with him in expressing my particular wanton desire for his touch and his body, and the appropriateness of it all. The age-old question of 'would he still respect me in the morning.'

"Please." The wantonness won out.

"The things I do for you. Ok." As I did, a sound of pleasure escaped my lips. I could hear his excitement growing on the other end. He knew that, if nothing else, he was lowering my emotional walls, which I had guarded for so long.

"Do it again." Again, I could not help myself but to utter my pleasure into his ear. "I want you to take your hand and bring your breast to your mouth and suck on your nipple and let me hear it."

"Really?" I was debating how audible this would be to him on the other end.

"Please." Again, I could not refuse him. I brought my nipple to my mouth and held the phone close so he could hear the suction created by my lips. The sensation produced was not as intense as it would be if his lips were on my breast, but it generated a pleasant tingle nonetheless.

"I love the way you sound. Touch your clit again lightly." I could not believe that there I was on the couch listening to him guide me in my masturbation when only two months ago or so, we had not even known of each other, and had never, as of that moment, actually seen each other in person. It was like an outer body experience. I was watching myself respond to him while a part of me was registering the throbbing his directions were generating. I felt powerless to stop it. My body had been so conditioned to his voice that I could not help myself but respond the way he wanted me to.

"Now circle your pussy hole but don't enter yet. I want you to imagine that that is my tongue circling you and licking you."

My own attempts at masturbation without a vibrator or a dildo had never culminated in an orgasm, but then again I had never utilized this particular approach before. I moaned in response as my body was slowly building up an electrical charge.

"Lightly tap your clit again. Tap, tap, tap. Just like that."

I cried out softly with each tap. I still could not believe what I was doing and how expertly he was guiding me in the exploration of my own body. It was as if he knew my body better than I did without ever having touched me.

"Now take a break and run your hands under your shirt again and caress your body and breasts. I want you to imagine that those are my hands on you. Touching you. My mouth against your neck ... kissing you ... tasting you."

He could hear my content sigh, as I was obliging his request and lightly ran my hands over my skin. I moved just the fingertips slowly across my stomach in a slalom-like motion, going from one side of my waist to the other, until I reached just under my breasts. Then, continuing my ski like path, I moved from the base of my breast, along the underside, up to the darkened areola before hitting the taut nipple eagerly awaiting the touch. It was unbelievable how powerful the mind could transform suggestion into reality. The hands I felt on my body, were truly not my own. He was taking control of me one word at a time until there was nothing left and I was all his.

"Bring your fingers to your mouth and get them wet, then run your hand back down to your panties and slide underneath them again. This time I want you to stroke yourself with your finger from your pussy hole to your clit."

It felt like his tongue was working doing the stroking instead of my wet finger. I could almost see his face there and wanted to put my hands in his hair. To touch him as I was feeling the intensity building inside of me.

"Again."

"Oh my God, you feel so good!" I exclaimed under my breath. Moans could no longer describe the exact extent of my reactions anymore.

"Again."

I cried out. I could feel the room starting to tilt on me and the walls fading back.

"I want you to slide one of your fingers slowly inside of you. That is my hand sliding up inside of you."

The room was starting to spin and not just tilt anymore.

"Pull it out slowly and slide it back in, but this time put one more finger inside."

"That is too much." Every man I had ever been with had always commented on my *'tightness.'* It would appear as if all those Kegel exercises during pregnancy and post-pregnancy truly did the trick because despite having given vaginal birth, my muscular structure in that area remained unchanged. I knew that it was not due to actual small construction, or otherwise I would be unable to accommodate the better-endowed lovers in my life, both in girth and length. The proximity and density of my vaginal walls became evident to me when I would observe dildos being pushed out unintentionally without my having an orgasm. As such, it did not take an extraordinary amount of width for me to feel stretched.

"Then just use the one. I want you to imagine me in front of you. My hand sliding itself in and out of you. First slowly out then hard back in."

I shuddered with pleasure.

"Ram it back in now."

"Oh my God!"

"Again."

I was getting dizzy even with my eyes closed.

"When I tell you, curl your finger towards your stomach."

"Charles. I want you!" This torture was getting to be too much. I was close to climaxing and he was there with me but not there.

"Again."

I cried out again.

"How does that feel?"

"It feels so incredible. You have my head spinning with so much want and desire. Please, take me." It was as if I was begging for my life, begging for fulfillment. Fulfillment I recognized I would not actually get that night, but without it, I knew I would die. If I did not have him, in whatever fashion, my body would just burst and spontaneously combust.

"Tell me how much you want me as you keep fingering yourself."

It had always been difficult for me to talk during sex, to the distress of some of my lovers, and even though it was not actually him doing these things, but myself, it still took a bit of doing to open up my mouth and speak coherently. "I want you more than I can describe. I want to feel your cock and your cum inside of me. I would do anything to make that happen." I paused for a moment and said the next thing that came into my mind. "I want to kiss you and never stop."

"I want you to squeeze down on your finger as you push it in and feel me."

I was so close to cumming, but my need seemed greater than just this one fulfillment. I could not imagine the impending orgasm to satisfy me. Not until I could actually feel him. Touch him.

"Again."

My body arched up higher with each moan.

"Again."

"Please, Charles. No more. I can't stand this anymore."

"Are you ready to cum?"

"Yes. Please."

"Squeeze!"

"What are you doing to me? How are you doing this to me?" I said as I cried out.

"Squeeze again!"

I could feel my climax taking hold of my body.

"Squeeze down on my cock!"

His voice enveloped me and created a direct connection I had never felt. It was as if he was right there, in the room with me, my hands were his hands, and my cum was covering his cock. He was more real to me at that moment, 300 miles away, than any other lover had been whose breath I felt on my skin.

"Tell me to cum." His voice was starting to sound strained. The conversation must have had an effect on him as well.

"Oh, Charles. Please cum. Please cum inside of me. I want to feel you."

"Squeeze!" My body responded without my even having to consciously instruct it anymore. He had taken complete control of me from 300 miles away.

"I am going to cum." I could hear the sound of his hands moving in rapid successions up and down his well-lubricated shaft. I climaxed again, right there on the phone with him, as I heard his voice like a rumbling volcano or a locomotive in a tunnel, yelling out "Oh my God!" Hearing him erupting over the phone only intensified my orgasm as I continued to climax with him.

This orgasm was different from anything I had felt up until then. It was incredible to discover and experience how dominant of a role the mind truly had when it came to sexual summits. While there had been some physical stimulation, true, I had never been able to get myself to climax like that with only my hand. The credit had to go to Ken and his expertise in weaving a world around us with his voice alone. I could see how people found a particular appeal for this type of sex. Once my vaginal muscles stopped contracting of their own accord, I felt like I could take a breath on my own again without him telling me to.

As the electricity seeped out of my body and into the couch and ground, it was all of a sudden replaced by crushing guilt, embarrassment, remorse, and mortification. I am not sure why I felt the way I did. Maybe it was because I thought that I had cheapened myself. Part of it might have been that allowing someone that deeply into my mind and them knowing it, was the ultimate act of vulnerability on my end. The vulnerability was usually followed up with self-hate anyway. So, I hung up with a terse goodbye and coolness that had never been there before and I could hear the confusion in his voice as he wished me sweet dreams. As close as we had just been, I could feel myself pulling away twice as much so as to keep myself safe from what I was sure would be his upcoming rejection of me. I could see the next email in my mind already: the email where he would tell me that he was no longer coming to Las Vegas. I went to bed with the steadfast resolve to never speak to him again. It would be difficult, but I could do it. I could never talk to him again. I could never think of him again. I knew I could cut him out of my life. The embarrassment of what I had done demanded it. I could not believe that I had allowed myself to do something of this nature.

I knew what I was feeling was an amplified version of what most likely would have happened after any initial sexual encounter. That expectation of no longer being of interest since the curiosity had been fulfilled. In any case, was this not the very scenario every girl was warned of while growing up? Once a boy slept with you, it was like a greyhound who had caught the rabbit in a race, he would never be interested in racing again, or in this case, seeing you again. Sex was every woman's ultimate holdout, or so we were raised to believe and many a cad of a man would confirm.

I had committed the worst sin of all, not only had I *'given it up'*, but I had done so in such a manner that required the least amount of commitment possible, he did not even need to be in the same room with me or look into my eyes. He had breached my walls with a minimal amount of effort, how could he possibly respect me now? How could I respect myself?

Those were my last thoughts before I went to bed that night.

The next morning I woke up to find an email of his in my inbox. Unlike my usual eagerness to seeing his name, I was hesitant to open it at first. I was reminded of my embarrassment from the night before, which I had hoped I had just imagined. I had never had a hangover from drinking alcohol, so I had nothing to compare it to, however, I recognized the tale-tell signs others had described. With a pounding head, nauseous stomach, and shaking hands, I grabbed the mouse. I took a deep breath for courage, closed my eyes as I clicked and opened them a minute later to read his letter.

Subj: hmmmm........a few thoughts......
Date: 10/18 8:40:00 AM
From: FinanceGuy
To: Pandora

You simply gorgeous creature:

Good morning......and I must say that I love the way the sunshine caresses your incredible face in the morning. I really cannot imagine what it would be like to greet a day next to you.....the way your hair must look......the soft glow of your eyes seeing through my soul.....the way your body must wrap around mine. These thoughts are a few I wonder about.

But this morning, I wanted to express a few things to you....a few things which kept me awake last night.

About yesterday, I have several emotions that I want to express. Some of these thoughts may actually sound strange in their context, but rest inside me with purpose and conviction with which I feel for you. As our thoughts wandered yesterday into a very personal area.....an area of passion and desire in its purest sense, I felt emotions that I have never felt before. As I continued to express the nature of my touch, I felt tuned into to you very clearly, beyond the walls that seem to interrupt our intensity. Maybe it is a phone call, maybe it is a package that needs to make Federal Express, and maybe it is a deal point that needs to be re-negotiated.....but yesterday.......time stood still for a moment. And for a moment nothing else mattered. Call it a sign........maybe...........call it an anomaly.........possibly...........but one thing I will call it is a very brief expression of me to you.....of how I care.......how I view us......and how the intensity of you affects me........every day.......a little something for you to digest.

Of course I daydream.......and I wonder about your thoughts........but to rest inside them for just a moment........was a very special gift that I will cherish. The reason? To understand this special gift........one must first understand you.......and to intertwine the two ....sets the memory in a rare room in my life.

Thank you.......thank you for you and the breath that you take......the thoughts that you possess and the warmth that you illuminate to everyone around you. But most of all......thank you for melting those walls around you.....for a brief moment........for capturing this passion.....this intensity in such a way that deserves recognition........that moves beyond reality. Please eliminate embarrassment from your thoughts.......and rest knowing that I hold you and your emotions......in a very guarded place that no one will ever disparage.......

You are amazing........you are a lady.........you are a gift........

Good morning........hope you got the sleep you sought last night.......

###

Far from the 'Dear Jane' letter I had expected upon opening, I was still hesitant to let go of my embarrassment. I had gotten comfortable with the idea of dealing with the impending hurt a break-up would cause me, and I was not sure if I was ready to let go of that notion entirely, for it meant that I had accepted the change in our relationship. A relationship that had most definitely changed that night and if I was going to accept this change, I knew there would be no reversing it. We had opened *'Pandora's Box'* and there was no way to put what we had released back. While I had been prepared to take a physical step in our sexual progression, what we had done the previous night was alien territory for me. It was foreign territory not so much because of the phone sex itself since it was not that different from flirting even, but because of the pure intimacy that had been created that night. I had never allowed someone that deeply into my psyche ... ever! Moreover, I was angry with myself for having allowed it.

Of course, then again, how could I hold on to any of these negative emotions when he had written such a caring and loving letter? I needed time to think. I replied to acknowledge his effort but avoided any contact with him for the rest of that day.

Subj: Re: hmmmm........a few thoughts......
Date: 10/18
To: FinanceGuy

Thank you for your kind words. I hope to talk to you tomorrow. Today, unfortunately, will be a hectic one for me.

P

###

All day and all night, I wrestled with his attempt to make me feel safe and accepted and my self-loathing for losing so much control. *'Good girls'* did not do these types of things. I was still undecided about the whole matter the next day when the flag in my inbox went up, signaling I had received new mail. It was from him.

Subj: Things I wanted to say..........but lost for words....
Date: 10/19 10:24:03 AM
From: FinanceGuy
To: Pandora

My love:

As you might imagine, with my affinity for words and thought, there are things that I think about in the normal course of my day, but seemingly never find the appropriate words to share with you during our conversations. Sometimes I think it is this overwhelming desire that I have to simply listen to your angelic voice, and other times I frankly sit stunned with the knowledge that I have the attention of such a complete lady. But I continue, reeling with anticipation of that first hello and the passion of that first kiss......the touch of your hand in mine or the possibility of just a glance across a crowded room. And regardless of my destiny in your eyes, or the amazing rhythm of how your heart races with us, there are these thoughts that I contemplate......and do so daily......

So with a deep breath.......these things I will share with you today.....

I wish I could find the words to tell you......

That I see every star in the sky within the glow of your eyes.......

That I marvel at your ability to succeed and drive for a future in this life......

That your motherhood is passionate and at the same time demanding of the very best of you......and the grace of how you handle everything you touch........

That my first and last thought of a day is how I wish I knew firsthand what it was you were thinking about......and if a time exists when we are thinking the very same thing together..........

That your thoughts and those that you have the courage to express to me are as important to me as they are to you to share......that I take pride in listening and protecting the delicate feelings that you harbor deep in the recess of your soul.....

That you carry yourself with a unique elegance that maybe only I see........but the mere fact that I see it gives me courage to continue trying my very best every day with the expression of what you do to me......

That I do want to dance with you......a slow dance........yes fully clothed and scented......if only to hold you and to look into your eyes......I wish I could find these words.......

That I crave to know feeling........to capture this penetrating emotion that you have allowed me to feel and express it without words.....from a simple kiss to a glance.........from a smile to a belly laugh.........from an animal passion to something sinfully erotic......I wish I had the words...

That you melt me.......this intelligent driven man........with beliefs and passions that I have always defined myself with..........for all of my life.......you have met every challenge......mental......physical and spiritual........and then........surpassed them in every principle........every time.....

That you have captured my ability to dream again........to believe in the value of a new day.

That I respect you........for who you are ....for your trials.......and your tribulations.........from your self-imposed faults to all of your wonderful successes..........I respect you...........and do so without reservation........

That you have grounded my feet with purpose.........while still giving me hope........with love and passion........and acceptance for who I am .....for whatever I am........for whoever I am ....and for this I thank you........

That you have given me a unique look inside a real heart.........real emotions.........with real feelings........you have shared you with me.......

That you have shared an unspoken physical passion that I have never felt before with anticipation and hunger that I have never known......but wonder about more than I should.......

That for all of these things to express love with you........in whatever form we are constrained with..........that I enjoy listening.......caring and believing in the woman that you have become..........you should know this...........

That you are the best of everything that I consider beautiful.......tantric.......and erotic..........everything that makes a lady a lady.........all that you have secretly worked on inside yourself.......all of those internal goals you have never shared with anyone.......your insecurities and your weaknesses..........I will not exploit them.........I will only enjoy the opportunity to share them with you........in the timeless elegance that is you.....

That regardless of our future.........thank you for being my friend........the lady that I desire........and the woman that grabs me to reach higher.......and strive further.

For all of these things..........I thank you. I am proud of who you are.......and all that you share with me........for accepting me......my faults......my attributes or lack thereof........for seeing in me what I don't see myself..........

For all of these things..........that is why I write..........and why your elegance courses through my mind and affects my heart.........

I desperately want to know what it is like to touch your life.........to make love to you in the only way I know how.......to lift your spirit and to touch your soul..........I want to feel your breath and experience your passion.......I simply have to know.........for I am sure of these very things.....for every dream I have.......and for all of the years I have dreamed.........I could never make out the face of the woman in my dreams.......that was......

Until I crossed your path..........

So here I stand.........

Good morning Love............hope your smile is bright today........

###

My plans of self-pity and loathing were effectively annihilated with his email. It was impossible to hold on to any remnant of embarrassment with such words. He had effectively not only filleted his soul for my inspection but took my actions and elevated them to such a level of respect I had previously thought unattainable.

It became apparent to me that I was truly in love with Ken (although I still knew him as Charles) and by accepting this change in our relationship; I would be forever unequivocally his.

There was a strange new emotion in the hodgepodge of sentiments that typically accompanied my romantic relationship. It took me a while to recognize what it was because it was such a foreign concept to me, but I felt safe with him. I could not remember the last time I had a notion of someone being protective of me. Jealous? Yes! Opportunistic? Absolutely! Protective? Not so much. With my height and capabilities, I was often looked to as the protector, but never typically seen as someone who needed protecting - even as a child. However, despite having shown weakness to Ken, his reaction was not to exploit. Instead, he lifted me up and sheltered me from the unfavorable opinion of myself. How could I not repay such kindness with love and the commitment to continue despite my discomfort from the other day?

I had a busy day of putting the mourning clothes back in my closet and cancelling the flowers for the mental funeral of our relationship. My plans for drowning my sorrows while running rampant through the town were also shelved for a more appropriate time.

In their stead, I concentrated on spending time, in whatever form I could, with the dearest man I had ever come to know. It must have been a turning point for Ken as well, for his seduction endeavors increased exponentially as he became emboldened with the change in our relationship status.

***

CHAPTER 20

Having spent 90% of our time together so far naked while in each other's presence, it was time to do something that normal couples did - have dinner in a restaurant. As such, Scott and I had decided to meet inside of a casino on Las Vegas Blvd., but still a few miles away from what was considered the Strip. I had just lifted the martini glass to my lips as I noticed his 6'5" frame walking across the central bar, one hand in his pocket, the other swinging casually at his side, and flashing a smile that could light up even the darkest of rooms. He had already seen me and was making a beeline for my barstool with a gate halfway between a soccer player and runway model. Sporting that infectious smile of his, my mouth smiled in return, making it difficult to finish taking a sip of the stirred not shaken, (shaking bruised the alcohol) gin and vermouth mixture in my glass, causing some to spill along the front of my shirt. Breaking eye contact I took the bar napkin and quickly dabbed the wet spot. Thankfully, the gin did not stain. Placing the napkin and slightly less full glass back on the bar, Scott had arrived at this point in front of my chair, leaned over, and whispered, "It's great to see you again" in my left ear as he passed it to kiss my neck. Feeling his breath cascading down my neck and shirt, I experienced the sensation one must when walking into an electric fence. It was as if I were being bombarded with a thousand tiny little lightning bolts. I could feel myself going from 0 to wet in 1.3 seconds. My back arched both from the shocking sensation and from the need to raise my face high enough to kiss him on the cheek and respond with "the feeling is mutual."

Sitting down on the barstool next to mine and watching him order his gin and tonic from the bartender gave me a chance to appraise his appearance. Scott had the fashion sense of a typical professor, which was to say that his wardrobe consisted mainly of jeans and T-shirts. This being a dinner date, he had opted to wear a golf shirt with his jeans instead of the *Star Trek* T-Shirt he had worn to our first meeting and loafers instead of sneakers. Thankfully, most restaurants in Las Vegas did not have a strict dress code or Scott would never have gotten past the maitre d'. His head appeared to be freshly shaven and his beard newly and carefully trimmed so as to be almost imperceptible. Outside of the height, I could not have picked a person more physically different from Ken and yet in other ways they were nearly identical. Maybe it was that fact that Scott and Ken both seemed to be able to read me so well. Maybe it was that both had a take-charge attitude when it came to sex and both had had challenging childhoods that had shaped their drives in adulthood.

It was an interesting exercise comparing the hologram like a version of Ken to the very real Scott next to me. Thinking back, I found it strange now how Ken had seemed gargantuan to me at 6'2" back when we had first met. In comparison, while Scott had him beat at 6'5", I viewed Scott as only slightly taller than I. Of course, considering how quickly things had moved from a vertical to a horizontal position during our first meeting and the continued preference for those particular body placements, Scott had left little room for any sort of thorough height appraisal or for any logical thought for that matter. Then again, I might have gotten more accustomed to being around taller individuals taking into account the average height of the people I surrounded myself with had also increased since that time. Part of the difference in perception could also be attributed to the fact that, Ken had more of a football player's build and Scott had the slimmer soccer player construct. Volume wise, therefore, Ken might actually be the larger individual despite being slightly shorter. Since my mind had strayed towards soccer players, I had to admit that Scott had the best legs I had ever seen on a man in addition to arms that any bull rider would have envied. It was no surprise, therefore, that he had a penchant for short-sleeved shirts such as the golf shirt in front of me. Ken had never been as muscularly defined as Scott was and despite his bulk had more of the white-collar executive look. This might have been principally due to his clothing selections as well as having a *Disney* clean-shaven, *All-American*, appearance. Even while topped off with a thick salt and pepper head of hair. Scott, being the polar opposite, had a shaved head and red facial hair and had more baseball caps than I had shoes.

Ken was elegant and ever so consciences of society and appearances, both in his choice of clothes as well as his demeanor. He knew how to play the power game and make an entrance when needed. While Scott could wear a pair of jeans as if they had been sewn just for him, showing off all his below the waist assets from butt to bulge, the only tailored suit he possessed was his birthday suit, best matched while romping around someplace like *Burning Man* and wearing his latest *Nike* shoes.

Before Ken had entered my life, my style, due to a large number of professional social obligations, was much more quiet elegance. After a few years of marriage to Aaron, however, and having amassed my own wealth of jeans and T-Shirts back then, my style had slipped unfortunately more into the casual realm than it possibly should have. Ken, therefore, not only wound up re-shaping my sexual fantasies and standards for love but also influenced my current mode of dress. He was a fan of *Tommy Bahama*, knew women's designers better than most women, and had a budget for clothes and accessories that rivaled most department stores. While I had always been well dressed and had an innate understanding of the psychology of fashion from a young age on, I had rarely purchased a shoe whose heel was taller than an inch prior to Ken, who himself had a penchant for *Ferragamo* when it came to foot coverings. Taking another sip from my glass, I had to smile as the thought crossed my mind that Scott had probably never even heard of *Ferragamo.* In stark contrast, ever since Ken's entrance into my life, I had to admit that I had invested what must have been a small fortune in high-heeled stiletto shoes. And, it all started just to please him. He adored the color white, and therefore to this day, I would catch myself looking for white heels when I passed by a storefront.

He had been my *Pygmalion* and I his statue in so many different ways. I had come to life under Ken's touch and breath. Aside from steering my fashion purchases towards the sensual, he also made me realize that dining out did not have to be a work occasion and could be a romantic Hawaiian candlelit affair and expanded my already well-rounded pallet to such joys as

Grand Marnier Soufflé. Scott, I would imagine, would have been hard pressed to know that foie gras was goose liver much less have eaten it.

Of course, while Scott could be considered in many ways uncultured and unrefined when it came to the upper echelon way of life; he also had a unique mixture of straightforwardness, gentleness and strength. After all, he had no need to concern himself quite as much with the politics that moving through those facets of society required. I was wondering if I was corrupting him or broadening his pallet by inviting him in my world, just as Ken had done way back when with me.

Despite all the differences, it did not change how well both Scott and Ken kissed. How both men had a way of electrifying my body by their mere presence. If there was one thing to be thankful for, it was that I had not met them at the same time in my life.

Finishing our drinks, Scott and I headed to the steakhouse where the waiter took our drink order and shortly after that started bringing out food. Scott gave me a quizzical expression as the waiter placed a plate of carpaccio down in front of us. "The chef knows me," is all I said and with that, we focused on the thin slices of raw meat in front of us. I gathered some of the seasoning, cheese, greens, and meat onto my fork and savored the tangy sensation on my tongue.

"So tell me more about Ken. You had phone sex about a month before you were supposed to meet. What happened next?" he asked as he took a slice of carpaccio and hesitantly placed it on a piece of bread. Bringing the bread and meat combination tentatively to his lips, he paused long enough to smell it first before closing his eyes and biting into it. He was probably saying a silent prayer hoping not to have to spit it back out.

"I was swept up in a whirlwind of seduction," I responded and smiled at his apparent surprised reaction at being pleased by the dish. "We started to have phone sex almost every day. Our conversations started averaging 3 hours while our email correspondence began to resemble instant messages." I took a sip of my martini as the next appetizer was brought to our table, bacon wrapped dates. Taking one of these perfectly balanced sweet and salty concoctions into my mouth and washing it down with another sip of bitterness from my martini I continued. "What the emails started to lack in word count, however, I made up for in pictures. As the days progressed, I would take easily 20-40 pictures a week just for him - including something I had never done before - nudes."

At this, Scott raised an eyebrow in my direction and asked with a wicked smile, "Any you would care to share with me? Purely for intellectual reasons, of course. Just so I can get a better grip on what was going through his mind at the time." Taking now a more enthusiastic bite of the carpaccio, he looked expectantly in my direction.

"A better grip? Really?" My eyebrows arched slightly.

"Well, it would help to complete the picture, don't you think? Kind of like a forensic detective or scientist. I would retrace his actions, picture by picture. Reconstruct his state of mind and all that." He picked up a date and tentatively lifted it to his mouth.

"State of mind? Hmmm ... I had no idea you would be willing to go to such lengths just to help me out."

"For you? I would gladly jump on that grenade." He said with emphasize on '*grenade*' as he popped the date into his mouth. I could see by his face that this culinary flavor card had met with his approval again.

"That is quite the sacrifice. How selfless of you. Does the *Secret Service* know about you? Because, you would be a shoe-in for protecting the President with an attitude like that," I responded as I lifted my martini glass for a long sip.

"That's me, selfless to a fault." He paused and then adjusting his look to be one of somber honesty, he continued, "For your information, they did ask me to join, but I had to decline the offer. Weather is atrocious in D.C." He had started out with such a great poker face and then could not help himself but to smirk while reaching for his water glass.

I decided to pick up the thread nonetheless. "Yes, so I've heard. One of the main reasons why people do not join the *Secret Service* after having gone through all the trouble of the application, screening, test taking and background check - the weather in D.C.," I replied while buttering a piece of bread and taking a bite. "They have tried to mitigate the fall out with their low-cost Florida retirement option, but they still have so many unfilled positions. It's sad really." This back and forth was one of the reasons why Scott was worth his weight in gold.

"Ok, I'll be honest. The weather was not as much of a deterrent as the dress code. They do that whole running next to the car thing, in loafers. Who runs in loafers? If they allowed *Star Trek* T-Shirts instead of requiring those dark suits, I'd have signed up," Scott declared by finishing the last bite of carpaccio.

"Yes, well. I am glad to hear that you have your priorities straight at least." I felt we had gone as far as we could with that bit of repertoire so I decided to get back on point. "Anyway, to answer your question, yes I am still in possession of those images."

The waiter arrived with the next dish, mushroom ravioli. As Scott realized that this was a dish he actually recognized, he brought the conversation back to Ken. "So, you sent him nude pictures which you will show me ..."

"I don't think I ever agreed to show you the photos," I interrupted and giving him a hard stare that was utterly ineffectual since my lips kept curving upward despite my willing them to frown.

"Which you will consider showing me? " he asked with a boyish grin on his face. He continued, "And, which you might have on your computer right now?"

Sighing, I took out my laptop, flicked it on, flipped it into a tablet state, scrolled through several file folders and picked one. "This is the first such image I sent him."

Unlike the wolf-like leer I had expected, Scott's demeanor became that of an art aficionado. I could tell he was pleased; after all, the upturned corners of his mouth were not a facial expression of disgust. His eyes though told the full story. There was gentleness in them. After a minute of digesting every curve and shadow, he turned to me and said, "The picture is fantastic. Truly. But it does little justice to the real thing sitting in front of me." I could feel myself blushing at the compliment and I had to cast my eyelids down. He continued by saying, "Although, Ken lost out since you are more beautiful in the nude now than you were back then." And with those words I could feel myself turning three shades of red darker. Scott had seen me fully naked more often than not, however being partially clothed typically made one sexier than fully nude could ever be. So maybe this is the reason why I had decided to share the pictures. Certainly, there was a bit of showing off on my end, however maybe I was also attempting to be a bit more seductive. Why I felt the need to seduce Scott more than I already had, I could not figure out.

I knew it would take me a moment or two to gather my composure, so I just slide the computer Scott's way so he could view the next batch of email exchanges.

Subj: hmmmm........
Date: 10/18
To: FinanceGuy
File: Nude.jpg (184680 bytes) DL Time (TCP/IP): < 1 minute

Of all the things that I have done..........

I never thought.......this would be on the list of things I thought I would do........

God be with me........

###

Subj: Re: hmmmm........
Date: 10/18 11:00:38 AM
From: FinanceGuy

To: Pandora

Regardless of what happens ......

and realizing that I have seen completely gorgeous women before even maybe touched a few....

ok, ok well touched them in my dreams...

you my love......

are the most of every woman that I could ever dream to desire.....

INCREDIBLE

###

"This just confirms what I have already said. You have a sensuality and sexuality about you that captivates a person no matter the medium. I do have to admit, as magnetic of a pull as your pictures create, it is paltry compared to the full effect felt in your presence," commented Scott as I looked for the next email file. "It begs the question since you have this effect on people every day of your life, what did you get out of your exchange but words?"

I had to pause for a moment before answering, "I didn't know."

"You didn't know what?"

"I didn't know I had that pull you are talking about. That sexual magnetism. Not at that time anyway. I felt like the ugly duckling and it was because of him that I was being turned into a swan. No one had ever responded to me quite as he did. Had spoken to me the way he did. Written to me the way he did. Because of him I felt truly beautiful and wanted for the first time in my life." I paused our conversation as the busser cleared our plates and the waiter brought our filets. "For example, during this exchange, the night before we had spoken on the phone while he was on his way to a hockey game." I positioned the tablet so he had a better view of it.

Subj: my day so far
Date: 10/19
To: FinanceGuy

Woke up at 4 a.m. tossed and turned until 6 a.m. .. decided to get up .. wondering what you are doing .. hoping you had fun at the game .. I need some sleep .. when am I ever going to get some rest?

###

Subj: Re: my day so far
Date: 10/19 8:02:17 PM
From: FinanceGuy
To: Pandora

Love:
Must be because I was tossing and turning as well.......all because I can't get you out of my mind.........yes........you......

I want you that much.........that bad......

You are so delicious.....you make me ache

###

Subj: Re: my day so far
Date: 10/19
To: FinanceGuy

I hope your meetings go well despite the sleep deprivation.

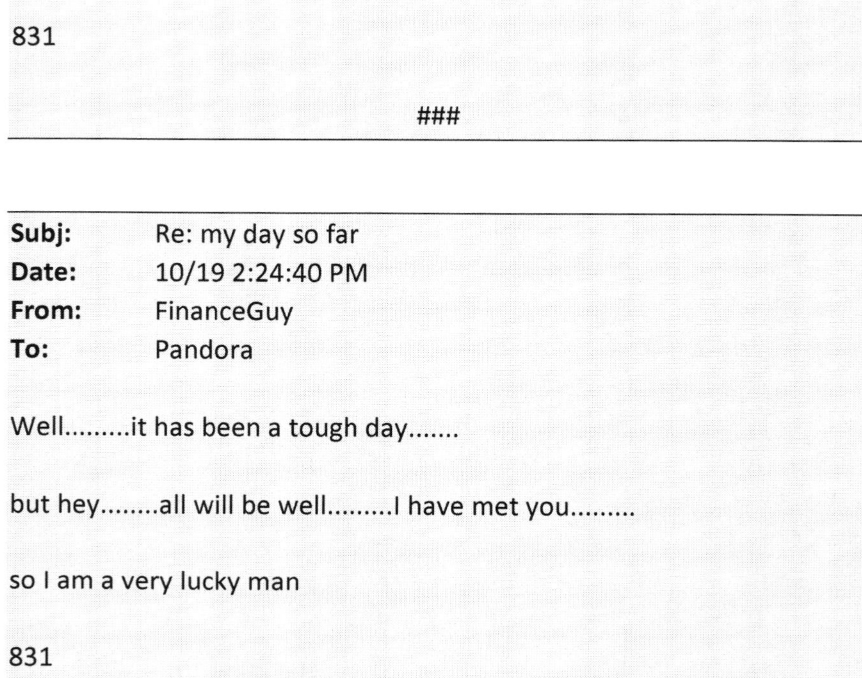
831

###

Subj: Re: my day so far
Date: 10/19 2:24:40 PM
From: FinanceGuy
To: Pandora

Well.........it has been a tough day.......

but hey........all will be well.........I have met you.........

so I am a very lucky man

831

###

"It looks like you guys were undeniably infatuated with each other," said Scott as he concentrated on his foie gras topped fillet and scalloped potatoes. "By the way, what is 831? Or is that some typo?"

"It was something that Ken had come up with." I could not help the wistful expression that crossed my face. "I always loved codes growing up and would practice breaking them. One day, out of the blue, he proposed this super cute idea of the '831' code," I replied as I scooped some spinach on top of my steak. "Much later, I found out that it was part of the general social speak much like BRB or OMG, but at the time I thought of it as our secret language."

"How disappointing for you I am sure," said Scott as I paused to take a sip of water. "So smart and yet so gullible. Were you crushed? Bleeding? Did you need a tourniquet?" he asked as he his eyes found mine over the rocks glass which he had lifted to take a sip of. Was that a flash of jealousy I saw across his face? Surely not!

I decided that it had been a trick of the light and instead picked up on the humor thread."Oh how funny. I wish I had a pen so I could forget to write that down," I replied with a sweet but slightly annoyed smile.

It was incredible to me how quickly he could turn on and off his charm as I noticed a glint of something in his eyes that did not go with his smiling lips when he placed his hand on top of mine and responded, "I was just observing."

I lifted his hand to my lips, placed a gentle kiss on his fingers and replied, "Well, in that case, just drill a hole in your head, set up a telescope, and call it a dome." This was more than just bantering, but I did not know what.

"I see that our bond grows stronger 'she-with-the-sarcastic-come-backs,'" replied Scott while he took advantage of the proximity of his hand to my face and caressed my cheek. There it was again. That expression I could not place.

Listening to his words instead of his face I responded with a sweet smile, "Is that my Indian name? Because on my license it says Pandora."

Leaning across the table he brought his other hand to my face, and with one on each side, as if holding a butterfly, gently leaned forward and kissed me on my lips. That was one way to change the topic of conversation and throw me off balance. Sitting back in his chair with a composed therapist/professor-like demeanor, he continued as if the kiss had not happened, "So, I am waiting with baited breath, what is 831?"

Trying to recover from the instant electrical jolt, I opened my eyes slowly still feeling the warm afterglow of his kiss. It was taking me slightly longer to regain my composure possibly due to the alcohol that was also coursing through my blood at this point. Clearing my throat, I responded, "831 stands for 8 Letters, 3 words, 1 Meaning. Do you need another hint?"

"What do I get if I solve it?" Scott shot me a smiling challenge laced with a hint of something or other.

"Nothing," I replied with a smirk.

"How about letting me slide a finger into you under the table?"

"No!" Did he really just ask me that?

"Please?" Was there anyone more persistent?

"I'll think about it," I replied. It was the easiest way to stop what experience had taught me would turn into a childish verbal tug of war otherwise.

"Good enough." Scott clasped his hands together satisfied with the bargain he had just struck. He could be so dominant at times.

"So what do you think the answer is?" I asked with a raised eyebrow, guessing he probably already knew or he would not have bargained to begin with.

It was as if I could see the sparks of his brain through his eyes as he gave his answer. "How about ... I Love You?"

"Yes, 831 is code for I love you."

"Great!" he was scooting his chair closer to mine.

"I said I would think about it."

"And I do love how you think, Pandora."

With a roll of my eyes, I took back possession of the tablet I searched for the next email file, which had a slew of pictures attached, in various states of dress. Trying to explain the reason for the number of images before handing him the content of the email I said, "Anyway, to get back on topic. The time for our meeting was drawing closer, less than three weeks away. But, he was headed to Alexandria, Virginia on a business trip and I might have had some twinges of insecurity and feeling a tad possessive of him."

"You?" asked Scott a bit bemused. "Possessive?" I could feel his hand on my thigh. I decided not to move it.

"Possibly a tad ... I was young after all," I replied. Scott just kept looking steadily into my eyes without blinking. There was just a hint of sadness there, or was that just determination? I could feel the heat of his hand through my pants and burning an imprint on my skin. "Ok, a lot."

Smiling he brought his hands back to his plate and took another bite of his filet. "Well, you were in your twenties." Pausing to adjust his slipped napkin on his lap, his hand wound up resting once again on my thigh before he asked, "So, what wild and crazy thing did you do to keep him out of the hotel bar and glued to his computer in his hotel room?" I pushed the tablet towards him in an answer. I had no idea how, but while one of his hands reached for the computer, the other had undone my zipper and one of his fingers was inside of me under the cover of my napkin, as he examined the images and emails with the same artistic appreciation I had seen earlier. He was more skilled than a close-up magician doing coin tricks. I could feel my chamber flooding almost instantly with warm, thick liquid and coating him where he was touching me. My walls were adjusting to encompass him and my head was pounding with the sudden circulation spike. The fear of discovery only augmented the adrenaline rush I was experiencing as I was losing the battle to try to keep my breathing steady. He had me trapped. Doing anything other than sitting there, being his personal finger puppet would have drawn unwanted attention to us and required a thorny explanation to the restaurant manager - who knew me personally. I was having a seriously difficult time finishing my fillet before dessert arrived. *Those hands should be patented.*

Subj: Re: A picture a day
Date: 10/22 2:31:31 PM
From: FinanceGuy
To: Pandora

You simply exquisite creature:

You ....with all of your beauty.......your amazing intellect........your captivating eyes........your heart of hearts.........

well........to put it simply........

captivate me.........

to say nothing else.........but............

OH MY GOD!!!!!!!

INCREDIBLE.....

And your desire reaches to the east coast as well..........

Endless........

###

Subj: Re: :-)
Date: 10/22 2:57:21 PM
From: FinanceGuy
To: Pandora

You are so mesmerizing.........

............have I used exquisite yet?

well then............

let me repeat......

EXQUISITE

###

Scott had a fantastic knack for knowing just where to focus the interior pressure. Leaning my arms slightly against the table to steady myself, my breathing became more belabored as I tried not to make eye contact and instead kept staring at a particular spot on the screen. As he was flipping through the exchange, it took every ounce of self-control and concentration to explain the next set of emails. "Of course,... the day would not have been complete ... without at least ... one phone sex session and this is where the first... lie came to light - his name."

I could see his ears perk up. Temporarily distracted from using me as his personal finger puppet, he gave me a respite and used both of his hands to hold the computer, one quite notably glistening with cum, as he looked at the next file.

Subj: If...
Date: 10/22
To: FinanceGuy

... I don't see you online remember to e-mail the phone number :-)

Thanks

P

###

Subj: Re: If...
Date: 10/22 8:53:26 PM
From: FinanceGuy
To: Pandora

Gorgeous:
The # is 703-XXX-XXXX rm 1525.......k cole

if you can't sleep.......call any time

###

Looking up from the computer with a somewhat distracted look upon his face, Scott asked, "k cole? I assume no relation to the fashion designer. What went through your mind when you saw this email?" The bus boy had come by in the meantime and cleared our table. The waiter had dropped off two Grand Mariners in front of us in snifter glasses and was preparing to bring us a plate of dessert selections and coffee. Thankfully, during this time both of our hands had been above the table.

"No, no relation, but he knew his fashion designers and had his finger on the pulse of fashion. That is just the way of people in the finance world, though. Knowing all about the status symbols from fashion to jewelry to electronics ... As to what I was thinking, I didn't know what to make of it at first," I said as I lifted the snifter to my nose strangely missing his finger inside of me. "I called him up that night asking about the initial K. He explained that Charles was his middle name and Ken was his first."

"How did you feel about that particular revelation?" asked Scott as the coffee and dessert plate arrived at our table. The alcohol must have started to affect his spatial judgment for as he pushed his cognac to the side, a bit more forceful than necessary, he almost spilling it in the process.

"I was trying to take him at face value. After all, the South had a longstanding tradition of people going by their middle name instead of their first. However, come to find out much, much, much, later, this was a lie as well. His middle name was not Charles." Dipping a spoon into the tiramisu and making sure to include all the layers into a single bite, I brought the spoon to Scott's mouth and said, "You have to try this! It's better than sex."

Smiling he took the proffered bite, swallowed, paused, and shook his head. "No, not better than sex, but pretty darn close." I leaned forward to kiss a dab of cream off his lips. "Now it's better than sex," he said with a wink and smile before checking out the east coast style cheesecake. I could not help but pause and luxuriate in the impression of the velvety softness of his lips mixed with the aroma of mascarpone cream.

Emptying a packet of the yellow sweetener into his coffee and following up with some cream, he bit his lower lip and said under controlled laughter and a bit of an edge to his voice, "He probably should have had a middle name starting with the letter 'O', like Ken Oliver Cole (KOC)."

I started laughing so hard I almost choked on the sip of cognac I had just taken to follow up the tiramisu kiss with. "That would have been a fine way to die," I said chagrinned as soon as I was able to catch my breath again. Sitting back up and taking his hand, which was holding a cheesecake topped fork and diverting it to my mouth I said, "I never would have thought of that one, but yes that would have been an apt acronym for him." Letting his hand go and allowing him to stab the cheesecake again and complete the trip to his lips this time I continued, "Fortunately, his parents were not that unkind. His full name, which I did not learn until years after that day, is Kenneth Michael Cole."

Scott had a faraway look on his face like he was trying to draw a parallel or draw a connection. Shaking his head slightly it looked like a *'never mind'* move, or a *'it'll come to me later'* move. Taking a sip of coffee to aid the cheesecake bit stuck in his throat, he asked, "Well, middle and the first name aside, what happened next?"

"I sent him more pictures of course!"

"Of course, and his response was one of disgust? Dismay?" replied Scott putting his fork down on his plate. His words sounded playful, I could tell though that he was still trying to figure out what it was that he could not remember.

Sticking my tongue out, I pushed the tablet towards him and said, "Yes, both of those. Here, read for yourself."

Subj: Re: More Pictures
Date: 10/23 9:34:45 AM
From: FinanceGuy
To: Pandora

My Hope:
You simply capture me..........

You could be.......quite possibly.......the most beautiful woman I have ever met........both inside.......and out.

My breath is gone

831

###

Sighing as if the world were on his shoulders, Scott took another sip of coffee and allowed me to take the tablet back. "You have quite the relationship with the camera. It's almost as if the camera were your lover." Putting down his coffee, he looked me in the eyes with unexpected sincerity, "Ken never had a chance the poor guy. I can see why he fell for you so quickly without ever having met you in person or why he preferred staying in his hotel room talking with you as opposed to hunting for the new game at the hotel bar."

Taken aback by the change in tone and evident sincerity in his voice I answered a bit stunned, "Thank you, Scott. I think that has to be one of the sweetest things you have said to me so far... Thank you." Leaning over the tablet to find the next email file I explained, "I flew home the next day and I was getting anxious about our upcoming meeting. I was not as nervous about the actual sex between us, but the clothes I would wear to meet him. He had such particular tastes. In our phone sex sessions, he would always ask me what I was wearing and incorporate it into the fantasy. I wanted the first time he saw me in person to be perfect."

Subj: Another Day Closer
Date: 10/25
To: FinanceGuy

I am off to get a workout in today ... hope your day has been going fairly well ... I should be back no later than 4 p.m. .... btw .. which color do you like better .. green or blue?

Talk to you later love

Pandora

###

Subj: Re: Another Day Closer
Date: 10/26 7:14:02 AM
From: FinanceGuy
To: Pandora

Gorgeous:
I have personally always been partial to white. Hope you slept well..........the team is now well rested and ready for another day of hell.......I mean life.........

Hope to see you later.........greet your day with one of those smiles I love......

831

###

"You do have a great smile Pandora, one of your many great features," said Scott as his gaze went from my face to my chest.

Lifting his chin with my finger and I said, "Why thank you, I have gotten quite attached to my smile as well."

It was then that the chef decided to come and pay us a visit. After all the introductions were made he chatted with us for a few minutes, asking if we had liked the food and, of course, we gave him stellar feedback. We talked about some of our favorites as well as touched on a few soccer game predictions, and then it was time for him to get back to the kitchen.

With dinner concluded, I motioned for the waiter and asked for the check. "Chef has already taken care of everything Ms. Richardson," was the waiter's whispered response. I had the most difficult time trying to pay for my dinner in this town. I reached into my purse, pulled out two hundred dollars and left them as a tip on the table. On our way out of the restaurant, we stopped by the kitchen again to give our thanks to the chef and headed out to the casino floor.

"What would you like to do?" I asked Scott as I turned my body slightly to face his, flushed with alcohol, carbs, and the lingering memory of his under the table antics, while walking out the restaurant doors. "We can go to the lounge and do some dancing, or hang out at the bar and drink and talk, or maybe enjoy a game of blackjack if you like."

Unlike the playful and teasing banter I had witnessed emitting from him for the last few hours, he had '*that*' look about him. That same look of intensity he always got when he was about to ravish me, but this time there seemed to be an extra ounce or two of determination. There was not a hint of playfulness in his tone or his eyes when he grabbed me around my waist, pulled me into him and leaned towards my ear and whispered, "I just want to take you to the room and fuck you until you don't know your own name anymore." His tone sounded like a man who had something to prove.

I felt a bit faint from the sudden rush of blood leaving my brain. The sensation of having walked full force into an electric fence when he pulled me completely towards his body had stopped all voluntary movement or contemplation of mine. I was caught up in the thought of what he had just proposed and could feel my nether region starting to pulsate as his cock pressed up against it, already fully erect, through his pants. Whatever he was trying to prove, my body seemed to be more than happy to go along with it. "Challenge accepted," was all I could barely whisper in response, and with those words, we walked towards the hotel elevators.

CHAPTER 21

Scott and I entered the elevator. As I turned to slide the hotel key into the security slot and pushed the top floor button, I could feel him pressing up against me from behind. I looked up and saw his hands on either side of me against the elevator wall, causing me to lose balance and pushing me into the display. Catching myself with my hands against the cool metallic wall, I regained my balance enough to turn around and face his eager mouth. We had just enough time for our tongues to find and savor each other before the doors opened to our floor.

I slid out from underneath his arms and tried to focus on the directional sign containing the various room numbers. I attempted to remember which way down the corridor we would need to go to get to our room. Then I saw it. The arrow was pointing right. Scott followed me out and as we made our way to our door, grabbed me again and spun me around. Kissing me while walking, he forwards and I backwards, we finally made it to the very end. Still having the key in my hand from the elevator floor selection; and with my back against the door; Scott, without ever lifting his lips off mine, deftly grabbed the key from me, reached behind, and opened the door.

The casino hotel building we were in was not your typical rectangular structure. Each end came to a point, much like a ship. Earlier that night I had checked into one of these corner suite points, which along with many other amenities came with its own hot tub in the room. I remembered thinking when I toured the abode prior to my heading to meet Scott, that it was larger than some apartments I had lived in. Two stories with its own elevator, the bottom floor had a full bar, sitting area, guest bath, and office. The top floor had the bedroom with a TV that lowered itself from the ceiling, a dual walk in shower with multiple showerheads, a bathtub that overlooked the strip, and a hot tub in the very corner tip that did the same. There were probably over ten TV screens throughout the accommodations, including those built into the bathroom mirrors. All the outward facing walls were floor to ceiling glass windows with motorized curtains giving a 270-degree view of the Las Vegas valley, from the mountains to the strip.

Most hotels in Las Vegas these days had a mirrored glass exterior, allowing the occupants of the rooms privacy during the day without having to draw the curtains. However, at night, much like most windows, it was easy to view the interior if the lights were on inside. The redeeming quality of our particular location was not only being on the top floor but also being on the top floor with no immediate neighbors to worry about looking in. Short of a helicopter taking a fly by or a car on the I-15 with binoculars, we could have turned on all the lights and left the curtains retracted without any fear of being seen.

Scott, while making what by most standards would be considered *'good money,'* had never been in a hotel room like this. Most people had not. A suite of this caliber typically went for several thousand dollars a night, and even then, was rarely available to anyone who was not a *'high roller'* or like me, had friends in high places at that particular property. While the room was not free of charge, it was well worth the money to see the look on Scott's face as we entered.

Being a single mother, my home was out of the question for these types of trysts, and I rarely felt comfortable enough to meet someone at their home either. Fortunately, my paycheck was quite adequate to fund my penchant for experiencing Las Vegas to the fullest whenever the whim struck.

Taking Scott by the hand, I showed him around the suite. When we got to the extreme corner of the room with the hot tub and the corner window seats, we both suffered from a bit of vertigo and walked back towards the bar. I took off my heels, turned on the entertainment system to one of the music channels, and proceeded to make us two gin and tonics.

I walked towards him with a drink in each hand. He ignored the glass proffered in his direction but took advantage of the fact that both of my hands were occupied. He reached in-between my arms and started to unbutton my shirt. Having a bit of a difficulty he asked, "Starch?"

"No, that is just how *Brooks Brothers* makes their shirts," I responded with a small laugh. Giving me a *'you-are-a-brat'* look, I placed the drinks, helped him with the first few buttons, and noted the look of appreciation as I kept the shirt on but in a completely unbuttoned state. His reaction proved my personal theory in regards to the ratio of clothing and skin and how it affected sex appeal. Having gotten glimpses of my bra all night long, now he could admire the full lace pattern before him.

As he slipped out of his shoes, I lifted his shirt over his head to expose the almost hairless but fantastically defined chest. He might not have the bulk of most of my conquests, but his muscle definition would make most plastic action figures jealous. *Why did he have to hide this body behind such ill-suited clothes?* Reaching to undo his jeans he stopped my hands and said, "You first."

I moved to unbutton and then unzip my pants showing the lacy front of my string underwear. Enjoying his lingering gaze, I pushed my pants slowly but smoothly down from hips to ankles without bending my legs. My forehead was almost touching my knees as I used my hands to keep the pants pushed to the floor while stepping out of them gently. As I straightened back up, I adjusted the thigh highs, which had an adhesive backing allowing them to stay up without the aid of a garter belt. I could hear Scott catching his breath. Closing the gap between us I walked two steps towards him, raised myself up on the balls of my feet to reach his lips, and while he was distracted with the kiss, I finished removing his jeans. Using the same smooth motion I had used on my own pants, I heard, "My God you are beautiful," as I helped him step out of the denim.

Straightening back up, he took his hands to cup both sides of my face, and kissed me. As the kiss intensified, he slid his hands down my neck and shoulders, never losing contact with my skin as his hands were now cleverly positioned under the fabric of my shirt. With one smooth slow motion, he slid his hands down my arms, undressed me of my shirt in the process and had it land on the floor. His hands dropped down to my waist, and before I realized what was happening, he bent down and forward, and had me tossed over his shoulder like a sack of potatoes. I was in shock. I was not a petite and delicate little flower and this had never happened to me before. Kicking and screaming, "Let me down!" he walked up the stairs to the second level with me slung over his shoulder. He was no more phased than if he were carrying a pillow. Finally, he placed me back on my feet once we reached the top of the stairs, which were located directly in front of the entrance to the open floor plan bathroom. "Holy hell! I cannot believe you just did that!" I said reacting out of shock and gave him a firm shove with both hands against his chest, inducing him to lose his balance.

"Took you by surprise did I?" asked Scott laughingly as he stumbled back a few steps to regain his balance and wrapped his arms around my waist, causing us both to wobble. As we accidentally careened into the walk-in shower, we bumped into the controls and inadvertently turned on the multiple showerheads in the process. Shocked by the cold then hot water, we both started laughing and I jumped out as fast as I could, but Scott decided to stay a bit longer.

Soaking wet I found a towel and walked over to the corner with the hot tub and window seats to enjoy the view while I attempted to towel myself dry. Listening to the water being shut off, the A/C kicked on as the vent hit me with a blast of air causing my nipples to stand up through the lacy fabric. I could hear Scott coming up behind me and felt the heat radiating from his body as he pulled my long hair to the side and said, "I am sorry if I threw you off balance." Water dripped down my front, one slow drop at a time, tickling my skin in the process. All thought of the embarrassment of being slung over his shoulder left my mind as I felt the heat of his breath brushing up against the chilled skin of my neck. I arched my back and neck leaning into him.

Feeling his lips and teeth creating a superficial suction on my shoulder, his hands circled to the front enveloping both breasts and moved down the center of my stomach in slight circular massaging movements until they reached hip level. His hands pulled me closer inviting my ass to meet up with his eager and ready cock. Not really being able to help myself, my hips started moving in a wave like motion, massaging it into an even harder state as my head leaned back onto his shoulder. With a sigh, I could feel all vestiges of cognitive thought leaving my brain and my baser instincts taking over.

Slowly, with our bodies pushed into each other, and still wearing my damp thigh highs, bra and g-string he noticed the chill on my dewy skin. He guided me towards the hot tub taking the small steps into the water. Once my foot reached the bottom floor, his arm reached across my chest and turned my body to face his. With my long dripping hair still across my breasts, he reached behind me to undo my bra. He lifted my hair up and over letting it cascade down as I extricated myself out of what now was an even flimsier piece of fabric due to the water and leaving it to dry on the side. With a hand firmly on the small of my back, he pulled me towards him, kissing me, feeling the wet, if somewhat chilled, bare breasts against his radiating chest, I pushed my hips into his. "I could stay like this for hours," is the only coherent thought that registered.

Leaning me back a tad, his hands reached for my breasts again. "Let me warm them up a bit," is what I heard as his mouth lowered down to engulf one of my nipples. Like a telegraph, I could feel the almost instant electrical communication between the nipple and my underwater grotto as a wave of pleasure echoed between the two body parts. It did not help matters any that his free hand was reaching for my clit and massaging it gently in slow but deliberate circles through the wet fabric. I could already feel myself starting to lose touch with my surroundings and having them fade into the background as the sensation was beginning to take over my mind and body. I did not want to cum so soon, though, so I pulled away, causing a bit of a stir in the water while breaking the suction seal of his mouth on my breast and interrupting the rhythm of his hand. Not fazed by any of this, and with a mesmerizing stare, Scott reached for my waist again and pulled me back into a stirring hug - optimizing on skin-on-skin contact. Slowly rocking against each other in the water with my head on his chest, almost dancing to the music being played over the multiple speakers in the suite, we felt the water lap against our skin. He leaned back, with one hand lifted my chin so as to look into my eyes, and said, "You are one of the most beautiful and sensual women I have ever met." My eyes closed again as he leaned in and hungrily started kissing me. His lips were completely bypassing my brain and despite my prior efforts, my body was feeling like a pinball machine on multi-ball play. There was no escaping the constant currents of electricity coursing through me at that point.

He took a step behind and up, standing on the lowest step in the hot tub, pulled me along with him. The water was now only hip high on me. Slowly keeping one arm at the small of my back, his other arm circled to the front as I came up for air from his kiss. Once it reached my chest, he pushed me at a 90-degree angle until my head reached the water level. Still keeping my hips pressed against his, and with both of my feet touching the floor, and my arms outstretched on the water surface, both of his hands trailed across my arched back and stopped at my butt and thighs. Not knowing what he had in mind while part of my body was still as taut as a newly tuned piano string, part of me was feeling completely relaxed. A beautiful oscillation from the heightened hunger that was all consuming a second or two ago, I took pleasure in the sensation of the water surface against my skin. The miniature waves felt like gentle caresses from another lover cascading from neck to waist playing a soft and light tune along my spine. I closed my eyes and focused on the delightful contrasting heat of the water against my back and the coolness of the air against my once again exposed chest. My nipples responded to the chilled air above by pointing thick and hard skyward of their own volition. They were the only physical betrayal of my body's keen level of sensitivity as the relaxed, but hungry state continued.

"I want to take you like this," he said lifting my legs up into a dead man's float. I drifted on the steaming water as he moved his hands to pull off my g-string underwear while keeping my thigh highs on my legs. Once he removed the g-string, his hands reached for my ass again and trailed along my legs. Starting at the lace top of my thigh highs, moving along the underside of my knees, then calves, then ankles, he spread my legs apart slightly. His caresses after the already intoxicating kiss were not helping to alleviate the anticipation building inside of my body. I was feeling a familiar ache from the rush of blood to my outer lips and clit as my hunger started to escalate once again.

With my body still skimming the water surface, he pulled me closer and lined up his cock with my pussy. I quivered with anticipation and he could feel me shaking as he put his right hand on my stomach to steady me. The edges of perception were starting to fade again as the blood supply was no longer being driven to my brain as efficiently as it had earlier that evening. Before I could stop my voice, I heard myself saying, "Please, I need you inside of me." My legs wrapped around his waist reiterating my request. I could feel the head of his cock brushing up against my clit, which was feeling as taut as my nerves at that moment. Then, he finally entered me. The instant I felt his cock penetrate my tight and swollen pussy, my back arched on the water, and I could hear both of our voices echoing from the walls. I could not think. He was just such a perfect fit from tip to base that I knew all it would take was a stroke or two for me to cum.

His hands reached for my waist, establishing the rhythm. I welcomed his fingers massaging my posterior side and my hands reached out to touch his. Grabbing his wrists and forearm, I grasped them tighter and tighter, just as my body automatically squeezed down tighter and tighter around his cock. I could feel the electrical storm of sensations building inside of me. The room started to spin with the force of passion that had taken over every nerve cell and before I knew it, I climaxed. My cum was mixing with the water around us and my body kept pushing out wave after wave of ecstasy. Typically, at this point, most men would be nudged out from the strength of the walls contracting around them; but not Scott. I could see that he was even more turned on after watching me cum. Unbelievably, his erection which had already been like steel just kept increasing in hardness. The plus side of being highly orgasmic and cumming almost as soon as entered is that it tends to pave the way for multiple orgasms for me. Scott already knew this and I could hear his voice as if from far away saying, "I am going to make you cum again," as his thrusts became a bit more intense, and my hands reached for the edge of the hot tub to steady myself. True to his word, the sensation built yet once again. It was unbelievable how effortlessly he was controlling my every thought and movement. How my body kept responding to him like a junkie needing more. Not only was Scott's cock an almost instantaneous pleasure delivery device for me, but it was also more addicting than any crack cocaine on the market. Maybe it had something to do with the fact that it had always been harder to get myself to orgasm than it was for me to orgasm during sex, particularly sex with Scott, but when he entered me, once was never enough. This time around, the magnitude had increased and by the time the wave broke again all over him, I was barely aware of any of my surroundings. Scott, however, was still not stopping and before the wave had finished crashing, another was already building up inside of me, stronger and higher than the last one. To think that there was a time, not so long ago, when sex was something I had done as an obligation. I definitely had no ability to put a grocery list together in my head while Scott was creating hurricane after hurricane of orgasms making me feel like I was being turned inside out in the whirlwind of ecstasy. As much as there was something about his shape or size or both that just kept consistently hitting my g-spot over and over again, burning through the haze of the storm of endorphins that were being created, I could also feel the heat of his hands leaving an imprint on my skin. Electricity can only flow once a circuit is complete, one of the reasons why kissing, for me, while climaxing heightens the climax. Right now Scott's hands were serving the same purpose as his lips had, closing that circuit of the electrical hurricane as it kept gathering strength while it crossed back and forth through my body, spinning between his cock and hands. The waves kept getting stronger as they were taking control and I felt like I was being lifted up 20,000 feet into the air. If this kept up, I would need an oxygen mask or suffer from altitude sickness. By the time this orgasm finally peaked and the energy was released all over him once again, you could have told me I was in India during a tsunami and I would have believed you. I was so disoriented. With my body reacting to heights it had not felt for an excruciatingly long time, I could only assume that it was the sheer iron quality of Scott's cock, vigor of his rhythm, and will power, that kept him surrounded by my wet pussy. I could feel it pushing harder and harder down on him with the ever-growing strength of my summits.

Fighting my way back to reality through the haze of the last orgasm, I opened my eyes and saw Scott watching my brown hair float around my face. Our eyes locked and if it were a tad darker, I think the arc of energy this created between us would probably be visible to the naked eye. Scott had never stopped his rhythm and my head was starting to spin again from the sheer emotion building back up. At this pace, if these were actual hurricanes instead of virtual ones, the National Center in Florida would have to come up with a different naming convention since the alphabet has too few letters to keep up with the "season" Scott was creating in my ever-growing electrically charged anatomy.

I could feel myself getting ready to crest the wave again. Before I descended from a towering swell into a million impulses all over his divining rod, though, I could see Scott starting to relinquish some of his tightly wound control and finally taking that first step to giving himself over to the moment. There was something different in his eyes. You could almost see the endorphins swimming around in his irises. He seemed to be looking straight into my soul and connecting with me candidly on a level he had never done before. He pushed himself a little harder into me, a little deeper, a little slower but more forceful with each thrust. It was as if he himself was no longer in control of his body either. His hands were holding me a little tighter and even his stance had changed. His voice was a bit rougher and his body was starting to tense. The feedback of his desire did something I thought impossible; it drove me even higher. There was a hunger and urgency in me now, of such a level, which had not been there a moment ago.

Despite having already climaxed several times in successive burst, seeing him getting ready to cum, however, focused me entirely on the gluttony of consuming him. All I knew at that moment was my body wanted more. It wanted achingly all of him inside of me, now! My legs gripped tighter around him, pushing him further into me until I could feel the base of his shaft at my entrance. Staring into my eyes, he called out my name and I could feel his balls getting tighter up against me. His cock was starting to pulsate and was working to move his cum up his shaft. Time seemed to stand still as I could feel the movement of his cum from base to tip and then, in a perfectly timed simultaneous explosion, I felt the sudden heat of him as he shot himself towards my back wall. He seemed to have an endless supply stored up as wave after wave was gushing out of him and kept being shot up inside of me. The heat of his cum alone was raising my body temperature a degree or two as I responded to every outpour of his by arching up and taking him in deeper. My body felt like it was being struck by lightning with such ferocity that I could almost picture myself disintegrating on the spot. I had him now. The evidence of his desire for me was trapped inside of my walls mixing with my own. After that, neither one of us could possibly have another orgasm left in us. *Or could we?*

Spent and reeling from the sheer force of our mutual orgasm, for a few moments, the only audible sound reflecting from the water surface and the walls, was our breathing mixed with the sound of the water itself as it moved expending its own energy in order to regain the calm and level surface we initially stepped into.

"So, what's your name again?" Scott asked jokingly.

Dreamily I responded, "Your *'mind-wipe'* mission is accomplished."

Legs shaking and still inside of me, he moved towards the edge until his ass found the other step and leaned back into an almost sitting position. My back arched and rose from the water with my hair trailing behind me creating a little waterfall as my head lifted up. With my legs still around him and making sure that we stayed connected like two Lego pieces, my arms wrapped around his neck and my head rested on his shoulder. My hips were adjusting against his in the position transition. Incredibly, he was still hard, and I was still wet. Unconsciously at first, and then as an idea dawned in my head, with a wicked purpose, my hips continued to move up against his ever so slightly. My lips found the soft spot on his neck. Kissing him delicately and distracting him from my hips moving against his, I could hear the sound of my kisses echoing back from the hotel walls and from the water on his neck. He could feel the water from my hair drip down his back while my hips never stopped their leisurely rhythm. I knew from experience that this is where the greater share of men were highly vulnerable. In this fashion, instinct was not being overruled by conscious thought. Relaxed and expecting to bask in the afterglow, all of a sudden Scott felt it! The aftershock brought on by my continued rocking after the fact! That last bit of cum rising from his balls coursing through his cock and splashing against the tight walls of my pussy. My plan worked too well, however. Not only had I triggered the aftershock in him, but, after what I thought was all that I had to give, I gasped and felt my own jolt in answer to his as my pussy was tightening down again. This time, though, I was able to gather my wits about me first.

"And this is me getting even for the 'mind-wipe,'" I whispered into his ear. I could feel his body vibrate with small laughter in answer followed up with a content sigh.

We stay that way for a while, our breathing echoing back from the walls, rocking against each other gently as the water was caressing our waists. The warm water dripped from my hair down his back, enveloping him like a soft blanket. Once the room finally stops spinning altogether, I lifted my head off his shoulder as my warm wet hair slid along his back and off. Knowing that Scott's erection would never soften as long as he was still inside of me, despite his two back-to-back orgasms, I lifted up from his still unbelievably hard cock, stepped out of the hot tub and made my way to the bathroom where I proceeded to take off my soaking wet thigh highs.

Finding a towel and a robe, I towel dried my hair and wrapped myself up in the robe. Heading back to the bar, I tossed the watered-down gin and tonic and made two fresh drinks. Leaving one on the counter for Scott, I took the other with me on the couch and curled up with my drink and my warm thoughts. I closed my eyes until I could feel Scott's lips on mine and heard his voice, "So tell me more about Ken. What happened next?"

***

CHAPTER 22

Subj: Good morning
Date: 10/27
To: FinanceGuy

I was thinking the other day when I grow up, I want to be just like you. To think that you got up at the crack of dawn, took a plane from D.C. to Phoenix, and then went straight to the office is a testament to your work ethic. Thank you for all the phone calls yesterday. I am just sorry I was not able to talk to you as you were driving to the office. After I had realized I had missed your call, my mind went racing for a good 20 minutes. All I could think about was you and the way your hands might feel on my body.

It is strange. I have so much self-control when I am on the phone with you. Yes, I know that you are trying to throw me off balance and cause me to breathe funny when you go from talking about the latest political news item, to running your tongue along my clit, and fingering me, and then curling your finger towards my stomach to hit that g-spot. <sigh> Thankfully, more often than not, I am able to hold it together and not to give you the exact reaction you are looking for. Damn it, I just refuse to have you listen to me orgasm for the 20th time that day <smiling>. How quickly do you think I can be manipulated by your voice? By your words? By your breath? Ok ... do not answer that. And while I pat myself on the back quite vigorously on my self-control during the daytime, once I am lying in bed trying to go to sleep, I am just a tad more challenged when it comes to keeping my thoughts and my reactions to them from running rampant. I might have a little more of an issue with my willpower during those late night hours. Ok, frankly, all trace of a semblance of moral fiber goes right out the window. My mind runs wild and there is no taming or controlling those musings anymore. I close my eyes and you invade my thoughts with the stealth of a Nazi Storm Trooper. Once that day's continuous video loop starts playing in my head, the off button cannot be found as I feel your voice resonate through my entire body. Last night's episode ... hmmm, something about going down ... just when I would want to ... hmm push your head ... you would come up and I could feel you just on the outside ... finishing off by going all the way back.<shaking my head>. It is exhausting trying to get any kind of sleep with you being projectionist, star and director of my personal and endless video loops. Early in the mornings when I know I have another 30 minutes before I have to get up it is not much better. I close my eyes and keep thinking of our soon to be first meeting. I can see your eyes staring into me the way they do in your pictures. The way your lips curve ever so gently when you smile and how my hand will reach out to trace the outline of your mouth. I think about how fast my heart will beat and how wonderful it will be to drink you in your scent, your sound, your feel. I wonder if that first kiss will be just as I have imagined it. What it will be like to lean into you and have you feel me press my body into yours. And, while all of these things make my eyes glaze with wonder, I have to admit that yes, I am scared ... yes, I am nervous ... but all of those emotions are also mixed with and an anticipation and passion I usually reserve for my work ... and now you. And then, I get scared.

I know that you think my hesitancy, fear and apprehension when I talk to you or reflect on you, must come from your speculation that I might be disappointed with you once we finally lay eyes on each other. However, that is so not the case. Yes, there is the general anxiety that surrounds meeting someone you have never seen before, but my fear is not you disappointing me. No, quite to the contrary! I am almost petrified at times thinking that the in-person me will not live up the one in my pictures. What happens when there is no make-up? No carefully controlled camera angels? No meticulously arranged clothing? Seeing my breast reduction scars. Will you still think I am beautiful? Will you still want me? I hope the answer will be yes.

Then, there is the whole concept I am still trying to come to terms with of having fallen in love with an electronic impulse. During my weaker moments, I sit and question my sanity and intelligence. I have taken a leap of off a cliff I thought I would never even find much less actually dive from, based on someone's voice, emails and chats alone. How can we honestly know anything about each other without having met in person? How can you be so sure that I am the perfect person for you? You are a tall, handsome, successful, single with no children. You are a guy with a voice to die for and could have your pick of anyone you meet. Why me? Me! Who is still technically married with a young son and so many miles from where you live! What sane person does this? But then again I suppose there is nothing sane about love. Our situation, though, is so far removed from anything that I have ever done, it is scaring me just a tad ... ok, maybe a lot. Again, just to clarify, I have no fear of you not living up to expectations, but I do worry and fret that I might not be able to live up to yours on so many levels.

I agonize not just about the appeal of my physical form to you, once presented in 3D, but my ability to maintain a relationship with you past our first meeting. I am so inexperienced in so many different ways when I compare myself to you relationship wise. I never had a high school sweetheart or that puppy love relationship that lasted for months or even years without any sexual intercourse. During those days, in my life, I was always working and any notion of romance was just that, a notion. Truthfully, I would not have known what to do with a boyfriend if one had even been presented to me. I was always busy with work even prior to high school. Work I know. Work I am comfortable with. Success in work I am familiar with and expect, but the same cannot be said of relationships and I. I doubt I have enough knowledge to even be considered a novice. Prior to my marriage, my longest romantic liaison lasted no more than a month. I have only failure as a history and no successful examples in my family to draw from. Therefore, if we look at the columns in my relationship spreadsheet, in one column, I have several month or less long relationships and a disaster of a marriage under my belt. The bottom line? A red number. The other column has you. I am hoping that you will not be moved to the disaster column like everyone else. However, I do not know how to keep that from happening. What do I do with you? How do I behave with you? How do I make this connection last? How do I make it last forever? How does love actually work? And then there is the most terrifying deliberation of all: How do I not feel devastated if this ends?

I have never been in love before and this level of emotion for someone who is used to logic is uncomfortable and unsettling. It is uncontrollable. I have been used. I have been hurt. I have been misunderstood most of my life long. But, I have never felt cherished. I have never felt wanted for all of me. I have never felt truly loved in return by anyone ... not even my family.

There is one more confession to be made when it comes to my insecurities since I am already bearing my soul to you. I know you might laugh at this and think I am joking, but it is a very real vulnerability of mine: my sexual inexperience and my ability to please my partner. I am grateful that my soon to be ex-husband has established he thinks the world of me in this area. My former partners have never complained and always given quite positive feedback. Nevertheless, there is still the gnawing insecurity that I am just not good enough. Granted, I am considered particularly flexible, but I am no acrobat. I love sensuality and experience my partner through my skin but would be unable to do a handstand while having sex for example. Heck, while I have confidence in my oral skills, as far as actual intercourse - *'Tab A in Slot B'* type of intercourse is concerned - I have rarely been on top and never been able to make my partner cum that way. One of the most normal positions in the world and I feel that I do not know how to do it properly. So here we are, and especially after all the conversation we have been having on the subject together, all the phone sex and play acting and making each other cum, not being able to possibly please you terrifies me. Moreover, it is during those moments, those moments when I realize sex is your biggest draw and probably my weakest link when I want to just chuck it all.

So there you have it ....

Do what you will with that info.

###

Subj: after this morning...........
Date: 10/27 11:03:06 AM
From: FinanceGuy
To: Pandora

My Love:

I have probably started and stopped this letter so many times to you over the course of the last few months. I have so much to say to you.....so much that I work on words to describe .....so much where I have difficulty expressing the wonder of how I see you and feel about you. All of these things exist without having ever touched you, or seen for myself if I take your breath away, or if the smile that I feel through your words is actually the same smile that would be on your perfect face.

I guess it is true that when we, as people, do finally fall in love and find ourselves unable to describe emotion, then that love......by its very nature.......elevates us to new heights and with new emotions. These emotions are of course uncertain and I think human nature also tells us that if we should discount them that the mental gymnastics that we go through on a minute or hourly or daily basis will somehow make the anticipation.....the fear......the worry.......the potential failure........or the wonder .....the permanence.......the ecstasy and the pure joy of what love ....a different accepting love.........could be.

Having never really calculated or charted a way to your heart........I find myself holding it. I hold it with care and pride........with intense emotion and with character that you are likely unfamiliar with. I have traveled many roads in my life........and I have endured more failures than I care to admit at times. I have lost millions and gained millions........but have always rested with what little character I have. I have over the years become a more and more closed person.......a person that does not open up.......does not share.........and does not allow people into the deepest part of my private life. I guess I do these things for many reasons.......it could be that it is because of my fucked up childhood......or the fact that I never had a teacher......or a mentor. Maybe it is because my first instinct is to survive......to exist. Maybe it is because friends have fucked me over.......business associates have been disingenuous...........and the like. But in the reverse, I have lived life.......good or bad......the best way that I knew how to. Making the most of the hand that God has dealt to me.......and even though in times when my confidence is shattered......I persevere because I know that he has a plan for me. And then came you.

Along the journey, I have been fortunate enough to meet spectacular people........and of course with life's great balance....I have met my share of less-than-desirables. From Reagan to Kissinger.....to Kirkpatrick to Muhammad Ali......I have been fortunate there. It is with this balance that I have become who I am when I present myself. My discerning eye simply tells me when a person is genuine and rare. You ask me constantly how I know anything about you.........and all that I can say is that I know.........I feel it. I sense it in your words.......and the way you carry yourself. The way you breath.......what you react to verbally and non-verbally. When I told you, that weakness is a source of strength......I will share with you why. When we are strong enough to share a weakness.......something that we alone might consider weak.......we in the end become stronger. Why? Well, if you think about it.......the total character of a person, the person as a whole, is stronger than one failure.....one weakness. And that is how I see you........what you see as a weakness......or a person that struggles......... or has scars that you are ashamed of or embarrassed with........that an area that you want to feel you are afraid to feel........if emotion gets the better of you at times........or when you simply feel like you need to let your hair down but don't.... even though you want to...........your childhood........your dreams (even though you say you don't dream).........all of these things are strengths..........because......they all make up the character of you. And together with all the wonder and magic that you have inherently in your soul.........your perceived weaknesses........complete you as a person.

In this light.......this is where my love is for you. I see you as something real........someone with shared journeys........shared experiences.......shared successes...........many similar in character with the journey that I have traveled thus far. And I am sure......without a shadow of a doubt that you feel like I do.......just when you think you have this life all figured out..........boom........God throws us a challenge to again rise above.....to further understand ourselves........and to ultimately realize that life is more wondrous and spectacular than even we imagine........or for that matter.......dare to believe in.

This is why I am captured with you........and why for very unique and wondrous reasons that I fall more in love with you every day. And it is with this feeling.....this confidence if you will that I am writing this letter to you today.

I told you that there are things that are better left spoken......than written. I also understand that it is difficult to grasp the deep emotion of private thoughts and feelings that each of us have as unique. I would have much rather waited to say what I am about to say, but.......I know that this will fester and likely overshadow our time........our moment.........should your courage rise high enough to share a moment with me. So here goes.....

All that I have told you......all that I have shared with you has been unusual to say the least.........actually unheard of in my life. You have brought me to this place of openness......and I firmly believe that the insecurity that we feel........is not just felt by you. Your concerns over who gets hurt.....how this will end up evolving........what is to happen.......are answers that I do not have.......I wish I did.......but I don't......please continue reading........

I am about to share with you the greatest part of my life........something that we share together.........something that should bind us......and my fear and my insecurity with telling you is that you might somehow feel otherwise. I am a father of two wonderful boys......Robert and Charles. Both of them are my life......they are the greatest light that carries me. They are why I survive on 4 hours of sleep.......they are what gives me hope.......backbone and perseverance. And with these boys comes a wife. A woman I have been married to for about 6 years now. Your situation with your ex-husband.......is exactly my situation with her. There are a few notable differences..........while we are separated... we are not separated in the classic sense of the word. We sleep in different beds........we communicate when it has to do something with the children........we have not made love in over a year.........and I am the sole provider of this existence. She does not work.......though very well educated..........she is a great mother but a terrible communicator.........and this is why I know what I know about you.

I have never strayed from this marriage........just like you. I understand the little things that you go through each day.......more than you think I do..... I am keenly aware of what a c-section scar looks like and what it is like to live with an eating disorder. I understand what it is like to support not only my mother........but hers.....for several years ago she had a stroke........now she is a dependent. I am familiar with premature births......Robert was born at 26 weeks......instead of 40. This is a long story that I hope to someday tell you more about.....if you want to know about it. But safe to say this.......it was the most difficult time of my life. I am familiar with every cartoon and *Nickelodeon* video ever made........the value of reading......the value of time. One thing, however.......I did actually help finance *Nickelodeon's* venture products several years ago........so my familiarity with "*Face*" and all those characters are more real than just on the TV set at home.

So here I am. I would have much rather told you this in person........and maybe with this full disclosure.........you will decide that my chance for that time is now past........I certainly would not blame you.........but I will tell you this......I would most certainly feel loss without you.

I have come to a level of trust with you........a level of confidence and strength that has prepared me today to tell you the deepest part of my life. I have a plan to extricate myself........maybe in 3 years........but certainly not more than 5. The boys, by the way, are 3 and 5. The cruise I told you about.......I am not going alone.......I am going with my sons........the 3 amigos.........and the three of us will have time.......share time.........create a memory.

So in the end this has been quite a year. I have lost my ass in the stock market........lost my father.........in litigation with my sister and brother.......my sister-in-law is pregnant.........I finally came to know the face of the woman in my dreams.........and I have taken this risk........to trust you with my deepest life parts.........to put them out there to be judged........observed and questioned.

Regardless of how you react........how you will look at me from this moment forward.........realize this. You are the first woman that has captured my attention for reasons that maybe now you understand better than ever........ So when I say.......you are beautiful.......with a great soul......and a real character about you...........maybe now you will understand. When I told you that this will forever be your choice........maybe now you will understand. And when I tell you how I feel and why I feel the way I do..........maybe now you will realize that it comes at a depth of a heart you have never felt before........

Maybe now......this will mean more...........for that is the last paragraph of disclosure.........you know everything now. Maybe this will be more sacred for you........maybe not........maybe it will mean less.........maybe you will say goodbye...........

But with all this I know........I have expressed my life to you from the heart........with my emotion and with a love that I reserved only for you.

So as you said in your letter this morning........

So there you have it........

Do what you will with that info........

And if you are to say goodbye.......always remember this........

I love you

###

Subj: So..
Date: 10/28
To: FinanceGuy

Good morning....

Wow! That was quite the letter, Ken. I loved the buildup prior to the heart and soul of what you were trying to bring across. Nevertheless, I do have say thank you. Finally, the truth is out! While it was not unexpected, I am a little hurt. Not even so much by what you had to say, but that, you had not mentioned it earlier. After all, I told you about my situation from the start. Did you think that I would not understand? That I would judge you? That I would think any less of you? It makes me question how much you trust me but thank you at least for telling me before our meeting. I am not sure how I would have reacted if you had waited until then.

Wow! As you know, I suspected something all along. It was difficult to reconcile such openness with your communication blackouts. Remember all those times I accused you of leading a secretive life? This is why. I was trying to get you to open up about whatever you were hiding. While I did not fathom a full-blown marriage, I did assume you were in some kind of relationship. That is why I kept asking you, what would happen if I should show up at your front door unexpected. I guess thankfully for both of us I have not.

I am curious, though. Now that everything is in the open, can we clarify some other questions I have had all this time, please? Did you initially contact me thinking I would be an easy conquest? Someone to fuck while you were in Las Vegas and just wound up getting in over your head? If so, you would not have been the first one and then wind up getting more than what you bargained for. LOL, I guess it is like the conman going after a mark and winding up becoming one himself. I cannot begin to count the number of emails I have received from people who would be looking to for a "*hook up*" while in town for whatever convention happened to be here that month.

I should be furious. And, I am. I should say that I do not ever want to talk to you again and certainly not see you in person. And, I feel those emotions. I should. Yet, I cannot help it. I have to admit that while I would rather have known about your situation from the start, at this point trying to maintain any kind of anger is a lost cause. You are anchored so deeply in my heart that despite the shock, anger, and disbelief, I am unable to hold on to those negative emotions for any length of time. Yes, I am saying that as much as I know I should not, I still love you ... even like you. Heck, reading your story, and in spite of everything that I should be feeling actually elicited strands of sympathy from me. You, much more so than I, have some serious golden handcuffs. I am truly sorry about the situation that you find yourself in. Supporting three households is a rough job. A lesser man would not have accepted all this responsibility. You should be proud of what you have accomplished. As you skillfully counseled me in your build up, forget the failures. You take what you can from those learning experiences and move on. I am glad to see that you have two boys to bring you happiness in your life. I cannot help but still see the good in you and feel that a man such as you deserves every bit of happiness he receives and so much more.

While I know that you were hoping for acceptance, which you have received and would have received earlier if you had let me know, here is something that you might not expect. We all have God-given talents and I know what mine are. Yes, I have a head for figures (hey watch it) .. yes I am good with computers and people .. etc .. but the one talent that all those others are geared towards is that I know how to bring out the best in people. I am a mom through and through .... long before I ever gave birth to my son. It is in my personality ... it is the way I relate to people. I foster, I encourage, I believe when no one else will, and when necessary, I let him or her fall and skin his or her knee. That instinct to nurture and protect, to provide hope and comfort, lifting and fixing, and taking my wants and desires always entirely out of the equation, is still at your disposal. My end goal has always been that people are better off for knowing (having known) me ... and that includes you. What that means is that even if what is best for you is helping you to reestablish a relationship with your wife and therefore quite deftly paint me out of the picture, then so be it.

I do not know what turns are ahead on the road for any of us. Your love for me at some point might fade to that of the fondness of an old friend .... or not. It might stay the same or it might turn into hate. But believe me when I say this, I will only do what is best for you, even after all of this. I have always been the confidante for almost everyone who has crossed my path. If you need a safe sounding board, another opinion, someone to make you laugh, or just someone to tell you how terrific you really are .... do not hesitate to call. I will never screw you over or be disingenuous and only provide you with unbiased feedback.

One quick note though while talking about communication and feedback. When you said in your letter that you know what it is like to be with a bad communicator, I was not quite sure if I was in that category as well. If the answer to that is yes, well then, I apologize and will endeavor to do better.

I am still mystified at my reaction as I ponder all of this and the only answer I can come up with as to why I am not more upset is because I no longer have my heart in my body. I think the best way I can explain it is with a fairy tale I used to listen to repeatedly. I always loved fairy tales growing up. I was so excited once I finally learned how to read because I could read as many as I liked. Do not read this as a need to be rescued, by the way, I am just making a point about the lessons I learned early on and how it applies here. To continue, before I learned how to read, I kept wearing everyone out around me. I would go from person to person trying to cajole him or her to read me just one more story. My mother got so tired of this that she wound up buying children's fairy tales on cassette tapes (did not have a VCR back then). I would play them on my personal Panasonic (yes I remember it well) handheld, portable cassette player/recorder for hours on end. Ahhh .. what a theater of the mind that was. Well, moving right along. One of the more obscure fairy tales involved someone who after a great tragedy, gave his heart to be carried by a bird (I think it was a bird anyway) so as never to get hurt again (forgive me .. it has been a long time since I heard it). Strange how stories that give us endless hours of pleasure as youngsters, take on a deeper meaning as adults. Anyway, later on, when that person had need of it again (although why you would want to feel emotion after a great tragedy beats me) the bird gave it back. I have to find that story for you sometime and send it to you.

Well, I said all that to say this. I have been hurt deeply in the past ... and the battle scars are not beautiful ... but I trust you. You are my bird and have my heart. Keep it safe. As long as you hold it for me, no one, not even you, can hurt me ... not really. If the day comes that the burden is too heavy for you, or I have need of it again ... just give it back and we will live happily ever after.<smiling>

I hope to see you soon ... as you can imagine .. I do have questions for you regarding what happened 6yrs ago ... 3yrs ago .. 1yr ago. What she is like ... what your sons are like etc. I hope to be an asset to you ... I know you are one to me. Remember ... you were born under a lucky star ... you are fortunate ... people take to you quickly ... and things do come to you easily. If they have not in the past, they will from this moment on. I will do everything in my power to make sure that they do. After all, it is in my best interest to protect the bird that happens to be carrying my heart.

In closing, and after microscopic ass chewing, let me say that I wish for you everything good you have ever desired for yourself.

831

Pandora

###

Subj: a quick thought....
Date: 10/29 2:38:03 PM
From: FinanceGuy
To: Pandora

My Love:

I do not have the time to write on this day but will promise to make it up to you.......but quickly.........I love you........and that means more to mean than anything else I could try to say eloquently......

I will hold your heart if you will let me .....and will hold it forever.......

Thank you for being the woman in my dreams........and the keeper of my heart........

I will prepare myself for a more proper ass chewing tomorrow........it is yours to kick.

Again......my words to you are profound and emotional........critical to me and important.......just as you......

I wanted to get online to express to you my sincere appreciation for you ....and only wish that I could give you one wish that you really wanted.........but until then........just know.....you are not just in my thoughts.......you are my thoughts.......

I love you.......831.......and however I can express it........

Until tomorrow.....

###

***

CHAPTER 23

"Had you know then, what you know now, would you have continued?" asked Scott in his most calm and collect voice while massaging my feet.

"Yes."

"Why?"

"Because I was ...," and I had to interrupt myself since I had never answered this in the past tense before, "because I AM in love with him."

"Despite everything?" I could see a change in Scott as he asked that question. While the question could have included more than just Ken and his acts, I decided to answer it as such.

"Yes," I replied thoughtfully.

"What would it take for you to fall out of love?" He had stopped massaging my feet at this point.

"I don't know. I have only ever fallen in love once in my life."

"What if someone else fell in love with you? Would that do it?" That seemed like a silly question considering I had remarried and divorced since then.

"I have had many men fall in love with me since then. It hasn't changed anything," I answered trying to follow his train of thought.

"What if you fell in love with someone else?" he asked contemplatively.

I laughed at the notion. "I've tried, but it has yet to happen."

However, Scott instead of mirroring my mirth kept his calm demeanor as he asked, "Why do you think you haven't fallen in love with anyone else since then?"

I had been debating this question for quite some time on my own. "I think for three reasons: No one has been able to capture my imagination quite like Ken did; no one has been able to convey the total acceptance he did, and no one has ever made me feel as feminine as he did."

"Do you feel completely accepted by me?" he asked with a mischievous if somewhat sad expression on his face.

"Yes," I answered a bit curious.

"Well, that's a start then." I could see the light come back into this eyes.

My eyebrows started to furrow. "What are you driving at Scott?"

"Nothing. Nothing at all," he answered with a wicked yet wistful laugh as he reached across the couch and pulled me closer and almost on top of him for a profound and intoxicating kiss. I could feel his cock standing at attention yet once again as his hands unknotted the belt from my robe. Before I knew it, he had a breast in his mouth as his cock was rubbing against my clit from underneath.

He had my body so finely tuned into him at this point, that I was no longer amazed at how quickly I was able to coat his tip with my white and viscous fluids. Neither was I amazed anymore at how easily he slid himself in, as he positioned me to straddle him while on the couch, a move that with Ken, I would have been highly anxious over. Having had some experience since that email I wrote disclosing my *girl-on-top* insecurity, now it felt like one of the most natural positions in the world. With Scott's hands on my waist guiding me and doing more than just sitting still underneath of me, I reached behind his head to steady myself on the couch, and just let the sensation run over us. After a while, the waves kept crashing so hard and so high that I was no longer aware of Scott, or the couch, or the room as a whole. My body kept moving as if of its own volition, as I felt Scott getting deeper and deeper inside of me. I had not realized that my eyes had closed until I heard Scott's voice saying, "Look at me." Slowly our gaze reconnected as I felt myself falling into his soul.

He was leaning back now, allowing the whirlwind of electricity to grow and take hold of his body. After what seemed like only a few minutes, our storms collided, feeding off each other and becoming stronger than either could be on their own. I could feel his climax not just due to the sudden rise in heat inside of me, but because I could feel his strong voice and soul vibrating through my body. It had been a very long time since I had connected with someone this fully - this completely during sex. The last time had been with Ken and the depth of it all was a bit daunting to me. I was not sure if I was ready for another Ken.

Taking the sudden shift of desire fully in, I gently kissed his neck as I typically did, before lifting myself up and off this *everlasting-gob-stopper* of a cock Scott possessed. Before I could get up completely from him, though, Scott pulled me back down. Like a starved man, and not one who had just finished having round 2.5 in two hours, kissed me one more seductive time while causing me to cry out slightly as he shifted his hips and pushed his cock up against my furthest interior wall. Satisfied that he had sufficiently thrown me off balance again by exerting his dominance over me, as the room tilted for a second, he then helped to steady me as I finished getting up. With a wistful smile on his face, he leisurely watched as I re-wrapped my robe and found my gin and tonic to take another sip.

"What would you say is the biggest difference between Ken and me?" asked Scott heading back to the bar. I noticed he was a bit wobbly as well.

"The attention to clothes! Definitely the clothes. Ken knew every designer found in *Neiman Marcus* or *Saks Fifth Avenue*. Could you open the bottle of champagne for me, please? I think we should have strawberries as well." As Scott went to search for the champagne and strawberries in the refrigerator, I continued. "He also had a thing for the color white. Which, considering it was after Labor Day, was driving me nuts trying to fulfill his vision of an outfit for our first meeting."

"White huh? As in *'all in'* or just accent?" he asked as he pulled out the champagne bottle and strawberries.

"As in *'all in.'* And while he was a fashion adroit, his fascination with women's shoes bordered on obsession. I would not go so far as to say that it was a fetish, though." I stood up to open the bottle after Scott had finished taking the metallic paper wrap off the cork. "Unless you have a sword like Napoleon did, this takes a bit of finesse so as not to put a dent in the ceiling or window," I said as I took the bottle and gently let the heat of my right hand expand the gas trapped in the neck and push the cork into my waiting left hand. With no spillage, just an audible pop, I tossed the cork to the side as I poured a glass. Offering him one, he declined, sticking rather with is gin and tonic. Taking a strawberry and dropping it into the champagne I continued. "Being 6'2," most women could obviously wear high heels around him, including me. He preferred the highest heel I could walk in, which considering I started on point at age 4, was relatively high." I paused to take a satisfied sip. "Fortunately, the platform heel was not in fashion at that time, but the super pointy shoes were. Neither look is something I am partial to," I said while putting my glass down, pushing myself up to sit on the counter, and picking the glass back up again.

"I am not the aficionado he is, I do have to admit, though ... that there is something sexy about the curve of a woman's high-heeled shoe," said Scott as he finished pouring the tonic and walking over to where I was sitting and standing directly in front of me.

Wrapping my legs around him, and once he was sufficiently close enough to also drape my arms over his shoulder, I said "Agreed, but trying to find a pair of white ones after Labor Day, that also had an appealing look was proving to be close to impossible." Just before I placed the champagne-soaked strawberry halfway in my mouth and before leaning forward to have him bite the other half out of my mouth.

Subj: Good Morning
Date: 11/6
To: FinanceGuy

I am starting to think that most designers have a conspiracy going. Do they just not make cute heels anymore? And, the designers that do seem to only have shoes available in sizes 2-3 triple narrow. I might be exaggerating a bit, but not by much. The only consolation is that I still have a week to go and have some backup plans in case Las Vegas turns into a shopping dud. I have to say, I don't think I have ever tried to please someone on a clothing level as I have you (OK let's be honest - most guys don't really think about this stuff anyway). Add to that my own strict requirements and you have the reason why I am having trouble sleeping at night. ARGH !!!!

Yes, as if I do not have enough to do already. Now I understand why most stay at home women truly do require most of the weekdays to plan their clothing.

Oh well, back into the fray. If I show up in a sweatshirt and jeans, you will know that I decided to give up.

Hope to talk to you later. Hugs and kisses sent your way.

Pandora

###

Subj: Re: Good Morning
Date: 11/6/00 8:53:10 AM
From: FinanceGuy
To: Pandora

Gorgeous;

Please, please, please..........do not worry about trying to please me with your clothing. I sincerely appreciate the effort that you are obviously putting in, but my vision of you will likely have little to do with what you have on, as much as it will have to do with the smile on your face........and the beating of your heart.

I already think you are the most incredibly beautiful woman that I have ever seen, so if it is blue jeans and a sweatshirt.........then I would bet you $1,000 seven days a week.......and twice on Sunday........that it would look just as fantastic as a *St. John* knit or an *Escada* elegance........

You are an incredible woman...........enough said........now it is simply time to show you..........without words.......how you make me feel.......

I hope to talk with you as well.......

Take care lover......

831

###

Scott finished reading about my clothing dilemma over my shoulder as I was still clinging to him like a *Monchichi* doll. With a bit of a bemused look on his face, he turned the tablet off and while looking into the depth of me said, "Tell me about the first time you guys actually met."

"I am not sure I am intoxicated enough yet for that story," I said with a laugh as I jumped down off the counter and grabbed another strawberry.

Putting my glass in my hand, grabbing the bottle of champagne and balancing it with the plate of strawberries in the other, he grabbed my hand and led me up the stairs to the bed. Topping off my glass, he then arranged the pillows to allow me to recline in a chaise lounge position, dimmed the lights and laid down next to me. As his arm went comfortingly around my waist while his head was propped up on the pillow next to me, he said, "Now tell me."

And, So I did.

***

CHAPTER 24

I had by no means ever done anything like this before. Despite multiple accusations to the contrary for years, I had never actually physically cheated on Aaron and while I was technically not cheating now either, it was the first time I would be with a man that had not been my husband, and in a way, it felt like cheating. There were many occasions where I wished I had taken advantage of offers made by men, but I never had indeed taken that leap. This day, *November 14th,* would be the last time I could make such a claim.

I was so nervous. I had arranged for a '*me*' day as my excuse to be out of the office. I was getting my hair done (true), a massage (a lie), and then just out and about (half a lie). I had chosen my outfit days before. White 4" heels, white thigh highs, white g-string, white bra, white bustier, a dark blue silk mini skirt, and a white button up sweater top which had become quite famous in the slew of pictures I had sent back in September.

I had booked the earliest appointment possible with the hairdresser after which I went to the hotel/casino where Ken was staying. Due to security measures, Las Vegas hotels on the strip typically required room key verification before allowing guests to access the hotel elevators. Ken had emailed me his room number the night before and once I entered the lobby, I located the house phone and dialed him up. My palms were sweaty and shaking I remembered. *Would he recognize me? Would I recognize him?* I sat down on one of the couches and waited for Ken to arrive. My eyes kept darting all around. Anyone of the people here could be him, and today seemed an exceptionally busy day at the hotel. I was wiping my hands profusely on the couch fabric to keep them as dry as possible, which was not very.

Worried that it would appear as if I was a *'working girl,'* which Las Vegas was known for despite prostitution technically not being legal, I was looking down at my shoes and skirt. I had never worn heels quite this high before or an outfit where my unmentionables would risk being seen by the casual observer sitting or standing. Making sure that my skirt had not risen too high and the lace top of the thigh highs had not peeked through, I was nervously smoothing down and pulling at my hem. Satisfied that I had not risked exposure, I lifted my eyes and took in a sharp breath. I saw him walking through the crowd. My mind went racing and the thought "It's him. Oh, my dear God! It is really him!" kept circling in a faster and faster loop through my frightened brain. Later I would find out that he was just as nervous as I was, but I could not tell any of that by looking at him at the time. He looked just like his recent pictures. He had an executive haircut, longer up top and tightly cropped on the sides and back. A white streak of hair, in otherwise naturally dark and thick tresses that started on the left side of this forehead, combed back into the forest thick head of hair. Piercing blue eyes that had zeroed in on me and a smile that was encased by the most adorable dimples on either side. His nose could have been used as a model by a plastic surgeon, both in size as well as shape. Straight as a ruler when viewed from the side, it had just the right amount of hourglass curve for attractiveness factor when viewed straight on.

His 6'2" football player frame was dressed in a typical resort cut and if somewhat muted *Tommy Bahama* silk shirt, loose fitting tan *Tommy Bahama* silk dress pants, and light brown *Ferragamo* square-toed shoes. With one hand in his pants pocket and the other swinging casually at his side, he was the epitome of casual resort style.

I do not recall actually standing up, but at some point I know I must have because the next thing I remembered was him standing in front of me and I hugging him hello. "You look even better than your pictures," he said. Nervous beyond belief, we made small talk as we ever so slowly (part due to the height of my heels, part due to his apprehensive state) walked back towards the elevators and took the next available one. The thought of meeting someone who, on the one hand, was a complete and udder stranger, and yet on the other hand I had orgasmed with, and who knew most every intimate detail of my life, brought out the skittish colt in me. I was not able to look at him for more than a second or two at a time. My embarrassment kept my eyes darting around while we were in the confined space, waiting for the doors to open again. After what seemed like eons, we arrived at the top floor and as I was stepping through the metallic doorway, it hit me that I was only a few steps from technically becoming an adulteress considering I was only separated and not divorced and a mistress to a married man. The panic lasted for only a moment as I misstepped out of the elevator door. Ken, being the supportive gentleman he was, instinctively grabbed my hand and steadied me before I could fall. When he did, it was as if the entire electric content produced by Hoover Dam at that moment was being funneled through his hand and into my body. Shocked at the sensation and with no room for thought other than how natural my hand felt in his, I gave him a thankful look and with a nervous laugh said, "Stiletto heels and elevator grooves just do not mix well together," before letting go and following him to his door. Each step closer seemed to amplify my pounding heartbeat in my ears. By the time Ken actually opened the door, I could barely hear what he was saying. I was only able to make it a few steps past the door before I stood as if rooted to the floor of the two-room suite.

With my back to the wall, I could see the king size bed with its leather covered headboard and flanked by two nightstands at the far wall in the bedroom which I could see from where I was standing. To the left of me in the corner was a sitting area with a love seat, couch, glass coffee table and its own entertainment center. Behind it, the outward facing wall would have been a solid uninterrupted stretch of glass had it not been for the column halfway in-between which served as a buttress to the overly large French door unit separating sitting area from the bedroom. Positioned on the other side of the column against the window was the entertainment center for the bedroom. I could see a set of doors to the right of the bed, which I assumed to be the closet since the door next to it was open and revealed the entrance to a spacious and marble clad bathroom. Directly in front of me positioned against the wall, and in the sitting area side of the suit was an ornately carved wooden desk and tufted leather chair.

I watched Ken put the hotel key on the desk and turn back around to face me. With his long legs, it only took two steps to be directly in front of me again. Reflexively, I stepped back and found myself colliding with the wall. "I cannot believe you are actually here," he said, as my eyes never left his smiling face. Then, slowly, very slowly, much like you would approach a frightened animal, his hands came up to cup my face. Smiling and gazing hypnotically into my eyes with his dark blue ones, he still had to lean down slightly despite my 4" heels to reach my mouth. Following the trajectory of his lips as they approached mine, my eyes began to close. However, shortly before they were completely shut, a sigh escaped my mouth and after months of talking and describing, what it would be like, we finally kissed.

No amount of discussion, dreaming or fantasizing could have prepared me for experiencing that first kiss. His lips were so much softer than I could ever have conceived while my fingers had traced the outline of them on my computer hundreds of times. All thought of infidelity, guilt, or nervous apprehension was annihilated, as our tongues met and I felt for the first time the thick velvety texture of his and how perfectly it fit in mine. Then something happened that had never happened to me before. My knees buckled underneath of me. Fortunately, my hands came up and clasped themselves behind his neck just in time to keep from a complete collapse. My sudden shift caused him to support me with his entire body, the length of him pressed against me as he held me up against the wall, effectively sandwiching me between his football player's build and the wall, and keeping me upright if a bit wobbly.

We had had many a conversation about what the first time would be like. What our desires and our hopes and wishes were, and true to his prediction, when we kissed, it felt like I had never been kissed before that moment. It was not just the meeting of lips and entwining of tongues, but a simultaneous conveyance of tenderness and yet unquenched hunger. It was a pleasant bite of the lip followed up with a soothing caress of the tongue where just a moment ago teeth had been. It was a deep penetration of our mouths, alternated with a whisper like breath over the lips. It was like dying and being reborn at the same time. I could not help but melt with satisfaction as a new Pandora was being brought to life.

As we continued the undulating exploration of our mouths, my hands, still behind his neck, kept pulling him closer while my forearms rested on his broad shoulders. His hands moved from cupping my face to resting on my hips, and pulling me firmly into him. Contained by what I knew to be boxer briefs from our random question sessions, I could feel his erection pressed up against my skirt through his pleated silk pants and almost fainted from the lightning strike sensation my groin experienced in the outcome. Thankfully, I was still sandwiched between Ken and the wall and able to stay upright for the time being.

What brought me out of my haze finally, was hearing the sharp intake of Ken's breath as his hands continued their exploration of my body and he felt the tale-tell-ribs of my bustier underneath my sweater and skirt. "My God! You did wear it!" is what I heard as it became apparent that up until now, like some wildcat, he had only been circling, and that his predatory instincts were getting ready to take over. I could feel his body becoming taut with desire and his movements more dominant in nature as he reached to unbutton my sweater. The static electricity was building inside of me as the urgency increased for both of us. Being fully alert now, my hands reached his and with both of our fingers going down the series of buttons, my sweater turned from a demure top to a sexy jacket, exposing my white bustier and bra underneath. With stealth and power, he took my hands and firmly guided them up and over my head until they reached the wall. Pressing my wrists together, and needing now only one hand to keep them pinned as, he proceeded to push his cock harder against me while his mouth went to work on the side of my neck.

I was helplessly trapped in his web of magnetized passion as my animalistic side answered his. This electrical charge seemed to surround us from head to toe like an aura. Between feeling his teeth on my neck, breath in my ear, and groin against mine, I forgot to breathe. Then, his mouth turned back to mine and the air finally entered my lungs again. I was writhing in agony and yet intoxicated with desire as my blood redistributed to more primal anatomical areas. He continued his sweet torture of my body as his mouth created a trail of gentle bites moving from my lips, down the front of my neck, and down to my décolletage, stopping just short of the bustier and bra. Then, using his tongue to force itself under the fabric of my bra, he reached my nipple and made me cry out with hunger as my fervor for him increased exponentially with every second. After he had teased both of my nipples while still fully clothed, I could no longer stay still under his body or the web of wantonness he was creating. I had to make sure that he would be just as taken by me as I by him, and the only way I knew how to do that was to push his ass against the wall and go down on him. I knew that when it came to blowjobs, I was in the 99th percentile (adjusting for margins of error and population demographics).

Willing my blood to replenish at least part of my cerebrum, I opened my eyes and was hit yet once again with the depth of blue staring back at me and the stunning nature of his smile. Shaking off the hypnotic effect before my knees would betray me again, I used a traditional martial arts move and twisted my hands in a circular motion of - in, under, and out - to not only to break free of his grasp on my wrists but also to take control of his instead. Next, I arched up and forward and created some much-needed space between our bodies. Taking advantage of his momentary loss of balance, I used my hips and my hold on his wrists to roll him over. Standing now with his back against the wall where mine had been just moments before, and my body pressed against his, I forced his hands above his head. It was my turn to make his world spin and have the rapture take him over. Using my entire body as a tool of pleasure from mouth to thighs, it was all I could do not to give myself over to the force field like sensations - even though I was the one in control.

Feeling his cock straining against his boxer briefs and causing the band to noticeably lift from his skin and create an additional ridge in his pants, I leaned forward and whispered in his ear, "I will bring your hands down to your side, but only if you promise to keep them against the wall." Nodding his agreement, I released his hands while mine reached for his pants. Keeping his button closed, I lowered the zipper, reached in, spread apart the slit indicative of all men's underwear, and pulled his cock through the now multiple layers of fabric towards sunlight. While all of our close contact within the last few minutes had given me some indication as to his length and girth, and indeed I had asked in our various phone discussion and he had always skirted the issue, little did I realize that his boxer briefs must have been the equivalent of a minimizer bra, because what came to light was much larger than what I had been prepared for.

With my sweater still undone and keeping one hand on his chest and pressing him up against the wall, I moved down to my knees by sliding along his body and felt his chest rise suddenly and sharply under my hand as I took the very tip of him into my warm and moist mouth. Leaving my left hand on his chest and bringing my right hand to keep the metallic zipper from coming into contact with some of the most sensitive skin known to a human being, my mouth slowly started working on his shaft. Imitating the rhythm of intercourse, and not the faster pace of masturbation, I kept my tongue broad, soft and relaxed as I took him in a little deeper with every downward movement. Slowly letting his shaft slide in and out of my mouth, never further out than just under the ridge of the tip, my mouth eventually ran out of room and yet my lips had not reached the base of his shaft yet. Keeping him in this position for just a few seconds, I moved my tongue in a wave-like motion up against his back vein as his hands, which he had until then kept at his side as instructed, moved to my shoulders. Preparing myself for what I knew would come next, I relaxed my throat, brought my hands down to his ass, and then in one smooth yet slow motion pushed his tip and a quarter of his shaft deep into my throat while my tongue continued its slow, methodical massage of the backside of his cock.

As his tip penetrated my throat, Ken let out a moan that could have woken the whole neighborhood if we had not been in a high end, sound insulated, Las Vegas hotel room. Seconds after, his hands moved reflexively to my face and cupped it as gently as he had during our first kiss. Looking down and into my eyes he whispered, "Pandora," as he saw himself sliding in and out of my mouth. I could only imagine the view he had watching the combination of his cock, my eyes, and the roundness of the top of my breasts appearing and disappearing depending on the depth of his penetration. Moving his hands from merely cupping my face to gently holding my long cascading hair back in a ponytail, I continued to elicit rumbling moan after moan from him for a few more minutes before he lowered his hands to my shoulders and pushed me and my mouth away from him. Giving him a questioning look he explained, "If you continue like this I will cum in your mouth and I do not want to cum just yet."

Understanding his reasoning, I allowed him to lift me back up by my shoulders as he stepped out of his shoes and moved to undo my skirt.

With my oxygen supply getting sparse again, I felt the silk slide along my thigh high clad legs down to my heels to the floor. There was another sharp intake of breath as he saw the stay-up thigh highs. Helping me out of my sweater, I stood in front of him now, feeling like a bride, dressed all in white, from heels to bra, as requested by him. His eyes lit up at the sight and he just kept saying, "so beautiful," as my hands now moved to undo his shirt and pants.

After I had unbuttoned his shirt and pants completely, he took over, and smoothly and quickly removed his clothing within a matter of seconds. Standing now completely naked in front of me, he pulled me into him again and whiles kissing me deeply and hungrily. My hands moved back to around his neck as he guided me backwards through the French-door partition and towards the bed. Once we reached the foot of the bed, his hands grabbed my waist, lifted me up and over, and positioned me in such a fashion on my back, so as to have my pussy within easy reach of his mouth while his hips were resting against the edge of the bed. Placing my legs over his shoulders, he paused and looked admiringly at my satin and lace underwear, just before he pushed it to the side and like a lion lapping milk, slid his thick, soft, broad tongue in one smooth unhurriedly slow motion from my entrance to my clit.

My back arched up involuntarily as my right hand came to my mouth to bite down on my finger to keep from making too much noise. He stopped for just a moment to look into my eyes before he recreated that same movement again, causing my back to arch up anew with incalculable pleasure. This time, however, I was unable to keep silent and a loud moan escaped my throat. Taking his hands, he gently caressed the outer lips, and a shiver built along my spine and shook my whole body. Like one of those toy cars that you wind up by stroking them across the floor, his tongue continued its slow and deliberate path along my canal, as the kinetic energy was building and turning tighter and tighter inside. Then, just as he had told me to do so many times over the phone, he took his right hand and penetrated me with his finger while his tongue never skipped a beat. After all that build up for so many months, then experiencing his exquisite touch in actuality, I had to release that wound up energy, and just like one of those cars, I felt like I was speeding across the floor of the universe and I came right then and there. While most men would have taken pride in this accomplishment and focused on their own needs now, Ken was not even close to being finished with me yet. His hand never stopped its penetrating rhythm while his thumb massaged my outer lips and his tongue kept traveling along my now soaking wet channel. His left hand came up to my lower abdomen, and before I knew what was happening, his right hand instead of continuing its rhythm stopped and curled up towards my stomach while his left hand pressed down on my abdomen at the same time. Between the two, my g-spot was being attacked from both sides. This time, I came so hard and cried out so loud, I officially fainted. Fortunately, my incapacity lasted only for a second or two. Ken, drunk with power now, repeated this move a few more times before allowing respite.

I was struggling to come out of the explosive mine that had just engulfed me for what I had lost track of but must have been already in the double digits. The darkness finally started to recede from my vision, and I could see his face as if far away, smiling at me. He carefully stripped me of my soaking wet g-string and unlaced my bustier. Kneeling on the bed, he appreciatively ran his hands along my right leg and brought my heel-clad foot to his face while keeping my leg in a straight line. Staring admiringly at the sensuous curve of my white stiletto, he gently removed my shoe and then went to repeat the process on my other leg. All I was left with were my thigh highs and my bra. Fully conscious again after my multitude of climaxes, he lifted me by my waist and positioned me high enough in bed so my head actually reached a pillow. In this position, as he was kneeling at the edge of the bed, I could see him in all his glory. He reached down and experimentally pushed a finger up inside of me again. Satisfied with the level of wetness I was maintaining, leaned forward, and paused to stare intensely into my eyes as if asking for permission to enter me. I took a deep breath, reached for him, and as he slid inside of my waiting pussy, my back arched up and both of us cried out at the same time.

The sheer sensation of his cock plunging itself deep into me was causing an electrical storm whose intensity I had, up until that very moment, been unfamiliar with. Once again, despite having been married and dated other people prior, it was as if I had never had sex before then. Certainly, I had never had sex like this. His cock filled me to the point of overflowing - both physically and emotionally. My pussy felt stretched beyond belief in every possible direction. "My God your pussy is tight,"

Ken said as he kept thrusting himself into me. However, I would have a difficult time imagining any woman not being tight for his cock. "Your pussy feels like velvet. I have never felt anything like this," he said as he kept thrusting himself deeper and deeper into me. I could tell he wanted me to talk as we usually did over the phone, but it was getting more and more difficult to hang on to my higher brain function and respond in any kind of coherent verbal communication as he kept hitting my g-spot with every stroke. The whirlwind of sensations was getting to be overwhelming as his deep-timbered voice was resonating through my body and soul.

Just before a tidal wave of an orgasm came crashing down around me and all over him, I had barely enough wherewithal to say "Oh my God Ken! ... You feel so incredible." Taking a pause I continued, "I just want to keep you inside of me forever!"

Not being satisfied with a mind-blowing level of the climax he had made me achieve, the equivalent of cresting Mount Everest and requiring oxygen gear, I could hear him say "squeeze" like he always did over the phone and my body without thinking squeezed down on him. "Aaaaa," I heard as my pussy was acting like a cock ring around his base, not allowing the blood to flow back and reinforcing his erection. I could feel him getting even harder inside of me. "Squeeze," he said again and once again my climax engulfed him, causing some of my cum to run down his balls and thighs. He kept telling me to squeeze each time he would thrust his cock inside of me, causing both of us to experience vertigo. Myself from forgetting to breathe due to the headiness of every thrust and him for channeling what, I would imagine being, all of his blood supply into this torture device that kept pushing itself past my ever-enclosing walls. His hands reached for my breasts, squeezing them hard while he was turning me into a mindless marionette of his passion, responding to his every word and touch. I must have cum 10 times from his penetration alone, by the time I heard, "tell me." This typically meant that he was on the verge of orgasm himself.

"Please cum inside of me Ken."

"Tell me."

"I want to feel you to fill me up until it drips back down onto your balls."

"Tell me."

"Please cum."

"Tell me."

I finally realized what he was looking for, and with a deep breath I said, "I love you, Ken." Knowing that this was just the start of what he wanted to hear I continued, "I belong to you. You have me mind body and soul."

And with those words, Ken let out a profound and compelling groan that could only be matched by the sheer ferocity of his cum. Feeling him ejaculate inside of me caused my pussy to squeeze down so hard that I was afraid of squeezing him out as I climaxed together with him. Instead of feeling sated for countless orgasms Ken had brought me to within the last hour or so, I knew I had to level the playing field and make sure he was as addicted to me as I was to him after this performance. The only way I knew to assure this was either to do something extremely well (like the blowjob) or do something he had never experienced before. But either way it had to be stunning.

I knew if I could accomplish what I had in mind, he would be mine ... forever.

Instead of releasing him and moving on to the post-passion cuddling, I locked my legs around his, arched up and took control of his body from underneath. Thrusting my hips into his, I kept him prisoner with my legs and unable from moving any of his lower body, including his hips. I reached up for his neck, pulled his head down to mine, and as my hips kept working in a circular as well as wave-like up and down motion, my tongue once again found his mouth. Knowing that just like every other man I had been with, Ken would never lose his erection while still inside of me, we kissed deeply as my hips ground out another load from his balls. I was not aiming for an aftershock but a full-blown orgasm. The intensity of the connection between our eyes and the hunger of our mouths only added to the ever-growing storm cultivating and churning in both of us. We were like two hurricanes merging into a super storm. It only took about another 15 minutes, but it was well worth the time! Orgasm number two for him, and in the double digits for me. Spent and satisfied with having accomplished my goal, I released his lower body. Despite being no longer shackled by my legs, he stayed inside of me, hard as could be, but not moving just staring into my eyes and said "I love you, Pandora," with such emotion I knew he was mine. Like a key to a door, his emotion was a floodgate for mine and that is when the full depth of the total destruction of my innocence hit me.

The betrayal I felt I had committed by being intimate with someone for the first time other than Aaron. The longing I had experienced and finally fulfilled. The desire I had to have him as my own, but the concern that he would never be. The sadness of having settled for the marriage I did because I did not know any better at the time. The mourning of everything I had been, and the panic of not knowing who I would be, all came crashing down around me. I started crying. Softly at first, and then uncontrollably after a few minutes. Confused by my reaction Ken pulled himself out, wrapped his arms around me and asked with a deeply concerned voice, "did I hurt you?" I could not answer verbally and just shook my head no. Maybe he had gone through a similar concern or maybe he just connected with me as a soul mate does, but either way, his whole body started radiating understanding without my having to explain. He hugged me closer while stroking my hair back as he soothingly kept saying like a mother to a frightened child, "It is going to be ok. It is going to be all right. I am here. I've got you."

As I was rocking against his chest having buried my face there, I slowly stopped crying, and with a deep breath, I allowed his hand to lift my face to his and he began to kiss away the trails of my tears. Once every clue of my emotional breakdown had been kissed away by him, he looked into my eyes for a moment and then slowly kissed my lips. With that kiss, all guilt and anguish left my body for good as I simply melted into him.

The rest of the day was spent talking, more lovemaking alternating with wild abandoned sex and utilizing every piece of furniture in his high-priced suite. We did take a stop for a leisurely meal at some point at one of the restaurants downstairs. However, even with the lengthy conversations and the lunch break, during those approximately 6 hours or so, Ken had a total of 7 orgasms and mine, well mine had probably climbed into the triple digits. Those hours became some of the happiest in my life. No tears or guilt-driven break-downs after that first round, and I even made him cum via oral a time or two. The bond we created that day was stronger than anything I could have ever imagined. We were completely taken with each other by the time it came for the muted yet heart-wrenching good-bye. As I prepared to go back to my life, I knew that the timer, which had been ticking already, had just been shoved into overdrive. If I had not been in love with Ken before that day, there was no doubt about my level of attachment after. As I walked back into my apartment, the main thought that kept circling my head was, "I want to be with Ken for the rest of my life."

CHAPTER 25

Scott was glad that the lights were dim as Pandora finished with her recounting of the first time with Ken. The look on his face could have been mistaken for desire when, in fact, it was a sincere appreciation for the skill sets of Ken's that Pandora had described. As much as he wanted to hate this guy, he had newfound respect for the man after getting to know him through his own words as well as Pandora's retellings. While her retellings might have been colored by perception and time, Ken's words were unaltered since he had written them, and as such, a great source of information. With each email his respect for the guy increased. Game recognized game and he had to give Ken props for that much at least. The only real mistake Scott could spot was that Ken had decided not to keep the winning lottery ticket he had been handed. Outside of that oversight, he sounded like a stand-up kind of guy. Had they met in person they might even have been friends.

He even seemed to be exceptional when it came to his sexual skills, not quite on par with Scott's own, but that was to be expected. Few people were in his caliber when it came to sexual capabilities. Most men, especially ones who had reached a certain age, tended to decline not just in frequency, but imagination. So many men and women stopped learning and looking for ways to improve. Scott, the eternal academic, did not look upon sex as a repetitive act with only one possible solution. He instead saw it as an eternal playground that allowed one to find new and interesting ways to achieve ever-increasing heights. His personal belief was that the very worst sex with a person was the first encounter. Most would not agree and those that did not tended to find comfort in familiar rather than exploration. Therefore, running across a like-minded individual, be they male or female, was rare enough to be a good enough reason to keep them in your life. With Ken, it would have been as wingmen and with Pandora; it was something closer to a soul mate.

What he had seen so far with Pandora was that she was what in sexual terms was called a *'switch'* and could get tired of people who had a lack of versatility in their sensual habits. What made her so attention-grabbing was how versatile she herself was. Most women liked it one way or another and it was rarely a mixture of the spectrums. It was usually either *50 Shades of Grey* or *Harlequin Romance*. Pandora, however, was the spectrum and the perfect spectrum of desires to match his own, all while staying within the exact same boundaries as his. It was the *'Goldilocks'* zone of sex - not too wild and not too tame. As a psychiatrist he understood the drive behind every sexual satisfaction sought, as a man, though, he had his own personal preferences. Due to his background, anything that included pain or humiliation felt inappropriate to him. Having experienced both in real life enough, he was none too keen to undergo more of it himself and his soul had become too empathetic to inflict those same negative experiences onto others. Taking control, giving control, multiple partners at once, all these things were perfectly acceptable to him as long as they were done with cherished consideration.

Given those parameters, Scott had been aware that he was a top-notch lover for some time now. *Numero Uno*! Not just 99th percentile but *THE BEST*! This, just like all people of success, had of course not always been the case. It had come about from one simple thing, having had a woman fake an orgasm and Scott knowing it. Therefore, while he had not necessarily always been the best lover, he had been the best sexual lie detector. He approached every sexual encounter the same way his favorite TV Character of all time did, by assuming that "everybody lied." Just like that character, he looked at every female sexuality as a puzzle to be solved, and only the most complicated ones held any interest to him. This, probably more so than any other reason, was why Scott had felt so drawn to Pandora at first. Long before, he found out all the other magnetic aspects of her personality. Scott looked at every experience as a learning experience and a reason to improve. As such, he learned how to adapt his tactics to whatever the prevailing mood required. Sometimes it would take a soft loving caress, such as the one that Pandora had described with Ken at their first meeting, and then other times it would take a rougher taking of control and being dominant. The verbal feedback when it came to his sexual skills had always been positive. However, he knew better than to gauge his personal ranking on verbal feedback alone. As such, he went by the physical responses. Getting anything by him was difficult. He would have a constant keen eye out for the physical responses during sexual interaction as well as take into account the desire from his partner to do it again - multiple times. . Sexual compatibility was an important part of bonding. It was after all an integral part of the relationship, and an integral part when it came to the building of emotions, as even Ken had discovered. While Ken had certainly built a connection on things other than sex - the sex had helped. The sex had helped a lot actually. It had helped not just during the physical interaction but all the times that he had had phone sex or close to it discussions with Pandora.

Scott knew that he could help her; he knew that with how perfectly they matched up not just in their sexuality (which was a colossal part) but in their histories, in regards how they had been betrayed, matched up perfectly. Plus, well, they just simply looked good together. An item that should not be discounted in importance. Someone of his height needed a taller girl, otherwise they were *spinners* and things just did not align properly.

The only thing that Scott was wrestling with was that the same loyalty, attachment, and worship that Pandora exhibited towards Ken, was what not only Scott sought for himself from her, but what she (and he) were looking to change about her. At least in the aspect that it came to Ken. The part that made him sleep a little better about what he was doing was that Ken had not been willing to return the loyalty that Pandora had shown, and as such, unlike Scott, was therefore not deserving of it. To Scott, not holding on to a person of this caliber and devotion who would look past every fault, was one of the gravest errors or hurts that could be inflicted ... well ... ever.

This was a woman who could help him as much as he could help her. Scott, despite having sworn off committed relationships, when he was truly honest with himself had to admit that, in the end, it was nice to meet someone he looked forward to seeing again the next day. This could not be a bad emotion, or him wanting Pandora to feel the same way. That life would be such an incredible adventure once they would start drinking from the same cup, as they had quite frankly even before this. This meeting of the souls. This amazing freeing emotion that could only be had with someone such as this. Life had to be lived with spice and gusto. He would have to handle it like a figure skater, with power while delicately balanced. He could see himself being inside of her for hours on end. Devouring her for hours on end. Needing to be fulfilled by her. Someone who was a kindred spirit who could match his intensity.

Many would have been daunted by what Scott had heard just a few minutes ago. However, he knew that it was a necessary spiel in the steps of Pandora's healing. He, unlike so many others, understood that facing your ghosts was typically the best way to exercise them. In the retelling of the story, particularly to someone else, the hold of the memory lessened. As such, Scott had never been intimidated by people's pasts. How could he? In many ways Scott was acting like a *sin-eater*, only instead of eating Pandora's sins he was eating her past. In the end, it was for a good cause.

Matching his breathing to hers, he whispered, "I love you Pandora." He did not know if her dream state would interpret his words for it was not long before they were both asleep and dreaming.

***

CHAPTER 26

It was unbelievable how much Pandora was on Ken's mind. With the months leading up to the signing of the divorce papers, she had increased exponentially in his thoughts. He had withstood the temptation to contact her while he was getting the legalities of it all settled. He had made her so many promises in the past that he knew he had to get this part of his life in order first. It was only fair. Not just to her but to everyone. There was no need to make it any more confusing by adding in unnecessary emotions into the mix. However, now he was finally free. Not just from his past but free to think about Pandora and their future.

He remembered Pandora saying something about their psychic connection back when they first met, and he wondered if possibly the fact that he was thinking about her affected her as well. Could it be that Pandora was thinking of him more so than usual because he was thinking of her or vice versa? Much like a mother knows when a child is in danger? If so, the thought of being in Pandora's thoughts in such a fashion was exciting him and causing his pants to feel slightly less roomy than typical. *Thank heavens for pleats.*

All this reminded him of the very first time that they had seen each other in person. She had sent him so many pictures prior to their first meeting that he could have carved her face into an ice sculpture. Was it any surprise that he had recognized her as soon as he had had a view of the lobby? Looking so apprehensive with her eyes darting and pulling at her hem. It was true that he had not fallen in love with her then. It had definitely happened before then. Strange how much the mind had control of these things and the body really had only a tiny amount to do with attraction. After all, if it were a purely physical concept, then orgasms would happen no matter the partner choice or quantity of intercourse.

Yes, he had fallen in love with Pandora long before they had met. It was nice though to have the physical beauty of her confirmed. She had looked just like her pictures from far away. The closer he walked, though, the more beautiful she became until he could almost not stand it and felt like me might just implode from the mere visage of her. And then she had raised her eyes and found him and it had been the very first time in his life (other than having gotten kicked in the nuts) when he knew what it was like to be close to fainting. *Those incredible eyes of hers*! Eyes that stared right through him and he could simply not hide from.

That last memory was what made him decide to pack an overnight bag right then and there. He didn't even need to schedule a flight. He would just drive his car from Phoenix to Las Vegas. It would only be about 4 hours and well worth it considering he would need a car anyway once he arrived in town to find her. He would call the office and tell them he would not be in for the next week. Anything urgent he could handle while on the phone or after his return. Should he try Scott again? He decided yes.

Humming to himself he gathered a few *Tommy Bahama* shirts and pants before turning off the TV that had had Penn Jillette debunking some magic trick or other.

***

CHAPTER 27

It was Monday morning, Pandora was sitting in her office thinking about the weekend, and the amazing night she had spent with Scott. Pandora did not make a habit of spending the night with anyone. In fact, that had been her very first time since - *well ... she had to think about that one for a moment* - since the last time she spent the night with Ken come to think of it. Of course, Ken would have to come to mind at such a moment, although she had noticed that he came to mind much less often than he had even last month. Why yesterday, she had not thought of him at all. The reflection came as a pleasant surprise to her since a slow day, prior to having her cathartic sessions with Scott, had involved thinking of him on average of once an hour during her waking moments. Which, when she did one of her stints of staying up 48-72 hours straight while working in the office, would amount to quite often. Moreover, considering that even on an ordinary day she averaged possibly 4 hours of sleep a night during the week, left still more than the average day to think about a guy who had disappointed her so many times. A guy who had disappointed her more than anyone else in her life. That was, other than the disappointment in herself. Taking herself to task was just one of those run of the mill things she did several times a day.

Ken had though also brought her some of her most exquisite highs. He had done it addictingly so. Well, that was until Scott had appeared on the scene. It was nice thinking of Scott. He had yet to disappoint her, but there was still lots of time to do so. She knew already about his lack of fashion sense of course. This, among some other minor pet peeves, kept Scott out of the perfect match category, it did not, however, make him a disappointment. As such, Scott had the perfect record of accomplishment to date. If I told him, though, I knew his ego would bloat to such immense proportions that it would take a full day to release all the hot air that would accumulate in his brain. His brain was the last thing she wanted to influence considering it was the most attractive of all. The body was quite nice too and the sexual skills were *blue ribbon* material. However none of that would be worth a darn, or well at least not worth thinking about while attempting to do some sort of work and surrounded by computers and needing to meet deadlines, if he had not that amazingly stellar brain.

Taking a deep breath and straightening herself Pandora attempted to refocus her gaze upon at least one of the three screens on her desk. She noticed that she had received five emails since her mind had wondered and her hand moved without any thought to the mouse so as to read and answer whatever questions were waiting for her.

Yes, there had been indeed a DDOS attack earlier that morning on the servers. However, it had gotten handled. As she went through the mechanics of conveying the information, 40% of her brain went back to daydreaming about Scott. The best relationships in her life happened quite quickly - both Scott and Ken were a testament to this. Although, Scott was more so than anyone else.

Pandora was debating in her mind if the amount of time led to a sense of acceptance or if one had anything at all to do with the other. The strange thing with Scott was that Pandora felt like she could tell him anything. Truly! Anything! She could not recall this ever having been the case with Ken. She could tell Ken a lot. Confide in him indeed any number of personal weaknesses and insecurities, however, Pandora could not imagine Ken ever being able to read through such email correspondence as Scott had and not throw the computer across the floor. Ken had made her feel feminine for the very first time in her life and secure and taken care of. However, it was easy to make Ken jealous.

There were many memories to choose from to support this impression. The first that came to mind was the afternoon during their very first meeting. After having spent already a few hours making passionate love together and laying in each other's arms, they had decided to go downstairs to one of the many restaurants and grab some lunch. On their elevator ride down they had shared the space with a man who never had a said a word to either of them and whom Pandora barely even registered as being in their vicinity, since like some schmaltzy 50s love song, she only had eyes for Ken. Moments after the doors opened to release its cargo onto the casino floor Ken had turned to Pandora and with an intimidating fire in his eyes had said to her "If that guy would have stared any harder at you I was going to take my fist and rammed it down his throat." Even though that moment happened many years ago, it was etched in her mind just as any shocking event would be. She would never forget that moment, just the same as she would never forget where she was when she found out about the two planes hitting the towers in New York City. It had been that much of a shock to her. Partially because Pandora had barely been aware of the fact that there were people in the elevator with them much less that the individual had been staring in their general direction. Unlike the look on Ken's face and the fervor in his voice, which she could describe with crisp clarity years after the fact, she would not have been able to describe the man who had shared the elevator with them even moments after having seen him.

There were other times afterwards when his competitive and protective nature came out. Like the time when they were walking in the airport together to another concourse and he commented about people staring in our direction. Or during another trip while they were again at an airport waiting at the gate. He had gotten up to go to the bathroom and during his absence several people, including a guy, had started talking to me. We were engrossed in conversation upon Ken's return and despite my making a big deal of his return and even throwing my legs across his lap; I could tell that Ken was not happy with me.

It did make me feel uncomfortable in a fashion since it made me feel as if I was being accused of something that had not even crossed my mind and would create flashbacks to other less than successful relationships. On the other hand, though, there was no denying how much he needed me and wanted me and yes even loved me. Part of me had to admit that I liked it when he was jealous. For, since my confidence was not the highest when it came to romantic relationships, and I also held him in such high esteem, high enough to wonder how he could not have every woman east and west of the Pecos dropping at his feet, I liked knowing that I could keep him off balance. It gave me a sense of power over him that I might otherwise not have had. It showed me that he was emotionally invested in me and in us and that was a nice drug to shoot up into my brain via my eyeballs.

This same jealousy, while empowering to me, just like every double-edged sword, also had its drawback. For example, this jealousy made it usually impossible to have the type of conversations, very candid and soul-bearing conversations, Scott and I had been able to have. These kinds of conversations usually could only be had with a stranger to whom you were paying $200 or more an hour. A stranger who also you were not sure of if they really cared or were just doodling on their notepad making grocery lists.

So, for all these things and so much more, Scott was the perfect man. Or as close to perfect as many could be. Pure perfection could be annoying and therefore no longer made a person as perfect as they started out being. Scott had just the right amount of flaws to make him perfect. He was perfect to fall in love with actually. That was where Pandora then had to stop and take an emotional inventory, yes; Scott was perfect to fall in love with. Pandora could feel the relaxed goofy state setting in followed microseconds later with the abject terror. Which emotion should she choose? She decided to go with neither end of the pendulum and just accept it as being a simple and concrete fact. Of course, now she had to figure out what to do next.

As if right on cue, she looked down at her vibrating phone and noticed a text message from Scott and it would have been impossible to wipe the smile off her face. Yes, she would love to spend his birthday with him and she knew just what presents to give him.

***

CHAPTER 28

Scott was in his office finishing the discussion with his grad student when his phone started vibrating for the 5th time that day. Needing an excuse to extract himself from the mind numbing conversation he decided to take this interruption and dismiss the grad student.

"Sunny, how the hell are ya? Haven't spoken to you ... in how long? Must have been years!"

"Hey! God, it's so good to hear your voice. I've been calling for days!"

"Yeah, well my voicemail kept getting overflowing full and people would leave messages expecting me to answer and they didn't know that I could not retrieve them and I tried constructively ignoring it in hopes of improvement, but finally..."

"Or you just take 30 days to return phone messages."

"Ok, that could be it too. You could have texted you know!"

"Yes, but the Bluetooth works better with voice instead of text while I am driving. Besides, if I texted then I would not be able to hear that lilting voice of yours," he said laughingly. "In all seriousness, though, I need to talk to you about something important and it is not the kind of thing that you say over text or maybe even over the phone. It really requires a couple of beers in front of us, although I might have to settle for the phone considering I am currently driving in."

"Wait! WHAT! ... must be a bad connection.. did you just say you're driving to Las Vegas and you did not lead with the information?

"I thought I had mentioned that already."

"No, you didn't. I would have remembered if you did anyway. Well, that's awesome! Can hardly wait to see you. You can, of course, stay with me although knowing you, you'd prefer staying in a hotel anyway .... "

"Yeah, it's easier in a hotel ... Listen. I think I need to tell you this before I arrive so it won't seem like such a complete and udder shock .. and well .. I am not sure how you are going to take this but ... "

"You're not sick are you? I know some great cancer guys if it is cancer ..."

"It's not cancer ..."

"Is it something else?"

"Yes, it's something else ... "

"Oh God! ... I knew it! ... "

"Nooo ... I am not sick. It's not something else in that fashion. There is a reason why I called you and if you will just let me get a word in edgewise, I will tell you."

"Ok."

"So, I have been thinking about you a lot lately and some of the conversations we had back in college ..."

"Sunny, I accept you."

"You accept me?"

"Yes, I accept you. Coming out is a difficult thing to do, especially to a male friend, but I am honored that I would be one of the first people you chose to call and share that information with. And I can even understand that you might have feelings for me of a romantic nature. And I am flattered beyond belief. However, you know that ..."

"Let me just stop you right there. I am not gay."

"You're not?"

"No."

"Not even a little bit?"

"No. Not even a little bit."

"Are you sure? Cause I have had this speech prepared for years now and it is such a great speech full of love and acceptance and demure explanation of non-reciprocation of feelings..."

"Scott, you need professional help."

"I think you just hurt my one feeling."

"I am sorry. I am sure it's a great speech."

"Can I still tell it to you?"

"Sure, just not now. Maybe over that beer."

"Ok."

"So now that we have that settled, can I please tell you that Vicki and I signed the divorce papers."

"I think you just did."

"Yes, ... uhm... wow.... yeah ... I guess you're right. Well, that was easier than I thought. Ok ... so anyway ... yes, it was strange how there was no fighting over the whole thing. It had been a long time coming so maybe that made the actual paperwork more of a formality than anything."

"I am not sure how to respond here. You know that I am your friend and will always be your friend and was never that fond of Vicki. However, you guys had been married for a very long time and there was a reason, well, quite a few reasons, that you decided to go through with it even though you knew that I would not be the most supportive of such a decision. So what made you decide to go through with a divorce despite all the sacrifices you went through to get married and stay married to Vicki?"

"I met someone."

"Wow! Mazel tov ... I think. So who is she? Do I know her?"

"No, you never met her. And ... well ... she is all wrong for me in so many ways. You know ... doesn't have the family name ... although she knows a lot of people and is influential in that way ... but going with her would require my hanging in entirely different circles. Nouveau riche circles instead of the traditional ones I have been in. Come to think of it, I did mention her to you once. Remember when we were on that trip and you asked me about my *Korum* watch? The one with the gold coin?"

"How could I forget! You had only been talking about wanting that watch for years and then you finally got one. So what about the watch?"

"Well, she was the one who bought it for me."

"Wow, you must have really laid down the pipe for her to warrant a $10,000 watch. Tell me again how she is all wrong for you?"

"Yeah, I know. I am an idiot sometimes."

"Sometimes?"

"Shut it. Anyway ... so the other thing is she lives in your town which is why I am headed your way."

"Oh, NOW the truth comes out. Here I thought you had long suppressed feelings towards me and instead it's a girl that has you calling me ..... Are you positive you're not gay?"

"NO."

"OK... well if you're sure. As to this girl that has supplanted me ... meeting her again should be fun. What if we double date for my birthday outing?"

"Well, that's the other thing."

"There is another thing? How can there be another thing?"

"We haven't seen each other in a little over a year or so."

"Aha. Any particular reason? Like was she in a coma and unable to have visitors? Or suffering from a highly infectious disease?"

"No ... I was just stupid and scared."

"Well, that's different."

"Thank you for thinking so."

"No, not you being stupid and scared. That's normal every day for you. I mean that's different that you would even admit that. Wait! ... It just hit me! You got divorced so you could be with this woman you met ... the woman of your dreams ... or whatever ... and you don't even know if she is still interested in you? Those balls must be made of iron."

"Well ... I already had the Porsche so I had to do something typical of a midlife crisis. I figured this was the easiest. Besides, who can really refuse me once I set my mind on capturing them?" said Ken with a self-effacing laugh.

"Balls of Steele and humble as shit you are! In the interest of actually helping you instead of having you self-destruct and then having to pick up the pieces, let me try to make it easier for you a bit. Call her up, tell her it is your best friend's birthday and have her meet us out. No muss no fuss. No fear of being trapped with the massive mountain of a man that you are. And she knows that you will behave since you guys are out in public. Besides, you know much I enjoy uncomfortable get-togethers. Would be the best birthday present yet!"

"I think I just might do that. Thank you, Scott."

"That's what I do! Oh and Sunny!"

"Yes?"

"If she gives you a second chance I want the first born to be named after me. Or at least have a dedication plaque on the bed with my name on it."

"Done!"

Scott was smiling to himself as he put his cell phone back in his pocket. What great timing! Here was a chance to introduce Pandora to one of his all time best friends and show her that he was ready to take this relationship to the next level without actually having to get down on one knee and propose to her. That would be just too much pressure and while he felt that he certainly had her 80% there, he didn't want to scare her just yet. Could life get any better than this?

Gathering his things he found himself actually skipping as he was walking towards his car and accidentally slid a bit on the slick floor. He had to laugh to himself for this was exactly how Sunny had gotten his nickname. Sunny adored singing and one day after lacrosse he was running out of the shower in a hurry to get ready singing "Get down tonight" by "k.c. and the sunshine band" and slipped and fell smack dab on his ass in front of the entire team. We tried calling him Sunshine, but you only did that once if you did not want to get your ass beat. Therefore, we shortened it to Sunny. That he was ok with and since then, to those of us who saw him "make a little love and get down tonight" he would always be called Sunny. So much so, Scott was hard pressed to remember what his given name was.

CHAPTER 29

I was getting ready to show Scott how a birthday should be celebrated when you lived in Las Vegas. His original idea had been to have dinner at some national chain restaurant or other, and while those establishments certainly had their place in society, and even I had been known to frequent them, I had something more extravagant in mind. Why else live in Las Vegas? It certainly was not to bake at 110F every summer and consider 99F to be the sign that summer was officially over and time to pull out those turtlenecks.

One lived in Las Vegas to partake of the impossible on any given night of the week and still be back in time to make pancakes for the kids in the morning before heading to work or to bed. Just like in the movie *Casino,* which was set in the mob days of Las Vegas. Joe Pesci's character, *Nicky Santoro*, would always be home in time to make his children pancakes ... no matter what. It was a nice hold over.

Scott let me handle the planning and fortunately, for both of us, he knew that it would take less than a day to get all the plans put in place. As I was going through my contacts, I ran across the email file that Scott had left open. The next email from Ken had been the one where he had written me a few days after our very first time of making love. I should just skip over it, but I had to see if reading the same email now would dredge up the same emotions that I had had for the last few years.

I decided it was worth the experiment.

Subj: a few things to say on this Morning.......
Date: 11/20 8:54:31 AM
From: FinanceGuy
To: Pandora

To my gorgeous lady:

Strange how you appear in my minds eye during a day and during an evening. I am not completely sure of what I am going to say here, but I know I have to find some way to communicate a few thoughts to you.

A few days have passed since I looked into your eyes for the very first time, since I was honored enough to kiss you, to taste you, to enjoy the beating of your heart, the pace of your breath and the magical energy of you. And now that I am back into my semblance of reality, this life that I have carved out for myself, you are there.......vivid as usual......but now with a hunger that I cannot describe. Though I will try, and God knows that I have tried, to express to you what I see when I look at you and what it is that I gain with having you...and however small a piece of you..... in my life.

Seemingly weeks and weeks ago, when I was first given the gift of your picture, I was utterly amazed that someone that looked like this.......would be interested, would even give a piece of time to, would take a second look at a guy like me. And slowly, we began to peel the onion of our lives and I discovered a few things.........a few things about you and a few things about me. I learned of the value of intellectual conversation and the appropriateness of respected career and effort. I learned of hidden passion and the desire in all of us to release it. I began to see in me what I haven't seen in years......energy and spirit........and I started see in you a new emotion of internal self-confidence......something I feel that you see now just in you..........not that which you project to everyone around you in your daily life.

And we advanced........advanced to a place where these emotions.....met with our faces.....our physical selves. This condition exists......and exists with an ease that I cannot explain.......I feel like I have known you before.....maybe a past life or something that unusual.......but nonetheless I have known you before. Now sure, maybe it is the fact of seeing you in my dreams and we are all aware now of how vivid this little boy dreams.......but nonetheless......I feel so comfortable just listening to you breathe.....just watching you ....just your presence alone is amazing to be a part of.

Touching you is like something that I am certain that I have never experienced before. Never in my life have I had this unusual feeling of pure voltage leaping through my body.......and experiencing this feeling with someone......feeling the very same explosions of passion. Prior to seeing the grace of you calmly walking next to me through some crowded casino, I would in fact stare at you, through your pictures, with some hope of preparing myself for the actual reality of that feeling. Would I say something stupid? Would I act as if I was all of about 3 years old? Who knows........but I had to know this feeling. Among the other emotions that I had to know......holding you in my arms......looking into your eyes....... simply kissing you........these things I had to know.......not simply wished to know. I dreamed of making love to you, but never counted on the fact that I ever would.......but now I know all of this things.......and I am lifted.

Today, I am a better man because of you. Maybe a man that is better understood.....at least in the spirit that our souls project.....but I am understood. I know that you will forever feel with me .... an emotional feeling of being naked..........having someone that actually understands the movements of your thoughts.........and the flow of your thoughts. Someone that understands this success-driven woman of business and this scared little girl........the one that I discovered........hiding inside you.

I hope that today.......you will feel like a better woman........and from this day forward........wherever the road leads........regardless of the twists and the curves........the ups and the downs ....that you will always have the ability and the piece of mind........to stop whatever it is you are doing.....close your eyes.......and remember.........whatever it is that is most vivid in your mind about us.........and all that you will ever be able to do is smile..........

For you see..........whenever I close my eyes........and think of you........I do the very same thing.

Have a wonderful day...........

831

###

As I finished reading the email he had written me after our first time together, I let the solitary tear that had left my eye drop to the carpet below. It was only one tear and it was shed in happiness. I still loved Ken, there was no doubt about this. How could anyone ever not love their very first love? And when Ken wrote, his compliments did just what he always said he wanted to do with me - to lift. His compliments were so free-flowing and well thought-out and above all else sincere. Dale Carnegie in his book "*How to make friends and influence people,*" had this as his second principle "Give honest, sincere Appreciation" and Ken had that part nailed - honestly. His appreciation would be not just plentiful but detailed in the why that it never came across as being manipulative or sycophant. And I could now appreciate that quality in its purest form because, unlike before, the hurt had stopped. I read the letter as it had been intended to be read: with joy and ease of mind. I would have to tell Scott and thank him for this miracle that no one else had ever been able to accomplish. I could look back at my time with Ken with fondness and put it in its place because I had someone else to look forward to now. Someone who had not disappointed me - yet.

It seemed that the old adage of "the best way to get over someone is to get under someone new" had some merit although not in the purest of sexual meanings. For, getting over Ken required not just physically getting under someone else, or that would have happened many years ago. No, it required an emotional bond and trust. It required falling in love with someone else. Finally, that I had done, or at least it felt like I had. Of course, I had not told Scott yet. *Wouldn't he be surprised?* Although, probably not anywhere near as surprised as I myself was.

It was as if a great weight had been lifted from my shoulders and it made the planning of Scott's birthday that much more joyous and added an extra zest to my resolve to make his eyes sparkle as they had never before. I was living the meaning of serendipity and would forever be thankful for having placed that wayward personal ad. For Scott was a godsend.

CHAPTER 30

When I first moved to Las Vegas, also known as the *'Entertainment Capitol of the World,'* the nightclub scene left something to be desired. Coming from South Florida, I was amazed that while every casino had at least one show as a draw, if not more, there were only about a handful of nightclubs, if that, worth going to. Fortunately, within the span of a few years, this changed drastically for the better. These days, every strip casino had at least one or more nightclubs on the property, in addition to whatever show might be headlining. Unlike the average city or even major metropolitan area, on any given night of the week, there were always several options to choose from in order to go dancing in this glamour magnet of a town.

In the beginning, casinos owned every part of their establishments, from restaurants to the hotel rooms. Everything that was offered in addition to gaming was all built for the purpose of increasing the gaming dollar. Hotel rooms, *Forbes* and *Michelin* rated restaurants, spas, and various other forms of entertainment were incorporated to allow minimal distance from the casino, where the real money was made, to the non-casino entities. As more space was needed to accommodate everything from movie theaters to mega-nightclubs, continuity had to be kept. As such, while having the appearance of a single building from the outside (for the most part), these resorts became actually miniature, self-contained cities on the inside. One of the many reasons why walking along the Las Vegas Blvd required ample time, comfortable walking shoes, packing lots of water, and maybe even a light lunch. A city block in Las Vegas was the equivalent of 10 most anywhere else. Just one of the many design features in addition to windowless rooms and circular floor layouts created to keep people and their recreational dollar contained in one spot. As these additions took on a life of their own and competed for the gaming dollar, the casino owners, to stay current, started leasing out those non-gaming spaces. Not casino spaces but areas such as restaurants and they entered into partnerships with companies with proven track records who could concentrate entirely on making those non-gaming aspects successful even when independent of the casino.

This was how the nightclub scene exploded in Las Vegas. The casino owners did well when the competition was low and created such trendsetters as *Club Rio* at the *Rio* or re-inventing a classic icon such as *Studio 54* at the *MGM Grand*. Bucking the infamous nightclub trend of mimicking the fashion industries saying of: "one day you're in and the next day you are out," Las Vegas nightclubs enjoyed an unheard of long lifespan with many turning a profit even as long as 10 years after opening. As such, patrons knew to expect spectacular light shows and aerobatics from a Las Vegas nightclub just as a high-end restaurant would have a wait staff instead of a walk-up window and trash bins in the dining area for bussing one's own table. Looking for partners to sustain and expand these operations, Las Vegas casino owners, having an already well-established connection with South Beach, Florida, started taking meetings with some of the better-known identities. The South Beach club owners began taking over the nightclub operations of many of the casinos and expanded their established world-renowned names by creating much larger duplicates and turning themselves into a brand chain. Competition for the nightclub dollar became fierce which created some of the most amazing nightclub experiences and elevated the DJ to mythic status. DJs started commanding wages of which most actors and even some CEO's would be jealous. Change, ever prevalent in the entertainment industry and, therefore, its capitol, started occurring in ownership as well. Owners moved and companies merged until a good portion of the nightclub scene was dominated by a single solitary corporation that did almost nothing but. Owning a multitude of clubs to cater to patrons from the Ultra Lounge experience to the 3 level - multi-room - restaurant/club, nightclub, revenue had started to rival the gaming revenue and the primary reason for visitors boarding planes, trains, and automobiles headed to this established entertainment capitol. Fortunately, being ever the networker, I had friends in this and other organizations.

I had always been one of these strange people that went to nightclubs just to go dancing. My object had never been to get drunk - nor to pick-up on anyone. It had always been just to dance. There were others like me, mainly locals, and while we did not know each other outside of the nightclub environment, and would have been hard pressed to recall anyone's name, there was a camaraderie between us as we recognized each other in the various locales. Sometimes we danced together, sometimes we danced apart, and sometimes we worked together and created dance space so we could take turns to have a place to show off. We melded and separated and flowed in and out of our respective dance spaces with the ease of a lava lamp.

With so many clubs to choose from these days, and my generally restricting my nightclubbing nights to Fridays and Saturdays due to my long office hours during the week, I would typically attempt to optimize my experience by going to three or four different nightclubs on any given night. This was not easy to do if you did not know the right people since the general admission entry into the more familiar places could be as long as a three-hour wait or more. Fortunately, I happened to know the right people. As such, the amount of time it took to go from one nightclub to another was essentially just the amount of time it took me to drive and get the car parked. I was just one of those people nightclub owners wanted in their clubs. I helped liquor sales and when bottle service could be as high as tens of thousands of dollars, comping my cover charge and fast-tracking my entry, was something they were more than eager to do.

While my purpose, when I went to a nightclub, was not usually to get drunk or have random sex with a stranger, that did not mean that I had never done so. Prior to our meeting and his becoming engrossed in the saga that was Ken and me, questioning me about the glamour of the clubbing experience and my threesome endeavors, which at times seemed to be more commonplace than the one-on-one ones, had been one of Scott's favorite topics of discussion. We had had quite a few ponderings about my dancing and how many indecent proposals I received on an hourly basis while out and about, both from men and women, that I knew showing him what I could do on the fly, would be the best birthday present yet. Besides, what man alive would say no to a threesome with two women? Despite the fact that, I characteristically did not like being tied down (or up) this way, preferring to remain fluid and changing clubs and people at a whim, I decided my lack of freedom for one night was worth creating a proper birthday night out with all the fixins'.

Since Scott rarely went to the Strip, other than to visit the occasional country and western bar, I picked a middle of the road resort for us to meet - or, what I considered middle of the road. Not too fashionable were Scott would feel uncomfortable, but also not too kitschy to where I would not be able to get the look of disapproval off my face. As such, for this endeavor I decided to pick an updated classic located smack dab in the center of the Strip, the *Mesopotamia* of modern Las Vegas. Not only had they been around since the 60's, but also much like the successful entertainers who had been around for longer than 10 years, this resort was constantly having a bit of a nip and tuck to keep up with the times. Most recently, a new hotel tower had been added, to the several already in existence, but under a different brand name. This was a trend that had started a while back with *Four Seasons* and *Mandalay Bay*. The suite was by all appearances decorated in an ultra modern style and touted the use of feng shui design in its welcome packet. The first thing I noticed upon walking in was the wood floor throughout. Lifting my gaze off the floor, I saw the regulation size pool table in front of the bar and next to the living room area. Scott had mentioned that he liked playing pool, so I thought it might come in handy at some point during the night.

Walking into the bedroom, I saw the bed straight ahead of me and another couch combo with chaise lounge ends on my right and the open floor entrance to the spacious granite bathroom on my left. The bathroom was more like a spa than a bathroom. My only regret was that my time was limited that night, but I made a mental note to ask for a late checkout and spend the next morning thoroughly enjoying the full unique pampering experience.

One of the many perks of booking in this particular tower was having my personal concierge checking me in while we were in the room and no long front desk lines to deal with. My concierge explained all the entertainment features to me before having some tea brought and set up before she left. I could feel the sensation of calm and relaxation taking over and decided to take a nap before Scott's arrival. I was not concerned about his access. I had added his name to the reservation and had told him to get a key so he could come up without having to coordinate a public meeting place. I closed the curtains, turned on the music, dimmed the lights, sprayed some of the lavender provided on my pillow, and went to sleep.

I must have been more tired than I had initially thought, seeing as what woke me up was the feeling of Scott's finger inside of my pussy and his mouth sucking hard on one of my nipples, as I was seconds away from cumming. Proving once again that I would be hard pressed to choose between which skill of his was superior: the psychological or physical? A bit confused and trying to make my way through the sleepy cobwebs, my body decided to continue with the process of climaxing, while my hands reached instinctively for his face to bring his lips to mine. Those lips were the nectar for my soul. Once his mouth had connected and completed the circle of sensations again, I reached back towards his pants to pull his understandably hard cock out as my walls closed down on his finger. *How was he able to achieve that level of hardness without any pharmaceutical aid?* I released his lips, twisted my body so my hips remained in the same place with his hand working on my second orgasm. My head was now almost over the edge of the bed and a lot closer to his cock and wide-awake. Judging by the amount of pre-cum already leaking from his tip, I knew it would take very little to have him shoot his load in my mouth. The room was starting on its familiar spinning rotation again as my body was building up another electrical storm for the next orgasm. My hand stopped massaging his shaft and instead brought him to my mouth. As soon as my tongue touched his tip, a high-pitched moan escaped Scott's lips, which changed into a loud exclamation of "fuck" as soon as I pushed him fully into my throat. I was feeling ultra self-satisfied with myself considering that I had woken up just minutes prior. It was maybe another two minutes before his finger curled up towards my stomach causing me to cum again, at which time he released the content of his balls into the back of my throat, as he could feel my sounds of pleasure reverberating through his flagstaff.

Fully awake now, I moved my head back to the pillow, pulled him down towards me, and kissed him deeply. If I had not been enraptured with him prior, acting out one of my favorite fantasies of waking up to an orgasm without having to ask him most certainly closed the deal for me. "That is an excellent way to wake up and it's not even my birthday week but yours," I said as he came up for air and stared deeply into my eyes.

"Oh, I think I made out ok on that deal," he said chuckling as he moved from laying on top of me to lying down next to me. Once there, he pulled me towards him and into a position that would have my head on his chest. As I adjusted my long hair, so it would not cover his face but the pillow instead, he asked, "So, what is on the agenda for tonight?"

"Make-over ... Drinking ... Dancing."

"Make-over?" he asked while twisting his head so as to look into my eyes.

With an evil laugh, I jumped out of bed and said, "Well, not a full make-over, but I do have a surprise for you." And with that, I walked towards the closet and pulled out the outfit I had bought him earlier that day. Not wanting to take him too far off the beaten path, I had decided to stick with classic essential elements and presented to him the French blue button down shirt with French cuffs, black Armani jacket and pants, and lace-up dress shoes. "See, I got you a birthday suit." I was tickled with my play on words.

I could tell that he was amused but less than overwhelmed by my surprise. With a sigh, he got out of bed and said, "Well ... I guess I knew this day would eventually come. Will wearing this outfit tonight make you happy?"

"Deliriously!" The fact was that, while he thought he was pleasing me, clothes were not just a necessary tool when it came to attraction, but also a declarative statement of belonging when moving in the circles I did. While I had the influence to get him past the dress code in the club we were going to, had he remained in his typical professor like clothes, he would have felt out of place. It would have been just one more hurdle to get over and I wanted his birthday present night to go as smoothly as possible.

"Fine, let's see how this stuff fits. By the way, I might have an old college friend, Sunny, stop by with his girlfriend tonight. Hope that's ok," he said as he got up. Walking over to kiss me, he successfully launched another lightning bolt through my body as he put his finger up inside of my pussy for a minute and hit my g-spot. I almost dropped the clothes as a result. Fortunately, he only tortured me for a moment before he pulled his hand out smoothly, grabbed the hangers from me, and proceeded to the bathroom to change as if nothing had happened.

"Bastard!" I yelled half-jokingly after him for not only knowing how to hit my buttons so to speak but for doing it so effortlessly. I could hear him laugh as I walked towards the closet. It still amazed me how he could get past my armor so easily. "And of course, that's ok. The more, the merrier. Just let me know and I will make sure that they don't have to wait in line." I would have done anything for Scott at this point.

I was not the classic female when it came to getting ready. Most of the stereotype involving the excruciatingly long waiting time in the female dressing process, was not just spent on the clothing decision, but also hair preparation and make-up application. I wore little make-up, even on a night out. My hair was long and easy to either put into a ponytail or use some clips to keep it back while long and down. Since I had my outfit hanging in the closet, I was dressed and almost ready to go in about five minutes. As I was grabbing my brush and clips for my hair, I nearly dropped both seeing Scott walk out in his new suit. He was quite the sight. Smiling he did a slow 360 turn and asked, "I hope this is what you envisioned when you bought it?"

Composing myself I answered, "No ... but it will do for tonight." I was not lying. It looked much better on him than I had imagined. Of course, I was not the only one with an eye full. After he had finished with his spin, Scott had a difficult time focusing on my face with my breasts appearing to at any moment, spill out of the French blue corset top that I had matched up with black yoga pants and my dance sneakers. One of my favorite eye-popping outfits since not only did it show off my dancer legs and bottom shaped by years of training but a cinched waist and top-heavy physique. Besides, the blue accented my eyes. That was, for those whose gaze reached that high.

It was funny how putting on different clothes aided greatly in putting on a different mindset - one that I would need to succeed at my nights plans. No matter the outfit or the persona, I would affect, at the core I was always the same person. I would just tap into the different strengths of my personality as the occasion would require. Tonight, I would need to become dominant. I would need to be director and author and know where to shine the spotlight. Some would call it being manipulative; I just called it being social. The vulnerable Pandora had had her indulgence and now the take charge Pandora that the public at large knew, set foot and walked out the very expensive suite and towards the elevators.

All told, it only was a few minutes walking from the hotel room to the nightclub, whose line was snaked through the casino already. I had told the manager what time to expect us and caught his eye as he was standing outside talking with some of the security personnel. Still a ways away, he walked past the ropes and down the hall to kiss me hello. "Pandora, so great to see you tonight. I have your table ready for you." Making small talk and giving Scott an approved once over, even if he had to strain his neck to make eye contact despite his 6' height, he walked us past the ropes and into the crowded club. All he had to do to communicate with his staff was a combination of looks and nods. Without a word spoken into his wrist microphone, a team of two waitresses and a bus boy mobilized and were in the middle of setting our table up for us by the time we arrived. I did not typically reserve tables in a nightclub, seeing how I hardly ever sat down, but tonight I had to make sure that Scott had somewhere to relax during the times when I just needed to let loose and could not be encumbered with a less than professionally trained dance partner. I was willing to make sacrifices for his birthday celebration, however even I had my limits, and to accomplish what I had in mind, I had to be able to use my usual means of attraction. While sitting and looking pretty had been known to work, being the center of the spotlight tended to work better.

Sitting down, it was my first chance to look around. I knew from past visits that the club consisted of three different rooms each with their own

DJ and dance floor. Antonio had sat us in the main room with only a rope separating our table from the throng of bodies trying to keep time with the beat on the dance floor. The club had only been open for 30 minutes at best but was already close to capacity with a slew of people still waiting to get in. Thankfully, Las Vegas clubs were open later than usual, or otherwise some of those people waiting in line would never see the inside of where we were. One of the many benefits of not having any blue laws was not knowing the meaning of *'last call'* and having the nightclub stay open as long as there were people buying alcohol.

Having stepped into my role of social hostess entirely by now, and wanting to get the partner dancing part of the evening over with as soon as possible, I said "Drink up," to Scott so he could get a bit more relaxed and less self-conscience while out dancing with me. I had to smile as I could see by his body language and facial expressions that Scott was not used to the amount of attention being paid to him. Part of it was due to my being by his side, but part of it was due to the clothing he was wearing. Just as my clothes had helped in my taking on my persona, his clothes helped to bring out the runway-model confidence not usually synonymous with professors. Scott finished his first drink in a gulp. The well-trained, hyper-attentive, and ample-bosomed waitress had already a second one at the ready for him by the time he lowered his glass back to the table. Another example that clothes made the man or Antonio just knew how to hire the right people. Too bad she was off limits. Antonio had already warned me not to poach his staff for my planned activities, and I was always a woman of my word. I turned my attention back to Scott and watched him take a sip from his second drink. Once Scott was sufficiently lubricated, I grabbed his hand and pulled him to dance with me. I decide the easiest partner dance to pull off would be dancing close together, with my mainly dancing and Scott mostly standing there. I used his body a like a stripper would a pole and never lost contact with him. There was some part of me, hands, hips, head, chest, etc., that would be touching him or stroking him in some fashion or other. I could be quite inventive in this way and all of which caused Scott's bulge to grow in size, as his hands wrapped themselves around the small of my back.

Once the song was over and while holding his hand and walking in front of him, I escorted Scott with his stiff cock back to the table but not before taking advantage of his being up against my back and reaching behind me and feeling him up. Guiding him back by both hand and cock I let go sufficiently to have him sit back at the table faced him to kiss him, straddle one of his legs while my thigh found his cock, and slowly slid down while our lips remained locked. Smiling wickedly, I pulled away and while walking back, I said hi to some of the regulars. I was now primed to let loose on the dance floor. As was typical, while the outfit was certainly eye-catching, something about doing triple pirouettes, splits, and back bends where my hand touched the ground and I came back up unassisted, tended to capture the attention of the eyeballs in the vicinity. Combining the classic ballet moves with hip-hop, jazz, tap, Latin and Arabic, and people would get the impression that I might have had a dance class or two. Halfway through the first song the compliments and questions from strangers started. Men and women alike would stop me and want to talk or dance together. The approaches would range from pure joy and appreciation, "You are an amazing dancer," to outright sexual advances, "I'd love to see you do those splits on my face." I laughed off the advances and graciously accepted the compliments, while I was on the lookout for the perfect girl for my plan tonight, and then I spotted her. Shorter than I, but just as top-heavy if not more so, she had short dark hair, a cupid shaped mouth, dark eyes, a silvery short mini dress with a V-shaped neckline. She would stare at me unabashedly and I would smile back invitingly. The predator in me came out now in full force. She was obviously there with a group of girlfriends but seemed to be solely interested in me and my movements. Her group was dancing near me and had asked me to join them. She, in particular, was dancing a bit closer to me than the rest. She was tipsy, although not drunk and kept *'accidentally'* rubbing her breasts up against mine as she looked into my eyes. I had drawn her into my web without her even realizing it. While there were definitely other choices and offers to consider, I decided that this would be the girl for the threesome tonight. In addition to the suite and the nightclub experience, she would round out the list of Scott's presents from me. Having made my decision, I moved in closer and danced with her outright. I took on the lead role and decided to run her through some salsa moves of spins and dips and fancy pretzel-like contortions - all of which involved multiple body-to-body contacts. By the time the second song was over, I could see that she needed a break and a chance to catch her breath.

"Would you like to come back to our table and have a drink with us?" I asked as I pointed towards Scott sitting at the table. It took a moment for her to focus on the right area. I could see her face change from the searching squint to the wide-eyed appreciation as she found the spot I had been pointing to. Her desire was palatable as I felt it encompass now not just myself but the handsome fellow sitting at the table staring back us. There was a sparkle in her eyes and I saw her sweeping up and down gaze as she was taking him in. She answered simply "Yes."

With my hand around the small of her back, I walked her back to our table where Scott and been watching us and we started talking. Come to find out she was visiting from California for the weekend with a group of her friends, whom I had met out on the dance floor, and was staying in the hotel. I would look at Scott from time to time to gauge his approval of her, and took pleasure in the amused if somewhat fascinated look on his face as the realization dawned on him that I might have more in mind than just drinks and conversation.

Whenever she would lean forward to talk to me, her breasts would, once again, rub up against mine. "You better be careful. You can poke an eye out with those," I said jokingly.

"I like yours, too," she said with a smile as her hand traced the outline of them showing above the corset top. "Let's go dance," she requested as she grabbed my hand and led me back to the dance floor. I turned to Scott and motioned for him to follow us. It was time to make Scott a more involved partner in all this.

The dance floor had gotten so packed that there was hardly room to move which seemed to be just fine with *California Girl.* Every time I tried to create a smidgen of space for a bit of breathing room, she would close the gap and press her body against mine again. It was obvious that it was time to prepare her for the nights activities and move from tentative flirting to outright sexual overtures. Running my hands over her dress, our hips kept meeting in time to the music as my nipples were getting hard from her constant rubbing up against them. As we continued to dance, I was struck with an idea and my dominant and manipulative side took over. My hands continued their exploration of her body and then they reached the end of her very short dress. My left hand circled to the small of her back while my right one traveled up the inside of her thighs, up to her panties. Once there, I barely touched the outside of her clit to make her gasp. I decided to take it a step further and right there on the dance floor, while surrounded by a throng of people, which was the best form of concealment there was, I pushed her panties to the side and started fingering her to the music. She pulled me closer. Scott was clueless to what was happening just yet, as I pulled him nearer by the front of his shirt to create a sandwich with her in the center. She leaned in to kiss me, and as she did, I pulled my hand out of her, grabbed Scott's, who was dancing butted up against her now, and guided his fingers into her pussy. I could see at first puzzlement, then surprise, and then an understanding smile as he continued what I had started. Her face showed that she was enjoying every minute of it, and since my hands were now on her waist, it was obvious that I was no longer the person fingering her. She reached above her head and behind, and pulled Scott those last few millimeters nearer to her, and with her other arm she reached in front to pull me further into her as well. The song was coming to an end, so I leaned into her ear and asked, "Do you want to feel his cock inside of you and my tongue on your clit?" She nodded her strong agreement. Scott instinctively slid his hand out of her and acted as if nothing had happened as we walked back to the table. "Why don't you kiss her?" I suggested as I settled the bill. They did. All told, we had only been in the club for an hour before we headed back to the suite. I had to laugh at myself for I could not recall her name even though at some point she had told it to me. However, for what I had planned, we didn't need any names and were probably better off not knowing them.

CHAPTER 31

Once I had signed the credit card slip and thanked Antonio, we all stood up. I wrapped my left arm around her waist and reached for Scott's hand with my right hand, as we walked back to our suite. Scott opened the door for us as I led her into the first room and pushed her up against the wall by the door.

It was funny how for me the girl-on-girl sexual interaction had nothing to do with emotion and everything with seeing if I could. If could make them cum. If I could make their eyes roll back. If I could touch them, intuitively like most guys would not. If I could know their bodies better than they did. For me, sex with a woman was a science experiment and not an act of an emotional bond. Sometimes an emotional bond would exist, a true friendship bond, and in those cases, the sex was 100% independent of anything that happened in our discussions. Sex with a friend, be they female or otherwise, was just another form of a hug with no desire for more.

Tonight, it was a purely physical act of *'if I could'* but times two. As I was pushing her up against the wall and kissing her while my hips ground up against hers, I was ever the director and creating quite the show for Scott. My cerebral mind was 100% in control and choreographing this erotic dance on the fly, choosing movements, positions and angles to maximize the view - the sensation - and the enticement. Guiding her to the pool table while kissing, I lifted her up and sat her on the edge and grabbed Scott by the hand. Pushing his hand up inside her pussy again I said, "Feel how wet she is." Seeing him fingering her outright and watching her respond to his long academic fingers, heightened my desire to make this as memorable of an evening as possible for him. Walking back to the bedroom I grabbed the box of condoms I had purchased earlier that day and removed one. Heading back to the pool table, I saw Scott still fingering her. She had changed positions slightly and had put her hands behind her and was leaning back to enjoy the particular skill at work as his other hand was massaging her breast. There was a bit of a jolt at the visual since I knew firsthand what she was experiencing and I could feel myself getting wet at the instant memory of that sensation. Dismissing my personal want, I went back to my director mindset. It was time to take things a step further and get her to a place where the room would spin on her. I moved behind Scott, let my hands travel down his shirt, to his pants, and reached underneath to massage his cock. I could feel it jump as my hands were working through the fabric, so I undid the zipper, pulled him out. I could just imagine how few women would be able to do what I was about to do even if they were the architect of the whole thing and in charge of the situation. How secure and confident a person had to be to let go and not feel threatened. I placed a condom on his cock, pushed her soaking wet panties to the side, and guided him into her pussy at which point he pulled his hand out.

Something about being the one to orchestrate this was as huge, if not more so, of a turn on for me than being the penetrated. *California Girl* being the stranger she was was the equivalent of a sexual toy in this scenario. Sharing her with Scott felt like some ancient ritual. This would be the bond that would draw us closer together, two friends - partners - taking control of another woman for the sole purpose of sexual experimentation and satisfaction. This was sex - not making love. This was taking control. I now moved off to the side grabbed her breast with my left hand and brought her head to my mouth with my right, and kissed her deeply as I was massaging her nipples and Scott was fucking her pussy. I would alternate between looking at her and him. When I would look at her, I could see the electrical storm of sensations in her eyes as he kept bringing her to the edge of orgasm. When I looked at him, I saw that while his cock might have been in her, his connection was with me and this was his way of showing off for me. His way of showing me how skilled he was. Just the way I liked it.

Despite having already shot out one load earlier tonight, I could tell that the visual of us kissing and my playing with her tits, was getting him ready to cum again. Before he did, I stepped in and pushed him back. The orgasm would be that much more heightened if he would get to the brink and have to pull back a few times before finally releasing. Knowing exactly what I wanted to do next, I took the opportunity to lift her down and lead her to the bedroom by her hand. Once there I started to undress her while, Scott removed his own clothes. I loved having my own personal life size doll to play with. As I was taking off her clothes, my mouth took advantage of the close proximity to her skin and I started to create slow, wet trails all over her neck, breasts, and stomach. Men could forget about the sensuality of sex unless they were emotionally connected. Gauging by her reaction to my tongue, it was a sensation not oft experienced by her, but one that she most definitely wanted more of. Pushing her up against a wall again, I ran my tongue along the inside of her thigh and just barely licked the outside of her swollen lips. She moaned loudly. The mouth could be such a tool for pleasure. I continued to run my tongue lightly over her lips and clit waiting for Scott to finish undressing. Once all his clothes were off I moved back up, pulled the girl towards me as I guided her to the headboard side of the bed. "I think it's Scott's turn to lick you," I said with an impious grin. She looked expectantly at him and nodded her agreement.

"Lay down on your back," I told Scott still in my director mode. As he did, I brought the girl over and position her so as to straddle his face. I could see the flashes of ecstasy going through her as his tongue worked its magic on her clit and alternated between licking her and tongue fucking her, as I got out of my own clothes. I was ecstatic at how well my plan was working out and how well the three of us meshed together sexually. It helped to have a knack for picking out the perfect sexual partners for these types of endeavors. Not the easiest of tasks to accomplish ever. Changing out the condom for a new one so as not to mix our floras, I straddled his dick, faced her and completed the triangle. With her riding his mouth and my riding his rock-hard pole, we would lean forward and while holding on to each others breasts, occasionally kissed while we were each getting our fill from him. Every time we did, the sensation of having a familiar cock but unfamiliar lips at the same time would cause me to climax again not to mention having my nipples stimulated at the same time. There was a softness about being with a woman that was exciting and enticing that could not be recreated with a man, and quite frankly was unappealing in a man. Getting to experience both the feeling of the yielding round squish of her breasts in direct contrast to the rod iron hardness of Scott's stud, was like having fried chicken and waffles or any sweet and savory combo at the same time. The dichotic experience was the only way I ever could climax when there was a woman involved. Otherwise, it was truly just a science experiment, however, having a woman involved while a skilled guy was present, heightened the ordinary everyday pleasure of the act just as double penetration would. Double penetration, while not something that I would put on my list of sexual musts in regards to every day or even every month, does feel absolutely incredible when done at the right time

After a while, I leaned forward and whispered in her ear, "I want to lick you out." She nodded her agreement. Scott and I switched places. She sat back down on my face while Scott continued to work on my g-spots with his God given talents. It was his turn to lean forward from time to time to kiss her and play with her supple bust. Licking her pussy instead of kissing her, though, required my actually concentrating on the movements of my lips and tongue instead of going with pure instinct. This would classically not be an issue, except that it was difficult to keep my awareness enough to lick her out properly with Scott doing such a thorough job with his shaft sliding in and out of me. I did manage to get two fingers in her and make her scream aloud as her creamy cum coated my hand. My mouth would alternate between licking her gently and sucking on her outer lip. However, the battle of which part of my brain would take over completely was giving me a headache. It was like watching porn and C-span picture in picture on TV. I was trying to keep the higher brain function to maintain the sexual control I had established over her, but it was at direct odds with letting myself go to the fiery build-up that Scott was creating in my lower body. Just as the wave would try to take me over, I would break the hypnotic control by focusing on the clit in front of my face.

Fortunately, I was not the only one who was battling letting the ecstasy just take over, since I heard Scott's voice saying, "I'm getting ready to cum." While this would, in general, have made my eyes roll back in my head, this time it served as the signal for my cognitive brain to slam-dunk my primal one into submission. After all, there was still one thing left to do before I could let him climax. When I had originally envisioned this night, I knew I had to orchestrate something that would push the memory of this event to an over-the-top different status. I felt that we had to do something that would not be possible in any other circumstance but as a threesome. Pushing her gently off my face, I said, "Not yet. I want to try out one more position. How would you like to alternate between our holes?" I could see the confused but *'willing-to-try-anything'* look on his face as I moved out from underneath him.

Placing a stack of condoms opened and ready to *'roll'* next to him, I got up on my knees, faced the girl while we were both on the bed and told her, "This will feel fantastic." Moving closer to her, I stroked her breasts and sank my teeth into her neck as she sighed with pleasure. Having control of her again, I never raised my mouth from her neck while I lowered her down and positioned her underneath of me. She was close to climaxing just from the suction I was creating along her jugular, which I knew would leave a mark in the morning, but neither one of us cared at the moment. She was already on the edge of orgasming again, so I decided to push her over by grinding my pussy up against hers. We were now lined up perfectly for a cock to enter either one of us from below. Putting on a new condom Scott came up from behind and slid himself first into her for a few minutes and then after changing out condoms into me for a few strokes. Every time he would push his cock in anew in one of us, a gasp would escape his lips as well as ours. When he was inside of me, she could feel his balls brushing against her clit and whenever he was inside of her, my pussy would grind against his washboard abs. Going back and forth between us a few times, the sensations kept rotating like a merry-go-round and drove our climax threshold that much higher. When he was inside of me, I was a glutton on overdrive and when he was in her, I felt the sweet pain of withdrawal being denied fulfillment. Not having him for those few moments created an ache that would push my ecstasy even higher than before when he entered me again. Between her soft breasts, mouth and body underneath of me and his hard cock inside of me at alternating intervals, I could not help but cum again, and hard, as did she. While Scott had the self-control to continue like this for hours, I could tell that *California Girl* was starting to get tired and sore from the change in her moans. Therefore, the last time he pulled out of me; I slid away. I grabbed his free hand and pushed it into my pussy while leaning forward and whispered in his ear "Cum for me." He started pumping her while he was fingering me and I leaned across to kiss her.

With her soreness forgotten as she was feeling his pounding, she moaned and screamed her orgasm into my mouth while Scott was cumming inside of her and she was cumming over his covered cock. Turned on not only be the varying rhythms of his hand and her mouth but also by the fact that Scott knew which buttons to press, I could not help myself but cum again all over Scott's hand as he curled that finger up towards my stomach. We had, at that moment, achieved the sexual trifecta - I had synchronized three orgasms at once! I was one hell of a director. I wondered if they handed out statutes for this sort of thing.

Understandably spent, Scott took off the condom, grabbed the pile he had created, and tossed them into the wastebasket as the three of us laid down on the bed. Stroking her skin, she kissed me then Scott and said, "It's getting late. I think I need to head back to my room before I fall asleep."

Scott, being ever the gentlemen, walked her back to her room. It must not have been very far away because he was back just a few minutes later. Taking off his pants, he slid back into bed and spooned me from behind.

I had been able to fulfill a goal he had set for us early on, but strangely, he was not satisfied yet. There had been a lot of sexual play but little deep seated fulfillment, just like watching a porno rarely fulfilled.

"How did you like your birthday present?" I asked in the darkness not able to see his face.

"The suit?" I could feel the suppressed laugh as his breath swept past my ear and neck. His hips were moving to reposition themselves to find a comfortable spot.

"No! The threesome silly." I smacked his arm as Scott kept trying to find a spot to settle in for his lower body.

"Oh ... that. It was ok." Grabbing my hands before they could smack him again, he said thoughtfully. "Thank you. It was better than anything I could have imagined." I could feel his cock getting hard up against me.

"I am glad you enjoyed it," I said somewhat appeased.

Changing his tone a bit he asked, "By the way, are you still in a giving mood?"

Confused at what he could possibly want after everything that I had already done unless it was to go back downstairs for more dancing which did not seem like him, I decided to answer, "Well, I would think that I have gone above and beyond, but ... what would you like?" In direct answer to my question, he slid himself into my sore but still wet pussy from behind.

"This is what I have wanted all day," He said as his cock was starting to build up the spinning sensation inside of me again.

"You being inside of me? But you have been ... almost all night," I answered somewhat confused as my back arched in response to his wave like motions.

He did not answer right at first. His top hand reached around to my breast while the other had circled around to the front and fingered my clit. The sensation of being struck by lightning besieged my body again and my walls contracted in response down on him. "No, feeling you and how wet and soft you are inside ... No condom ... Just you and me. I want to fill your pussy up until it brims over." With my ass pressed against him, my back arched and my head leaned back to kiss his mouth. Just as our lips met, I could feel his cum shoot unrestricted and all hot up inside. The volume of what I felt was not of someone who was climaxing for the third time in the last few hours; it was the equivalent of someone who had not had sex for days. I found it amazing how much the mind was a sexual partner in the overall experience. It proved that while sex was sex, having an emotional bond made sex better for both men and women. Moaning into each other's mouths, I could feel the last drop pushing itself into the depths of me. With his final thrust, he wrapped his arms around my chest and kept me there. Not moving. Not pulling out. I felt so comfortable that once the adrenaline of the night's activities had subsided, relaxation covered me like a thick blanket and my limbs became almost instantaneously heavy. The combination of all that alcohol and physical activity, despite it still being early by Las Vegas standards, was beckoning me to sleep within a matter of minutes. I had one last action left in me before the darkness swept me up completely. "Happy Birthday Scott," I whispered as I could feel myself falling asleep on my side with his cock still inside of me.

"Hmmm" is what I heard in my ear as he squeezed me a little tighter.

The haze of the twilight must have been playing tricks on me, though, or I must have already started to dream because I thought I heard his voice in my ear saying, "I love you, Pandora."

I mumbled back, "I love you, Scott."

***

CHAPTER 32

Judging by the bedside clock, I had been asleep for less than an hour before I woke up to the sound of pool balls clinking against each other before making what I imagined was a satisfying thunk into a hole. Most hotel rooms took great pains to ensure that each room was as soundproof as fiscally reasonable. Neither wanting to break the bank nor wanting a bunch of angry patrons who were upset about the headboard banging going on next door. Considering that the suite we were in also contained a media room, short of keeping the doors open from room to room, sound insulation was top notch. As such, I could only make out that there were human voices laughing and having fun in the other room but could not hear to whom those voices belonged. I could only assume that one of them was Scott's.

Remembering that Scott had mentioned a friend named Sunny possibly stopping by, I assumed that this, therefore, had to be him and maybe a quiet lady friend as well since I could not pick up on a higher pitched female trilling. Knowing hence that there was company on the other side of that door, I took advantage of the close proximity of the bathroom and closet to the bed. I did not think it would be necessary to get back into my corset top and such, however, I assumed something more socially acceptable than a hotel robe was warranted. Maybe arranging my hair into something other than bird's nest chic might be a good route to take as well. I opted for a pair of jeans I had been planning on wearing the next day and a clingy white t-shirt containing lycra and skipped the bra thing altogether. So what if they saw my darker areolas through the light colored fabric? I could always change if our plans required our going downstairs. Not wanting to be completely dressed down, though, I had decided to not only run a brush through my hair and pull it back with a pair of clips but to swiftly slip into a pair of white heels. Giving myself a quick once over in the mirror, and opting for a light gloss on my lips with some mascara (thanks for the blond eyelashes mom), I opened the door to the main living area of the suite. I felt I was ready to meet Scott's long time friend for the first time and hopefully make a halfway decent impression.

As I opened the door, I was looking down on the floor to make sure I would not trip over anything. What had been significantly dampened laughter while the door had been closed, greeted me in full volume with just the smallest of cracks and I almost fainted. I had not looked up because there was no need to. I could recognize that voice and in particular that laughter anywhere. There was only one voice that sounded like that. After having spoken for hundreds of hours on the phone together, having had phone sex together, I did not need visual confirmation - I knew that voice belonged to Ken.

Neither one of them had noticed me yet. With some morbid curiosity, or maybe because eventually I would have to look anyway, I cast my eyes upward and in their direction. Yes, it was indeed Ken standing there next to Scott - playing pool. Ken was about to walk around the table to get a better angle on his next shot and in so doing looked towards where I was standing. As our eyes connected, I could almost see the electrical arc in the air. Indeed, if the lights had been dimmed, all of us would have seen it. Maybe it was just me, my vision, and my perception, nonetheless, I felt the electricity as our eyes connected. At the same moment that recognition cascaded across his face, I went from almost fainting to actually fainting. The last thing I had remembered before the darkness closed in on me was seeing Ken sprinting to try to catch me.

I woke up on the couch with a dull ache in my head and Scott's face worriedly hovering over mine. Embarrassed that I had behaved in such a typical female romance novel manner, I tried to sit up and paid the price for moving too quickly by having the room spin on me. More gingerly this time and only nodding in answer to Scott's "are you all right?" I raised myself up to a full sitting position, swung my legs off the couch, and let my heels touch the floor. I felt set up somehow and could not decide if I was angry, embarrassed, or relieved. I still could not bring myself to speak as Ken handed me a glass of water. The look on Ken's face was priceless and Scott apparently still did not know. After drinking the water down in four big gulps, I handed the glass back to Ken without looking at him. Scott still concerned about my well-being lifted my long hair off my neck and brought it to the side, thinking that I might have overheated for some reason. I looked into his eyes and smiled and Scott's face lit up.

I could tell by his body language that he thought the worst was now over and was just about to introduce me to Ken. Not wanting him to go through that particular embarrassment, I turned my head towards Ken and just said "Scott, meet Ken." and now it was Scott's turn to put the puzzle pieces together. Having known Ken simply as Sunny for most of his life with some vague knowledge that there was a real first name that he had just forgotten about, it was an almost audible click as the tumblers in his mind aligned.

Now it was Ken's turn at feeling left out and not knowing that Scott had been privy to a great deal of our initial communication, however, that was not something that needed to be brought up just yet.

Ken, not knowing what to say, only started with "I see you are still wearing white heels."

I could feel the heat in my neck rising and it took every ounce of self-restraint on my end to not take the heels off and throw one or both at him. Imagining him with the heel piercing his heart and bleeding on the white fabric I responded. "Old habits are hard to break," and left it at that.

I wasn't sure what I was more upset over, the fact that Ken had appeared out of the blue - once again - like he had done every other time we had gotten back together, or that the headway I had been so proud of making just earlier that week had immediately taken 20 huge steps back.

Before I had ever met Scott and during one of my more self-pitying nights that included a liberal helping of wine, I had sat down with my computer staring at my spreadsheet program. In my drunkenly aided decision, it seemed to me that the best use of the spreadsheet for me for that night would be to calculate: out of all the time that Ken and I had known each other, how many days had we actually spent together as a couple? It came out to be just short of three years or 1,001 days and nights total (adjusting for margins of error and daylight saving time). How did fate keep bringing us back together?

Ken turned to Scott and said, "She is the reason I came to Las Vegas."

"I assumed as much. Not when we spoke on the phone mind you, but yeah ... a few moments ago I kind of made that connection." Scott was struck by the irony of the situation. Not too long ago when Scott had determined that Ken was a rival to be vanquished, he had quite accurately assumed they might have been friends had they met under different circumstances. There was a certain sense of schadenfreude in being proven right - yet once again. Of course, it had been quite easy to feel superior and competitive when the rival was a faceless individual. It was quite another thing to know that the *'cock fight'* so to speak was between you and one of your best friends. All his old insecurities had come back in one huge anvil dropping like cartoon moment. Speaking of, where had all the anvils gone? Faster than any time machine possibly could, he was transported back to when Claudette had left him back in college. He could see Pandora rejecting him just as every other woman of importance had. There was only one thing left to do, get drunk.

Ken, for his own reasons, had come to the same conclusion when it came to the alcohol and had already prepared a round of rum and cokes for everyone from the bar. Proffering a glass towards Pandora and then Scott, after setting down the bottle of rum and bottle of coke on the coffee table, Ken took his glass and downed it in seconds. We all followed suit. Not waiting to be asked, Ken refilled everyone's glass and after three very quick rounds, the tension eased. Not knowing if it was the alcohol or no longer being flooded with the *'fight or flight'* chemicals, maybe it was both, I was able to fill Ken in on how Scott and I had met while skipping over the bit where I had opened up my email attic to Scott. Ken and Scott in turn gave me the *CliffsNotes* version of how their friendship came to be. As we continued with our intake of alcohol, we all marveled at how small the world really was even though there were over 300 Million people in the

U.S. "Out of all the gin joints in all the towns in all the world, ..." and we had found each other, in Las Vegas. For me, this was easier to accept as commonplace, possibly since life had tended to be just such a string of coincidences, ever since I could remember. And well ... Las Vegas could be considered as a modern crossroads.

Scott, feeling the effects of the rapid infusion of alcohol into his bloodstream and combined with the already alcohol soaked hours prior, and not having had the opportunity to sleep it off as Pandora had, could feel himself losing the battle with his eyelids. Moreover, even without his degrees, he knew it would be a good time to exit to allow Ken and Pandora some private time. He excused himself and stumbled to the bedroom where he promptly passed out from physical, emotional and compound exhaustion.

***

CHAPTER 33

I looked at Scott's exit with both relief and trepidation. While I knew that Ken and I had things to discuss without being hampered by Scott's presence, the selfish part of me wanted him here as my mental safety net and emotional buffer just like he had been for the last few weeks. I was not sure if I could face Ken alone, even though I knew that I had to.

"You look as fabulous as ever. Even more beautiful than I remember," Ken said with a smile.

"Thank you. Although, that sounded like something I would hear from Santa Clause and the Easter Bunny combined ... Very charming but just as fake." I regretted the sting in my words almost as soon as they had left my lips; however, I also knew that I could not just jump right back in. As much as I could feel that, my body apparently was still tied to his energy, my brain was still in control. I could not just give in and pretend nothing had happened - that the last year of silence had not happened. I could not act as if I had not been hurt by his repeated acts of abandonment. I had a life damn it. I was important. People adored me! Next, he would tell me that he was planning on leaving his wife.

"For the last few months it has been difficult to think of anything else but you. It seemed ...," he trailed off trying to find the right words. "It seemed ... as if everywhere I turned ... there was something there that would remind me of how magical things are when we are together." There was a strange almost distressed look to his eyes as he said those words.

"And I realized that I had to do something about it." His voice was steady and even keel. "That while I have been trying to do right by everyone, I am accomplishing the exact opposite. That the one person who was the reason why I could do what I needed to do for everyone else ... I repaid by pushing her away." It was strange listening to him. I was both listening intently and yet felt like I heard the words while in a faraway place. "I kept thinking of how much I wanted to show you what you mean to me and how important you are to the very essence of my life ... so ... I got into my car and drove north. Once I hit the Hoover Dam I called one of my oldest and dearest friends to enlist his aid in trying to figure out ... not only how to find you .... but to tell you that ... I am in that spot ... that spot where I realize that life has no meaning unless I get to spend it with you ... and that is why I came here ... to tell you that I signed the divorce paperwork ... for you." There was no embellishment in his voice. There was just the steady patience that I had gotten to know well over the years. "So... therefore ... I am not sure that fake is something you could accuse me of."

I had not expected this. Granted, I figured he would lead with promises, but having actually signed the papers? I was still trying to digest that information and was unable to believe him just yet. He had said many things to me in our time together, all which had been for the purpose of roping me in. Although, I had to give him credit. He had stated his case well. *Perry Mason* would have been proud. This was also the first time he had gone to such lengths to find me, and that he had said that it had been done instead of something he was planning on doing for me. I felt slightly chagrined, only slightly, though. I did have the injustice of years to which to cling.

"I am sorry. When I think back ... I have to admit that your compliments have always been genuine," I said with a calm and even keel voice. "It's just everything else that I have had to question about you." I could feel the emotion welling up inside of me. I took another sip from my glass and pushed the knot in my throat down with the rum, allowing my voice not to break with emotion as I continued. "My mother told me this story about my very first steps. I had been holding onto the coffee table ... all unsteady as toddlers are wont to do, and the very first step that I took was in her direction. She saw that moment as a tug-of-war between desire and fear and desire won. That my desire to be with her over-rid my fear of letting go of the table." Taking another sip from my glass, I thought for a moment before I continued. "And I think either this story or her interpretation of it colored my life expectations ever since." I had to catch my breath for a moment and will myself back into a robot mode before saying, "And I cannot respect anyone who would not do the same for me. Whose desire for me does not override their fear of letting go of whatever that may be. Table ... wife ... whatever." I had to look away and force back the tears that I knew were near the surface. I would not let him see me cry. There was no way that I would let him see me cry. Not tonight! Not ever again. I was struggling to regain control. Damn the alcohol that was making it difficult to remain even keel about this whole thing. "And I am not sure if I can ever trust you again. I know you said you are done, but I just can't believe you just yet. Not after all the broken promises. Not after all the heartache I went through with you ... oh ... so ... many ... times ... before!" My level of niceness had reached rock bottom and the alcohol in my blood stream made it so much easier to no longer teeter on the edge of an emotional breakdown, but to dive into it as if I were on a 100-meter board and Greg Louganis was up next. And maybe it all happened because I was not sure if there would be another such opportunity to share with him how I really felt about all of it. How much I was hurt by all of it. So, I dove off the high dive board like an *Olympic* gold medalist. "I hate you," I whispered. It was like that little bounce divers did to get on the balls of their feet before launching themselves into the air and trusting that their body would not be destroyed by the elements. As such, my voice became more forceful and built to a crescendo saying, "I hate you, hate you, hate you." It was like the arc in the air and now for the double twist. "I want you to go away!"

Ken had to pause for a moment. I had not responded quite the way he had expected me to upon hearing the news. Listening to my sudden detonation of emotion he attempted to digest the full content of what I had just said. He knew that he had hurt me even though it had been I who had suggested breaking up. My words had been in response to his actions, my pain was real and raw, and it needed addressing. If he were to have any hope of having more than this drink with me. If his four hour or so drive was not going to be for naught, this was the hurdle that had to be overcome. Ken, however, had skills most motivational speakers had yet to know.

"I deserve that one." He paused for a very long time before continuing and I could hear the wistful longing in his voice, "You know the funny thing is that as much as I have tried to stay away from you ... as much as I am aware I am no good for you .... I can't help but seek you out," he said with a sidelong glance in the direction of the bedroom to which Scott had exited. It was the first time he had acknowledged that on this go around there might be complications when it came to our reconciliation. That it might not be as easy as saying "I'm back" and pick up exactly where we had left off. It was also the first time that he had admitted to possibly not being the right sort of individual for me.

He was saying all the right things. Things that I had wanted to hear for years, although my brain would require more than a split second to reconcile the new-and-improved-Ken, the willing-to-give-Ken, with the Ken I had experienced off-and-on for the last few years. How could he truly love me and stay away from me for all this time - even if it had been my suggestion? How could he lie to me repeatedly? *Moreover, how could I not think of those things every single time his lips moved?*

I leaned back and laughed, and then I did something I had not expected. I shied away from it since it would always elicit a feeling of wanting to just die and burrow into the ground and not stop until China had been reached. I cried! In the rare occasions, such as this, when I had given in to this natural function, I had never been able to dig my way to China. I had, in general, hid behind the closest pillow or covers that could be pulled over my head. Without a pillow or cover to hide behind, and feeling emotionally naked, I broke down.

It was a single tear at first through the laughter. Then, I was sobbing outright. The dam had cracked with all the pent up hurt for all those years of feeling not good enough for him, of feeling discarded and like I was second best. The anger, the pain, the love, the dejection the every emotion I had ever felt just broke free and started coming out in waves of slightly salty water. *How could he have not loved me enough? How could he have stayed away from me for even a minute?*

Ken, perplexed at first by my laughter, saw that first tear slowly finding the path of least resistance across my cheek and reached out for my face to wipe it away. It was an automatic reaction with no need to consult any of the higher functioning lobes in his cerebral cortex. It was driven by the pure instinct of who he was as a person. Although, who that person was master-manipulator or comforting-caregiver, had yet to be decided. Anyone who had a mother knew that often there was no difference between those personalities.

After wiping the tear, his hand went to the back of my neck. He was manipulating it the way a jaw would grab a newborn puppy's or tiger's neck before carrying the young to safety. I could feel my body exhaling as his hand mimicked an ingrained behavior. Grabbing me by the small of my neck, he moved my face closer to his, to the safety that his physical proximity had always radiated. He first kissed the new tear on my cheek before he slowly moved to kiss my lips ever so softly. That was all I needed to lose complete control and my face turned into a version of the Niagara Falls as my body was driven by the elemental need to release all those toxic thoughts.

Instead of shying away as many others would, he brought both of his hands to the back of my neck and forcefully brought my mouth to his. Demanding my lips further apart with his tongue, I could feel it enter my mouth and stifling my sobs. His hands were so strong that I could not move my head. I had to kiss him back timidly and after what was only a few seconds, but might as well have been an eternity, I kissed him back in earnest. I had hungered for his complete love and affection for so long that his entry back into my life was just like a *Borg* taking control of *Captain Picard* in *Star Trek* and I was experiencing a *'resistance is futile'* moment.

I wanted him! Despite all the headway, I had made with Scott. Despite just hours before declaring my love for Scott, I still wanted him. This man who had taken my virtual virginity. The man who was like an anaconda and after refusing to give him my love just grabbed hold and squeezed until he got what he wanted. The energy was unlike anything that had ever happened between the two of us. Our interactions had always fallen in line with lovemaking. There had never been this rawness to our contact by incorporating such anger or hurt typical of make-up sex.

Just as that thought had crossed my mind, Ken grabbed my wrists with an undisciplined strength that I thought for sure would leave them bruised the next morning and placed my wrists behind his head. Not understanding at first and only able to process the microsecond I found myself in without the ability to guess at the next step, I was not prepared for his next move as his mouth continued to assuage my emotional state. He swept me up in his arms and almost crushed my ribs in his forcefully tight grasp of me. My hands with a reflex ingrained by millions of years of evolution held on tighter to his neck without our mouths separating. I had such a lack of awareness of anything as he pressed me into his broad body. Being held by him in such a fashion had me freefalling into the universe that was Ken. I saw stars, although it might have been the spotlights hitting my retinas. *I just wanted him and damn the consequences.*

With my eyes closed and my every fiber absorbed into Ken's body, I had not realized he had carried me to a different room until I could feel the sound and air change around me and he had thrown me roughly onto the bed. With my eyes closed until the moment of impact, my squeal of surprise was shortly squelched once I felt the mattress move up and down a few times. At least I knew I was not actually free falling through space and there was something solid beneath me. I had never been handled quite like this in my life. Even more surprisingly, I could feel Scott's body next to mine in bed, stirring slightly due to the ruckus carried out by Ken's actions and my mind started oscillating again. What was I doing? How could I be in love with two men at the same time? The love of my past in direct competition with the love of my present? The history with Ken certainly had an excruciating and unwanted hold over me. The love for Scott was so new that it had a difficult time competing with my deep-set feelings for Ken. Maybe this was what Ken wrestled with when it came to his wife and me. I had to remind myself though that he had told me - several times - he no longer loved his wife, unless he had lied. Which, knowing Ken, was ever the likely answer. *I was in an excruciating blender of emotions with the setting set on frappe!* As much as my body wanted to reject him, it responded with a fervor I reserved for high-profile business deals. I just wanted him. At the same time, I knew I wanted Scott. I loved Scott. *I needed them both!*

Ken, despite his blood-deprived state of being, acted like a man with a singular plan, reached down, and jaggedly relieved me of my shirt. Having to raise myself so as to avoid death-by-strangulation-of-lighting-fast-removal-of-shirt, I landed briskly again, only this time a little further up and with my head hitting Scott's stomach. I could hear the "oof" coming from his abdomen as my head found his chiseled and engraved midsection. The room was completely dark except for the light peeking in through the bottom of the door. As my eyes looked in that direction, I felt Ken's hands working with expeditious speed. He took my jeans and g-string off me in one hurried swoosh. In the process of it all, I had to reach above me and grab hold of Scott so as to keep from sliding off the bed and achieve enough leverage to lift myself up to allow him to remove my jeans and such while my legs were still dangling over the edge of the bed from my knees on. Once free of my garments, I could feel the air moving across my body from the sharp intake and expelling of breath by Ken. The visual effect of his handiwork became perceptible to him.

I could feel Scott stirring under my hands. His body moving in a wave from shoulders to hips and what I knew would be his toes. My touch was waking him. I did not have time to think much less observe Ken removing his own pants as I was feeling Scott's body move under my hands and head. I also had not noticed the additional weight on the mattress or Ken having moved his hands on either side of my waist until his breath greeted my skin and his cock moved smoothly over my soaking wet entrance. I opened my eyes to see Ken's face hovering over me above the bed and without so much as a *by your leave*, he pushed into my wetness and my back arched higher than it ever had. Grabbing onto Scott for safety, I did not even catalogue that Scott would be completely awake now. My head on his chest and seeing my breasts heaving in his direction as one of his best friends was parting my pussy with expert precision. Scott thankfully was no stranger to threesomes, having even had one or two with the very person in bed with us now. As such, instinct took over as his brain was still attempting to awaken fully.

Scott's breathing changed and he shifted his body. The only reason I noticed was that my head was all of sudden flat on the bed and no longer on his abdomen. Moreover, while my back was arching up repeatedly from the excruciating and yet welcomed and familiar torture Ken's rod was inflicting on me, Scott leaned down to kiss me with one of his mind-altering kisses. A kiss that rivaled Ken's and made me forget that there was anyone else in the room with me - much less two of the most influential men in my adult life.

This was not at all anything like the MFF threesome from earlier that night. This was aggressive sex combined with aggressive emotional attachments between three people. The situation had all the makings of a nightmare. However, whatever fairy godmother was looking out for me, or whatever lucky star I had been born under, it instead became a fulfillment of a fantasy. A fulfillment of a fantasy I did not know I had until I was smack dabbed in the middle of it. With Scott's tongue and Ken's cock in me at the same time, I entered into a consciousness that made me think I had never actually climaxed before. I could typically orgasm in such a fashion that most women and men could only hope to attain. However, none of those times could compare to *the out-of-world* existence these two men had put me in. How could anything compare to having the love of my lives touching *every - single - part - of - my - body?*

Scott's hand reached for one of my breasts as Ken's hand reached for the other and my torture was intensified. My love for both of these men was intensified. The conflict of not wanting to fall into the same trap had left my mind as the electrical impulses generated by the two of them dominated my brain and the dopamine/epinephrine mixture was reaching levels in my bloodstream that crack addicts could only hope to connect with.

Ken's movements, rough and forceful, more so than I had ever known him to be, took on an even more compelling rhythm as his body started to tense, inches away from letting himself cum. I could sense though that this was not the plan he had formulated. Of course, how or when he had actually decided on how tonight's activity would progress, would have even most sports books clueless on what line to set. As such, and with my head having traversed the universe and back several times already, Ken pulled out just as the first drops of pre-cum had leaked from his tip. Taking a deep breath to push his animalistic urge back down, and while, on his knees, he slid further up on my body. Scott sensing the presence lifted up from my mouth. I could feel the shifting of the mattress underneath me, as

Scott got up and took advantage of the break to remove some of this clothing. Like a well-rehearsed scene, Ken now placed his stiffness on my lips and without a second thought, my mouth opened to take him in. It was evident that Ken and Scott had done this very same dance a few other times together and it seemed like they were falling back in the same tandem they had created while in school.

Ken, regaining control over his testosterone driven need, slid back down and into my pussy as Scott with a knowing glance took his place straddling my face. It was difficult to move my head in this position or anything else for that matter as my arms were also pinned. I was lying like a sex doll unable to budge and just feeling the inundation of sensations as Scott and Ken were using my respective openings as their own. Ken, moving like a *rock-n'-roller* in my lower region and Scott slowly entering and exiting my mouth, conscious of my innate need to breath.

My crying had long stopped, however my sounds had not. Scott could feel my reactions as my moans reverberated through his cock every time Ken would reach deeper inside of me with his torture device. It was almost as if Scott was unaware of Ken, having his back to him and all. As he looked down, he saw my eyes on either side of his cock and could feel my breasts under his butt cheeks. Scott shifted slightly allowing me more freedom of movement than just my tongue and freeing up my arms and hands while everything else was still under one or the others control. Making use of my newly released hands and feeling the need to get circulation back into them, I moved them to the only available place I could reach outside of the bed sheets, his rump. My fingers grasped his muscled glutes and slid down to caress his balls. The only way to reach them though was to apply pressure to the bridge between balls and ass. That move hit some sort of instant cum button for Scott as his hands came to the side of my face to steady himself and look into my eyes. I could feel the classic gathering of his sack, just like an octopus that was getting ready to propel. Unlike the jet of ink that an octopus would squirt to create a cloud of confusion to escape from, his one-armed octopus moved, jumped, and propelled the essence of him into the back of my throat. No ink or cloud, however, there was lots of choking on my end and breathing was getting to be difficult. Even if I were to die right now due to suffocation, though, it was well worth the price for having made him lose control in such a disadvantaged position as mine. Sex was eternally the battle for control. Sometimes you lost and sometimes you won and sometimes you did both.

Sensing my discomfort, Scott, ever the gentlemen moved off the bed and I was able to take my first deep breath in what seemed like forever. I could not see Scott, I could, however, feel him laying on the bed in such a fashion as to have his breath hit my neck from behind as I was still trying to catch mine.

I had no chance for respite though as I could hear the locomotive sounds of Ken's orgasm building just seconds after Scott had lifted himself off me and I was faced with the object of my longtime obsession again. I was faced with the man who had shaped such a huge part of my psyche. Despite it all, though, I could barely recognize him as he was using my body to achieve his own ends. It was difficult to recognize him, not only because of what he had come to Las Vegas to admit to, but the energy of the moment seemed to transform him physically somehow. This intensely focused dominating and vampire like energy. It was Ken, but it was a different Ken. It was still the same broad shoulders. It was still the same chest big enough to view a movie on. Those were still the same arms that had lifted me with ease. Despite the physical similarities in front of me, he looked different. Maybe it was a trick of the lighting but I doubted it. There was an edge to him that had never been there when it had only been the two of us before.

Ken, being a typical male, responded in a visceral way as he once again had a clear view of my face and chest. *How did I deserve to be this lucky?* Scott began kissing and biting my neck while Ken changed his rhythm to a slower but more insistent pace. It probably had something to do with wanting to enjoy the palpable reaction surrounding his maleness. With each touch of Scott's lips or gentle digging in of his teeth, I could feel my walls pulsating in response and Ken could in turn feel the glove-like constrictions. How unfair to be this easily manipulated. How unfair that my body temperature could be affected by the breath of air and my muscles would involuntarily contract with the touch of lips. It explained all those vampire tales of seduction by suctioning on the skin of this erogenous area, the neck. Scott's skills in dexterity did not stop at my neck, though. His hands, sliding like a fallen ice cream cone would on a hot summer's day, reached from the back of my head, along my shoulders down and then covered my breasts with his basketball size palms, mercilessly pulling on both of my nipples. *Once again, my body reacted*! However, it was much stronger than it had by the biting on my neck alone, all of which was bringing Ken to near his apex. I could see Ken's face as we both came together. I could feel the searing heat of his cum hit my back wall heightening my own sensation. I saw stars once again. All the benefits of space travel with none of the exorbitant costs. Green certified.

Staying inside of me and leaning closer to the point of almost crushing me with his body weight he slid his hands under my back, and staying connected like two puzzle pieces, he rolled quickly onto his side and back forcing me to be now on top of him with his cock still pushing cum inside of my pussy.

I could see Ken look to the side of me at what I guessed to be Scott since the closet would be an uninteresting focal point and the TV had not been turned on. He gave Scott a nod. With my upper body still touching Ken's after the upsy-daisy-like move, he had just performed, my pert butt was pushed up in the universal animal world indication of being ready to be mounted and penetrated from behind. Similar to the position I had been in just a few hours ago, however, this time my pussy was a bit more occupied than it had been the last time. Scott took up the challenge put before him by backside. Still hard despite having just cum and being blessed with an almost non-existent refractory period or at least one where it was just a change in level of hardness and not hardness itself, either way, I could feel the weight of his body shift the mattress underneath and the heat of him as he approached me from behind. With Ken's cock still inside of my pussy and Ken now just moving ever so slightly inside of me, just enough to stir the mixture of our cum together like a cocktail, I could feel Scott's head at the entrance of my ass. I had done a lot of things, and while double penetration in the form of cock and fingers or very small toys and fingers had been amongst them, two live men separated only by the thin wall between one biological system and the other, would be a first for me.

With Ken still moving ever so slightly inside of my pussy, staying hard, and keeping me relaxed and focused in the process, I now felt Scott's head push itself further into me, slowly inch by inch. Here they were, two men as close as brothers, and now closer than most brothers would ever be. They could feel not just my arousal but their arousal as well - and then Scott took control. Like a train engineer, he set the pace as he moved himself in and out of me. Ken kept pace at exactly half the speed. A necessary measure so as neither party would find themselves pushed out. I was unable to move or assist in any form or fashion. Ken had his hands around my waist while Scott had grabbed my arms like a rider would grab the reins of a bridle. Had either one of them been even a millimeter thicker than they were I would have been in excruciating pain. As it stood, my brain was still trying to decide how to best interpret the signals from my lower region. It would be either pain worse than childbirth or pleasure more intense than any I had felt prior. My brain decided to go with pleasure and my mouth let out a moan that rumbled through Ken's chest.

While both had climaxed, as had I, statically the amount of time to reach climax again for a guy, if the refractory period was short lived, increased with each event. The sensation of being stimulated in every direction, not just up and down but round and round as well, created a shortcut through the woods of the excitement and plateau stage of the sex cycle for us all. The best and most advanced sex toy could not duplicate all the points of interests that were being visited in this erogenous tour of my body. Neither could it have duplicated how overwhelming it all was as my neurons were attempting to keep up with all the stimulus.

It was not long at all before I could feel Scott tensing behind me and shooting what was left of him into me just as Ken's chest heaved as well and fired his second load of the night into my depths. The cacophony of sound as I heard both of them push forth such primal noises shook my body to the core. The room started spinning for me like it never had before in my life. Just as I could feel the infusion of heat from Ken and Scott enter into me, my own exploded in response. My mouth echoed their mating ritual noises and I could feel my body officially reach a level of simply too much. My neural system was so overloaded by the emotional release of reaching the pinnacle of sensation once again, that tears came to my face and all the pent up hurt left my body. And then ... the room went dark on me ... *again.*

***

CHAPTER 34

I came to with the feeling of a cold washcloth on my forehead and a concerned Ken holding it in place. Scott was also there sitting next to me. Embarrassed at having passed out for the second time in one evening I sat up.

"I guess the excitement just got to me tonight," I said sheepishly. It was strange. I should have felt more discomfort and ill at ease, not just by having both of them in the room with me, but maybe because I had been trained by so many one-time encounters, which threesomes usually fell into the category of, to leave as quickly as possible. Pure sexual encounters - when it came to threesomes certainly - were generally about get in and get out. This situation did not have a quick exit as an option - even if I would have wanted it to be. I should have felt ill at ease, and yet I did not. I felt safe surrounded by the two men that cared most about me. Also, there was something even stranger, I felt feminine. It was as if the three of us were the perfect grouping of individuals. There was even a name for it, trupple. I had to laugh at myself as a thought crossed my mind.

"Now I know what *Wonder Woman* must have felt like. If this is what it was like to be an Amazonian woman and living in a matriarchal society. No wonder, they had super-powers attributed to them. You would have to to survive a night such as this."

"Well ... if I said it once I said it a hundred times Pandora, you are quite the sexual athlete," replied Ken with a smirk.

All three of us were lying in bed now with myself in the middle, matching my breathing to theirs. I had an arm wrapped around Ken and a leg draped around Scott just staring at the ceiling. Why was it that that I felt so comfortable around both of them? Maybe it was that in addition to having established my own history and relationships with each, they had already a much longer established relationship and knowledge of each other that I was just tapping into. However, the mere fact that I could tap into it and that it existed calmed my typically overactive mind. It calmed the questioning side of me and even if I could not trust Ken ultimately I could trust Scott and between the two of them, they would keep each other in check enough to allow for an ease unheard of in most couple relationships ... much less threesomes.

Scott, who had been silent all this time, chimed in.

"Yes, and I can, of course, agree with Ken .... although I personally think your best trait that you're like a sexual magnifying glass. I know I am a one-percenter when it comes to sex ... as we all are here ... but you somehow amplify and just bring out an even better performance. It's like you can just elicit sensuality from a person. Speaking for myself, and while I definitely know I have the ability to, I don't typically have this many orgasms in a row with ... well ... anyone!"

"Or back to back," said Ken. "Reminds me back in college and some of the wild and crazy situations we wound up in."

And then we started a game of "Do you remember when ..." recounting all the silly funny and great things either Ken and I or Ken and Scott or even Scott and I had done. We shared our stories until our voices gave out and we fell asleep in each other's arms. I remembered having my head on Ken's chest, happy to have him back in my life and Scott spooning me from half behind and half beside me and happy to feel the steadiness of his body. I fell asleep with no thoughts or plans for the future and instead taking joy in having reconciled the past. Scenes flashed through my brain while in that hazy twilight. Scenes that were preambles to the happy dream landscapes brought on by sleep.

***

CHAPTER 35

I woke up alone in bed with what I assumed was the sun shining high, or the part of the sun that was able to peak through the blackout curtains. There was a note on the nightstand next to me, which read, "Went to the casino for a few. Be back soon," signed Ken and Scott.

Stretching lazily in bed, the details of last night's events started to come back to me one by one. With each recollection, my marveled appreciation of how things had turned out built upon the one before. Never in my wildest dreams could I have ever imagined this scenario as a possibility. I could feel my stomach rumbling and as such pulling me out of my lazy mental daydream and propelling me into action. Hunger after all was one of the primary human drives for everything. Walking into the luxurious bathroom I made use of the steam shower and was enjoying the purifying aspect of not just the shower ritual, in general, but also feeling any toxins that might have been leftover from last night's festivities, bid adieu to my body via the steam induced sweat. It felt like the steam entered through the pores and then escorted anything that was not supposed to be there out.

Finally, I took hold of the various soaps and washed off anything that standing under the steam and then the water had not taken care of already. Once I felt like a newborn babe, I stepped out to greet the world as my own. I went through the process of drying off and running a brush through my hair, which was to a large extend my full beauty routine. I had never been one for extensive curling or drying or plastering of make-up. I appraised myself in the mirror in my naked honesty and noticed something different about me. My cheeks had a newfound pink brightness to them and my body just glowed. Amazing what a steam shower and being in love could do for the body. Bringing back all of the youthful exuberance and not just in mental but in physical form as well. Before walking out to get dressed, I decided to check out the bathroom scale and regretted my decision almost instantly. Consoling myself that the weight gain must be due to the water in my hair, I finally walked to the door and left the steamy comfort of my new found inanimate friend of a bathroom to get some clothes and meet up with the boys. As I walked out, I noticed something that had not been there before, rose petals on the floor creating a trail to the door that opened up the sitting area of the suite. The scent of them was lingering in the air so I knew they had been freshly plucked and scattered.

Had the boys come back already? And if so why would they have done this? Just to celebrate our new found three-musketeers-like relationship? I grabbed the robe from the back of the door and with bare feet, wet hair and fresh face I opened the door and was greeted by an overwhelming scent of flowers. It was so intense that despite the size of the room I almost became nauseous. The suite was filled with easily several hundred flowers of varying sorts. I recognized the Sterling Roses and the Casa Blanca Lilies but not much else. Some of the arrangements were as tall as I. What drew my gaze though was the smallest bouquet of them all and the one I knew to be the most expensive. There, lying on the dining room table, were my all time favorite flowers and nearly impossible to purchase in the United States, or during this time of year and most certainly in the West, Lily of the Valley. Sitting next to them was a black velvet jewelry box with the word Pandora written across it by hand in paint pen. There was also a decorative bowl of water with floating votive candles arranged to form the numbers 15. Lastly, I saw a Surface computer propped up and displaying a draft of an email that had been saved but not sent just a few minutes prior from Ken to me. I picked up the tablet and started reading.

Subj:	Moments in Disguise ......
From:	FinanceGuy
To:	Pandora

My Love:

It is rare to be aware of a life changing event as it happens........ It would be amazing if there was a way to have road signs of what the future had in store as the fateful moment that was disguising itself as a mundane day occurred .... During those times when paths cross in our lives that change us forever.

The day.... well the day I ran across your profile was one of those .... and I wish I would have known then how much that action would change me for the rest of my life ...... how big of a crossroads I had stumbled across. ...... Looking back now and everything that happened thereafter .... I see that our times together ...... while they have had their challenges ..... have always encompassed happiness. True happiness .... happiness that cannot be found by the consumption of a martini or the view of a sunset .... it is happiness that stays .... that is unchanging ..... no matter the circumstance .... no matter the distance .... and I hope that when you look back on those same moments that you have come to the same conclusion as I.

You and I have never been hampered by such things as space or time .... our existence our union has always transcended that .... look at how we keep meeting ..... time and again...... without effort ... our paths cross ... again and again .... without any intervention of ours .... and even the most hardcore skeptic has to wonder if this might be proof that fate exists ... call it god .... call it the universe .... that you and I should be together ... not just for a moment ... or a day ... or a month ... but for a lifetime ...... and while it took me a while to admit it to myself .... even though I knew from the first moment I laid eyes on you ..... I want to be the person you have your happily ever after with and the person you dreamt about so many years ago ...... I want to be ..... well your everything.

I could go on and on here .... and write about things that you know ..... things that you have felt and we both have felt ..... and discuss the concerns we have had ..... the mean things we have said to each other over time ...... none of which mean a darn thing anymore because at some point we just have to raise our hands and stop fighting the fact that we are meant to be together .... no matter how many obstacles we try to put into the path ....

Pandora ....

Will you marry me? Will you do me the honor of being my wife and making me the happiest man on the planet?

I know there are hurdles to overcome .... I know though as sure as I know that the sun will rise in the east again tomorrow .... that if we are together we can triumph over any situation ... we always have in the past.

Please say yes for you already have me: mind body and soul .... I will be waiting for you ...... dreaming all the while in the *Lobby Bar* with Scott waiting for your answer ......

831
Ken

###

I was stunned. I re-read the email again, and then again, just to make sure I had understood what Ken had asked. My brain had not quite decided yet how to digest this information. Putting down the tablet my hands were shaking as they moved towards the little black velvet box. I had dreamt of this moment for years although had never envisioned it quite like this. Indeed, I had never expected to be proposed to via email, although, considering our relationship from start to well - everything - it was the perfect - maybe the only appropriate way - to propose. I knew that for years I had been waiting for just such an admission, invitation, and dedication from Ken. However, I was not sure if it was something that I really needed or wanted anymore.

It took me trying three different times to open the box, for my hands were so weak with emotion. Once I did, there was a perfect heart shaped, 5ct., blue diamond set in platinum with diamonds filling every available space in the metal. The prongs and band had small diamonds in them on every side possible. I had to remind myself to breath and my hands were shaking uncontrollably as I tried to do anything but stare at them.

I tried the ring and it fit. *Of course, it did!* Ken would not have let any detail go unplanned. How he had been able to pull this off within the amount of time, I had no idea. Of course, having money helped. Having money helped a lot - especially in Las Vegas. I could not even begin to calculate how much this must have cost him or the small army of people he must have hired to get everything just so. He had always had the most exquisite taste and for this reason alone I should say yes to his email.

Still shaking I made my way back to the bedroom and turned towards the closet where, upon opening, hung the most beautiful *Armani* dress I had seen. Princess seamed, knee length and completely in white except for the blue accents, I noticed shoes sitting just below. Yes, I would wear the dress and the heels and even the ring. And I would meet Ken and Scott downstairs.

There was part of me that wanted to scream "YES" from the deepest part of my lungs to accept Ken's proposal. There was also the part of me that was logical enough to know it was not as simple as just saying yes. I was not going to become a "*Sister Wife*" for one and would have to reassure myself on the finality of the divorce. There was also the part of me that saw Scott in my mind's eye and frankly was not ready to let him go just because Ken had finally come to his senses. We had built such an incredible rapport last night, and I felt that between the two of them I could have my total fantasy. They could be "*Bother Husbands*" maybe I mused. I had to laugh at the thought, even though it was not really all that farfetched. It was something to consider.

Putting on some mascara and a dab of gloss, I left my hair down and walked out of the hotel room and taking my first step towards my modern happily ever after.

***

CHAPTER 36

Scott was sitting next to Ken inside the Lobby Bar. They had woken up and decided to leave Pandora to sleep. Leaving her a note they made their way downstairs to the casino. They had had quite the conversation. Ken, as usual, did most of the talking.

Scott was thinking back to the last time he had seen his mother. There had never been an expression of remorse, guilt, or anything that could be considered in the same family of an apology by her - ever. His mother kept her motives for her abandonment and her affection to herself for the rest of her life and was unmoved in giving her son closure, even while he stood vigil at her deathbed in the hospital. Scott, having seen the same pain in Pandora's eyes had thought that she had undergone a similar experience with Ken. However, Ken, unlike his mother, had decided to make good on the havoc he had wrought. Scott was not sure if he should feel jealous or happy for Pandora.

If nothing else, watching Ken's face and demeanor during the fast-paced planning and avalanche of people he had hired to get the impossible accomplished, deserved Scott stepping out of his way and at least pretending to be happy for Pandora and Ken. After all, Scott was the one who had vowed to remain a lifelong bachelor and had made quite a life for himself as such. Whereas Ken had always been the marrying sort anyway and Pandora ... well, Pandora was just built to be loved. Scott did not really need anyone in his life. He would be just fine on his own. Just like he had always been. No one could hurt him.

Scott had been absentmindedly shuffling the deck of cards he had picked up in the gift shop. As he was listening to the music over the sound system and Ken reminiscing about the college days, he had taken the Ace of Hearts and ripped the card almost in half. Stopping just has the tear had reached the heart. Much like his own heart was feeling at the moment. The only smile he had in him was looking up and seeing Pandora walking across the casino floor looking like an angel dressed in a white dress and white shoes. Seeing her face and connecting with her eyes even from this far away, he smoothed out the tear in the card and wondered if maybe there was hope for him yet.

CHAPTER PREVIEW
(EMAIL PEAK TO NEXT BOOK)

Subj: this moment in time.........
Date: 11/22 11:55:05 PM
From: FinanceGuy
To: Pandora

My Love:

This time of year means so many things to so many different people, and tonight.....as you can tell by the hour of my writing, that this time of year for me.......has me adrift. My family has assembled.....or almost assembled....and yet I am not here. I am in thought over today.......not distracted so much as distressed of my choice of words to you earlier in this day......for the things that I have not said, for the things I have not shared with you, words that maybe will remain without meaning to you, but will forever have meaning to my life.........for the remainder of my life here......is this place.......in this world.

I have tried without being too dramatic to express to you what it is that I feel with you, how I revel in this new discovery of you, how you tempt me into yet another brighter day, another belief that in some measure.....this new emotion is one that will continue to grow and not drift.......as most of my personal emotional life has.

I guess you have said it best when you said that of all the relationships that you have encountered or experienced.......have never had this temperament.....this emotion.......nor for that matter this distraction. I realize that life is simple when we always have a certain level of control over it, when we live life with a basis of anticipation that is always met, or at least controllable. But, the life that I have lived has never been like this. I have lived the majority of my life wondering when the next pitfall is coming, instead of enjoying the next gift of joy.....the next good thing......the next higher emotion. I guess this stems from the basic insecurity in all of us.

I am the first to admit, and do so freely and without reservation that I am insecure. I am insecure about letting people into my life, into the sanctum that is me......to truly have the opportunity to know me, to grow to become a part of my life. I am a doubter of how I appear to the world, if I dress in such a manner that suggests an ease about me.....or a stuffiness about me.......if I speak with intellect......and if when I speak......do I say the right thing. These, of course, are moments in time.......moments in time that can either linger.....or change the very character of the people I touch. Sometimes I am stronger than I might actually be in a given circumstance.......and other times ......I am just stronger. But in the end......I am one thing......convicted in my beliefs......convicted in my thoughts.......and those things that drive this man that you have met......have touched.......and in my immediate memory.....loved.

I have never asked of you anything than for your complete happiness. I have done that which feels right to me with you. I have not hidden my emotions behind some rock for you to guess about.......I have just expressed them. When I look back on the conversations that we have had and shared through this journey.......I remember the evening when I finally decided to lay it all out to you.....I pined and pined and pined........about disclosing what you guessed did not make sense about me. I pined in fear of losing you.......and I pined in fear of what my heart was telling me to do. And the bottom line in this ......is this..........I completed my truth to you........because I am in love with you.

This is fact. This is why today and the comments of today have kept me from any holiday joy.....other than trying to write these emotions and thoughts for you......because of you.......because of how you make me feel......not just as a man......but as a man should feel for a woman......for a lady. A man that is in love..........a man that is in love with you.

I dream of you each night.......and I do so freely. I freely dream about making love to you with an uncommon ease......with elation......with satisfaction.....with a pure joy that I have never known before. I know that I have stressed that I have traveled a block or two more than you.......but this for me is new as well. I hope that you ....when you take the time to read these words.... understand that what I am telling you in words......are not just words on some computer screen.........from some distant keyboard.........they are emotions.......raw......honest......and from the depth of me as a man.

Tonight......I feel a deep loss. I fear that I have lost a friend.......a mate.....yes, perhaps even a soul mate........a love........and in this life.......for this man.....maybe even the greatest love. I keep hoping that maybe this is some bad dream.....but each pinch that bruises the arms that you have kissed.......are stinging.
But in addition to these feelings.........I feel mysteriously.......even more in love with you. I do my best.......as I do in most things........to try to put myself in the other person's shoes.......whether it is a business associate......or a rival......a friend.......a child......or a loved one. I have learned that in my trivial life.....the journey has never been designed under one story and under one ending. Life is an evolving microcosm of experiences........two sides to every story......so tonight as I attempt to regurgitate ideas that are racing through my head about you......I will try my best to walk a mile in your shoes......to maybe touch on those

things that you are struggling with........coping with......and the change that I have caused inside your function as one hell of a woman.

Only months ago........you were driving a ship in life. You are the captain, the purser and the engineer.......you chart a course......and you drive the boat there. Life.......for all practical purposes.........was easy. Every problem was met with solution........every challenge was met with success.......every strategy.......had purpose........every emotion had a box.......every tear was never seen.

And then........I arrived. ....and then you asked why?

Your heart was almost flipped in reverse of how it has beaten for the years before you ever knew I existed.
Temptation......passion.......integrity and character........were all mixed into the person that you had the courage to meet in your hometown. I know that a part of you felt that the guy in that picture..........would never show up........would not.......could not.......ever be reality. And then.......I arrived......

And every roadblock........every pent up emotion........every doubt.......every fear and level of distrust........escaped you. THIS OF COURSE WAS NOT NORMAL IN THE GENERAL COURSE OF YOUR LIFE. Then you kissed this man......then you said goodbye and you left changed. And then......we lingered.......I .....quite frankly linger today.......even after today.......right this moment......I linger. I sit here in my home office.......surrounded with overpriced Disney art and memories........and I miss you........

For every dark place that I have touched inside you.......you have touched that same dark place inside me. For every fear that was met with joy.......for every insecurity that was and is accepted........for every scar.......for every lost love.....for every shattered emotion........the opposite emotion has been experienced with this man...........and why?

Because.....I accept you without reservation. I hold your friendship.......your womanhood......your love.......and your expressions of these things.......with pride.....with trust and with honor. Funny......when was the last time that someone......let alone anyone......said anything like this to you?

For this......this is what loving without reservation means. I can take your hits....dish them out......and your doubts ....and your ill-fated attempts to break me.......but I will still stand...........fakes crumble..........I stand. You can drench me and spit on me......and kick me in the stomach.......and I will recover......but I will still stand. You can make every attempt to undress me.......and you will see what it is you see.......but it will never be what you are looking for........that certain whatever.....that allows you to say.......AH HA!!!!!.........."See I told you so".

For you see......you have been issued a ticket.......a ticket that few people have received.....and for that matter few people that I want to see. You have seen behind the walls of me.......you have gained insight into my emotions.....your emotions.......emotions that you have always had........just never thought they held any reality or place in your life......or your heart.

I guess when it is all said and done..........you and I are the same breed of cat. We circle.......we contemplate.......we think. We purr.......we hunger......and we hope........(and yes......one of us dreams). Inside of us.......we pursue.....and we strive.......but to what end. Your end is my end and vise versa. In other words.......in our lives we have discounted what we have always hoped for........worked for........in exchange for comfort......for wealth.....for material objects.......for status........for recognition. At least know that I know this. But this is what I also know........

Regardless of the exterior presentation of you........inside that enormous heart of yours........behind the perfect surface that my eyes see.......the face that I could re-create in an ice-sculpture........is a little girl.......a little girl with hopes and fears.......with boundless love and pure ecstasy that has been kept hidden since forever.........until your eyes first met mine.

Now I am not bespeaking ego.......nor am I bespeaking trepidation........no.....I am explaining the honesty of how I feel.......when I see you........how I feel when I dream about you..........how I feel when I remember your voice........your touch........the way I melt when you look into the soul of me.

For all of this........I love you.

While I am certain the sun will shine tomorrow..........I will dream again tonight of you.......in a fashion that I have grown accustomed to. I am here to tell you that you have touched me........thank you for this. Regardless of how you take that.........regardless of the discount you choose to give my thoughts and my emotions.........you have touched a depth inside my untapped heart.

God has a purpose in how we live our lives........and each night.......I pray for your safety.......I pray for your heart........and I thank him for blessing me with the strength and the purpose that gives me the courage to chart new waters with you......to feel new emotion with you........to gain a certain gift to express these thoughts that I possess inside of me.......for you.

I rest confident in these emotions.......and I cherish them. I was taken aback by your thoughts and words today........but I nevertheless respect them. I understand them......and I will accept them. But in the same turn........I will also smile in this lonely and desperate place in my heart.....that piece of me that has your name on it........for today I also realize.......that today.......the deepest of your fears......have surfaced......you can no longer fight what has become obvious to you.......obvious when you look in the mirror........when you get dressed.........when you walk into a room........when you breath..........when you close your eyes.........this is what love is.

Love is growth........love is not hindrance. Love is forgiving........love is not ignorant. Love is the dealer of passion and the keeper of faith. Love faces darkness of the soul.........and shines a light on it. Love only emerges through understanding.......and benefits those who believe in the power of faith........and the principle of perseverance. Love is not success........but success tastes sweeter when love is shared along the way. I am a firm believer..........in that old saying.......life is not a destination.......but a journey.

I will close with this. You are a woman with gifts that my eyes recognize at a level unknown to the rest of the world.......and you should know that I see them........feel them........want them. You are a woman that has surpassed any level of kindness and acceptance that I have experienced...........and you are the woman that has been present in my dreams........that faceless woman that only gained recognition after I saw you. These are all great gifts.........gifts that I have received from you..........gifts that I have always searched for........but never thought I stood a hope in hell of feeling.......

So in a season of thankfulness............thank you for you.........thank you for taking a moment of your life........and sharing it with me. I hope that my every tomorrow...........will include you within it...........and I hope that you will find solace in the fact that you have not only my emotions.......but my heart.........and the reservationless acceptance of the only gift in life that I know of.......that money can never acquire....... The gift of my love............
I love you..................

PS.......I am now going to attempt to find something to get me asleep.........maybe a martini...........sleep tight

###

Subj: and just one more thing...........since I cant sleep
Date: 11/23 1:13:15 AM
From: FinanceGuy
To: Pandora

My Love:

If one dream that I consistently dream.........I wish that would come true.......

it is this........

On New Year's Eve..........I have the first dance........and the last kiss........and the first sunrise.........with you.........

And then.........just maybe........my life might be complete........

Sleep tight........

###

***

DEAR READER

Subj: Happy Birthday!
Date: 11/02 1:10:20 AM
From: Angelique St. Chase, Jr.
To: You

Dear Reader,

You are the reason I wrote this book, so hearing from you is important to me. Truth be told, I can barely contain the giddy excitement every time I see a letter in my inbox wanting to talk about characters that are near and dear to my heart. Just because it says "THE END" does not mean that they stop living in my mind, and hopefully not in yours either. So please drop me a line on my website or on Facebook.

Book reviews are better than chocolate and coffee combined to an indie writer such as myself, especially one who is as involved in every aspect of the book creation as I have been. I can't begin to tell you how much I savor each one. If you can spare a moment, I would appreciate an honest, heartfelt review from you. Thank you for being a part of this creative world of mine.

831
Angelique St. Chase, Jr.

###

For more Information about the next book and to inquire about signed books, please visit my social media sites:

http://www.angeliquestchasejr.com • http://www.novels.vegas

Angelique St. Chase, Jr.on: Facebook • Instagram • Twitter

***

ABOUT THIS BOOK

Truth vs. Fiction • Cover Model

TRUTH VS FICTION

One of my favorite quotes from Mark Twain is: "Truth is stranger than fiction, but it is because Fiction is obliged to stick to possibilities; Truth isn't." I am sure he said it more than once and in different ways. I know I have heard other variations throughout my life. As I mentioned in the book, this quote personifies Las Vegas, and since this book is set in Las Vegas, it personifies the book as well.

The irony and one of the biggest *'Easter Eggs'* in this novel(and there are so many that I might have to write an accompanying reference book after the trilogy is finished) is that the parts that sound too incredible to be true actually are, while the parts that sound like they could plausibly happen are actually fiction. Every sex scene I wrote about, from how unbelievably fast things would happen, to the settings to the number of rounds, are a detailed description of actual events in my life as they occurred while living in Las Vegas. The storyline, the characters, and all the words between the sex scenes; well, that is the actual fiction. Don't get me wrong, yes, I have dated online, I have been catfished, I have traveled the world, and on it goes. As such, I had a lot of knowledge to pull from when I created the world for Pandora.

In regards to that world, keep in mind I am an avid mystery reader, inspired by the likes of John Grisham and Dan Brown and prior to them I read fantasy novels purely because of David Eddings. As such, most everything in this book has double and triple meanings and there is a reason for pretty much everything.

For example, Pandora has the last name, Richardson so her initials would be P.R. since her job is in marketing. Scott's last name is Himmel, which is German for Heaven since his job as a psychiatrist is the equivalent of being a sin-eater.

The characters themselves were actually inspired by other fiction characters with which I had identified strongly with. *Polgara*, a character created by *David and Leigh Eddings* was ever in the forefront of my mind when I wrote for Pandora and *Dr. Gregory House* from the TV Series *House* when I wrote for Scott.

COVER MODEL

It be me on the cover of this book - to the right of the glass (in case that needed clarification). I am the blue shirt-wearing person with the long hair. There were six different cover images I experimented with, and this one was a fluke, which wound up testing well. So, for those of you that saw ads prior to publication where the cover looked differently, you were not hallucinating. And yes, I also designed the cover, and did the layout, and built the websites, oh and I guess I wrote the book, too. :-)

***

ABOUT THE AUTHOR

Living a life many fictional characters would be jealous of, Angelique St. Chase, Jr. was named after the romance series Angelique before she was even born. Residing in Las Vegas and entertaining her friends for years in the detailed descriptions of her life events, she finally decided to give in to her destiny. Knowing first-hand about the alluring, if sometimes heartbreaking life, that Las Vegas and online romance has to offer, she revels in being the book's cover model, going to celebrity chef restaurants, and speaking 7 languages.

Sign up here for her newsletter plus get insider info, author's chapter extras and exclusive giveaways!

WWW.NOVELS.VEGAS

Made in the USA
Middletown, DE
18 December 2015